Turn or Burn

Boo Walker

Also by Boo Walker

LOWCOUNTRY PUNCH

OFF YOU GO (Novella)

This book is a work of fiction. Names, characters, places, and incidents are either the product of the author's imagination or are used fictitiously, and any resemblance to actual persons, living or dead, events, or locales is entirely coincidental.

Copyright © 2014 by Boo Walker
All rights reserved.

Published by Sandy Run Press

www.sandyrunpress.com

Library of Congress Control Number: 2014900164
ISBN: 978-0-9913018-0-5

For Mikella and Riggs, la mia ragione per esistere.

Turn or Burn

I

"I went to cover the war and the war covered me."

- Michael Herr

"Within thirty years, we will have the technological means to create superhuman intelligence. Shortly after, the human era will be ended."

- Vernor Vinge

CHAPTER 1

Saved a lot of money on therapy bills the past couple of years consulting my German shepherd mix instead of driving to some bland office with a still life on the wall, telling an overeducated, underexperienced, credential-burdened wannabe doctor that my life was fucked, and paying their ludicrous fifty-minute fee, so that they could afford their yoga dues and their Vespa payment and their organic, local, *blah blah blah* cuisine and perhaps even a cute little Argyle sweater for their seven-pound dog.

Not that my overexperienced, pissed-off, and jaded monkey mind had gotten me much of anywhere, but at least I wasn't diving in the dirt anymore. The vineyard I'd planted and was currently meandering through had certainly been part of the healing, too.

I still had a lot to get done before the sun fell much further. The temperature had already dropped fifteen degrees, though that was nothing out of the ordinary for the desert in the Columbia Valley of Eastern Washington. And that's what it was: full-on desert. A lot of people don't know that about Washington State. They think, Seattle and rain. Well, once you drive east over the Cascades about two hours from Seattle and get close to Yakima, you're *lucky* if it rains. You're in the desert. And I'm talking the coyotes, rattlesnakes, tumbleweeds, and dust devils-kind of desert.

It had been an especially hot May, and I welcomed the cool evening breeze and a dip into the low sixties. I could hear Roman coming up from behind, weaving his way through the rows of grapevines, as he loved to do. He caught up with me and nudged my leg with a dried-up cane left on the ground from when we pruned the vines in February.

"Hey, buddy. You can go all day, can't you?" I rubbed his neck and pulled the cane out of his mouth and tossed it south. "Go get it, Roman!" He shot after it. Nothing could make me smile like he could. If I had to put my finger on one reason why I hadn't put a gun to my head and painted my bedroom wall with blood and brain, it would be him.

I went back to work. I used drip irrigation to water my vines—the only way any of us did it up on Red Mountain. Heck, most of the Columbia Valley, I imagine. There's good and bad to having a meager five inches of rain every year and being forced to irrigate. There was an upside to being able to control the amount of water our grapes drank, which allowed us to fine-tune some. Play God with the water. Have consistent vintages. But I wouldn't have complained if I didn't have to dig another hole to fix a leak for a while. I've sawed enough PVC pipe for a lifetime.

Every couple of days, I walk down each row and make sure all the vines are getting water and that everything's working properly. That's what I was doing today, just having a good stroll down the rows, taking it all in, breathing and trying to find peace. It's in those walks that I'd found a path leading me to some kind of normalcy. Soldier normalcy—not quite civilian-style.

A soft thunder began coming in from the west, rolling over the treeless hills. My senses became very acute; my skin tingled. I dropped the shears in my hand and looked off in that direction. I couldn't see anything but the sound became clearer. It was a

TURN OR BURN

helicopter coming toward me. It didn't feel right, what my body was going through. Beads of sweat. Increased heart rate. Tensed fists. A sensation close to tunnel vision but not yet totally out of control. I analyzed the scene around me with precision and speed. No other cars or people in sight. The closest building was my tractor shed one hundred yards up the gravel drive. I had no weapon; I had left it back at the house.

"Roman!" I yelled. "C'mere, boy!"

He was by my feet in seconds. He must have known there was something wrong. The helicopter came into view, climbing over Rattlesnake Mountain. Roman started growling—a very defensive, guard-dog growl. The helicopter drew closer, crossing over the Yakima River. It looked like a four-rotor, single-engine Bell. Probably a 407. Police issue.

Roman began to bark.

"Shhh," I whispered. "Don't do that." I bent down and rubbed his neck. He quieted. It was me that was anxious, though. I was the reason he was barking. He was protecting me. We humans release smells when we're experiencing emotions. Millions of pheromones. Dogs pick them up. I'm sure my body was spraying scents of fear and anxiety like a busted fire hydrant. He had picked it up quickly, like he always does.

The helicopter flew directly over our heads. I stood tall and watched it move past us and told myself to be calm. My instincts attempted to override the message, told me to run, but I wouldn't let that happen. I kept myself from moving. I told my mind first—then my body—that it was okay. That I was safe. I wasn't in a war zone anymore. My body understood. My heart rate slowed; the tension loosened.

The helicopter moved on and its sound started to fade. I took a deep breath and slowly knelt in the sandy loam soil. Roman wedged himself between my legs. I closed my eyes and began to meditate, something I'd taught myself after reading a few PTSD-related books I'd discovered over the years. I'm not hardheaded about whatever the hell is going on with me. I want to get better. I want to change.

And I was changing. It had been six months since I had reacted to a trigger. Sure, I could still feel them, but I was proving that I could control the urge to physically react. For a while there, the triggers had the best of me. They were deeply ingrained. At a Fourth of July get-together the year before, I was in the backyard with a group of old high school friends standing around the grill when the neighbors started shooting fireworks. This was earlier in the day, long before sunset. Before I had prepared myself. As soon as the first one exploded, I hit the ground and yelled, "Incoming!"

There were embarrassing moments like that. I hoped I'd be able to laugh at them one day, but not yet. My illness was deadly serious, and it hurt more than someone who has never been in combat could fathom. I'm glad my parents didn't have to see what I'd been going through. It would have been too much. In a way, dealing with my PTSD alone made me feel more comfortable.

The helicopter was gone. My mind was calm. As is the mission with meditation, I wasn't stuck on my thoughts. I simply let them pass by. An inward smile started to rear itself. I was getting somewhere with this shit. I wasn't Buddha yet, but I had tasted a bit of Nirvana. Just enough to have hope. I was starting to feel my confidence coming back, like I had this thing licked.

There I was thinking again. I pushed away those thoughts, even though they were positive. I needed to get back to the stillness. Stroking my Buddhist ego wasn't exactly leading me to an orange robe and slippers. Things began to calm.

Nothing. Nothing. Nothing.

A breeze. The sound of leaves blowing. Warmth of sunshine. The first taste of this year's lavender in the air.

My cell phone, left in my truck, began to ring. The sound

TURN OR BURN

pulled me back to reality and thoughts flooded in. I pushed them away and tried to ignore the noise. I let the call go to voice mail.

Back to the silence. Back to purity and form and emptiness.

The phone sounded again, and what a bad chirp of a ring it was. I gave up. Enough spirituality for one day. I stood and dusted the dirt off my jeans. Roman followed me down the row and right along the drive to my old Ford diesel. The phone had stopped ringing. I reached for it and looked at the screen; I didn't recognize the number. Just as I began to check the message, it started ringing again. Three calls in a row. *Give me a break.* I opened it up and answered.

"This better be the president," I said.

"Harper Knox," said a familiar voice. It was Ted Simpson. I'd known him since Fort Bragg, which felt like hundreds of years ago. We were like brothers, though we hadn't spoken in a while. Ted hadn't stopped fighting. Not once in his career. While I was out there crushing grapes, he was over in the desert crushing Al Qaeda. "How are you, bud?" he asked.

"Was doing okay until my damn phone started yapping."

"Wow. I thought this vineyard mumbo jumbo was supposed to mellow you out. Where's the love?"

I leaned against the driver side door of the truck. "It doesn't happen overnight."

"Well, while we all eagerly await your transformation, I have a job for you."

"That right?"

"Yep. And I need you tomorrow."

"Can't do it," I said. "I'm up in Canada for a couple weeks."

"You serious? Where?"

"Banff."

"What for?"

"A vacation."

"I don't buy it."

"I'm not selling it. It's the way it is. Got a cup of coffee in my hand overlooking the Rockies. Let me ring you when I get back south. Talk to you later, Ted."

"Wait a damn minute. I'll fly you back. This is a good gig. Good cash."

"This up here is what I need right now. I am done with battle."

"I don't believe a word you're saying. You're never done with battle. And besides, you haven't left Red Mountain in months. Banff...come on. Can't you do better than that?"

"Whatever."

An SUV started coming down the gravel road that lines the southern side of my vines. The rocks crunched underneath the tires and dust rose up in a whirl behind it. I hadn't had a visitor in a while. I don't have that many friends anymore. "I have to go," I said. "Call you when I get back in the country."

"Wait a minute."

"Later, Teddy."

I closed my phone and looked up the hill.

As the car drew closer, Ted's face became visible behind the wheel. *Damn it.*

I turned and started running.

CHAPTER 2

Ted's shadow appeared first. I was standing on the ledge outside of the second floor of my white stone tractor shed, directly above the back entrance. One hand kept me from falling. He'd followed me in, but I had already scurried up the ladder and worked my way out the window. I heard him looking around inside, moving things, looking for me. "Tofu," he was saying, using my Army call sign. "Toooofuuuuu," he said again, drawing out each syllable. "Show yourself."

His shadow appeared. I breathed slowly and quietly. Didn't move at all. Waiting for the perfect time.

The sky was darker now. Colder. One 40-watt lightbulb that I'd accidentally left on the night before swung from the ceiling inside the shed. It lit his shadow and then his body as he stepped back outside into the night. Directly below me.

He hadn't changed much. Still six-five—four inches taller than me. Built like he was training for something. I noticed a little balding circle on the top of his head, the size of a cup holder. That was my target. He turned his head left and right, scanning my property. "Tofu!" he yelled.

I let go and jumped. I landed feet first on his shoulders and he dropped hard, knees to chest to the gravel. He grunted as the breath left his lungs. I fell on top of him and went straight for his neck. I threw my forearm around and tried to cut off his oxygen. He didn't give up easily, though. He got to his knees and kicked my shin with a nasty sideswipe. Just about broke my leg. He flung me off, and I hit the side of the shed and dropped into the dirt.

Ted stood and looked down at me. I pulled myself up before he could kick me again. I stood a foot from him. Looked him in the eyes.

We smiled at each other and opened our arms. Both exhausted, we embraced and broke into hearty laughter. "It's been too long," he said, letting go of me.

I put my hands on his upper arms and looked at him very seriously. "Oh, Teddy boy, I wish I could say the same. I thought I'd be fortunate enough to never see you again."

"Nothing changes, does it?"

"Everything changes. Last time I saw you, you weren't losing hair. That has to be eating you *up* inside."

He tried not to laugh and shook his head.

"Where have you been?" I asked. "How long have you been back?"

"Mostly Africa, protecting some DOD kooks. Dumb work. Got back a couple months ago. Been in Seattle ever since."

I hit him on the back. "Let's get you fed. Pump you full of greens. Try to grow some of that hair back."

"I didn't know greens did that."

"Clearly."

"You're still not eating animals?" he asked me as we started toward my house.

I'd been a vegetarian since I was five. "Nope. I'm still not eating animals."

***

TURN OR BURN

"When are you going to learn you can't lie to me?" he asked later in the evening, both of us still ignoring the elephant in the room, the catalyst of my self-destruction, the thing that had brought us both such terrible pain. Someone we hadn't spoken about in a long time. His dead brother.

"Same day you learn it's best to leave me alone. Can't you see I'm trying to get away? You know I love you, brother, but...you know." I pulled at the corkscrew, and the cork popped out of a shiner of Syrah a friend down the road had given me. I poured an ounce into my glass and sniffed it to make sure it wasn't corked, then shared it with Ted.

We were sitting at the long wooden table on my back porch. I'd showered. This wasn't our first bottle. The sun had already done its thing for the day, and the great and mighty night sky of Eastern Washington surrounded us in its terrifyingly humbling way, giving us a glimpse into the unknown, reminding us that we were nothing more than a tiny little part of it all. I'd seen more constellations on my porch than anywhere else in the world.

For the better part of an hour, we laughed at old war stories. Ted could tell them better than anyone. Like the time in Honduras, one of his first missions, when he and another Green Beret were sent to a beach to build a defensive barrier with sandbags. They'd been given four days to complete their mission. The day they arrived, they hired one hundred Honduran boys for a dollar apiece, and the barrier was done in a couple hours. They spent the next three days lying on the beach drinking beer and getting a suntan. That's the Green Beret way: delegate.

And the time he almost got caught with marijuana in his system. I never smoked much but a lot of Green Berets did. Instead of *Be all you can be,* it was *Be all you can pee.* Ted took part in the ganja from time to time, especially in his twenties. He grew up on Bainbridge Island west of Seattle; how could you blame him? Back on base in North Carolina, while firing his M-16 on the range, he and the others were told that they were to be tested directly after leaving. Luckily, one of the food trucks that rode around base was coming by. Ted bought some apple juice. Just before he got in line for testing, he took a big sip, swishing it in his mouth to warm it up, holding it there until it was his turn. They handed him the pee cup, and he somehow spit the juice in without them seeing and went on to pretend he was peeing into it. Well, he passed. Who would have known? Of course, that was back in the old days; I'm not sure that would work anymore.

Roman had his head on my foot. The vineyards sloped down toward the Yakima River in front of us, and we were looking beyond that, out over the sparkling lights of Benton City, which was really more of a village than anything resembling an urban community. One bank. A hardware store. A tire store. A damn fine diner called the Shadow Mountain Grill. That's about it. Come to think of it, Red Mountain, where I lived, was more of a hill than a mountain. Perhaps those of us from around there had delusions of grandeur.

Good, simple people, the ones that lived down the hill. Farmers and rodeo types. People like my mom and dad, here long before the winemakers discovered the vineyard potential.

In fact, I lived in the house my parents had raised me in. I'd done some renovating, but my dad built a strong, timeless stone house back in the sixties. Tall ceilings. Fireplaces up and down. Giant windows that looked out over the vineyards and orchards in every direction.

"That's good wine," Ted said, setting down his glass. "You got the life, don't you?"

"Life can be good out here. It's supposed to be. That's what they tell me." I stabbed a piece of Comté cheese with my knife and stuck it in my mouth.

"Still feeling sorry for yourself, I see."

I gave a half-assed smile.

He rubbed his face. "When'd you start wearing a beard? Is that the farmer coming out?"

TURN OR BURN

I touched my patchy beard. "Something about being back on a tractor makes you feel like you need one."

"It looks good. In all honesty, man. You look good. Better than before, I mean. Much better. I thought I was losing you for a little while."

"You were." I decided to change the subject. Green Berets don't do emotional real well. "What is it that you want, Ted? Let's get this over with, so I can say no."

"Don't get ahead of yourself. You ever heard of the Singularity?"

"I've heard of it. The end of the world. Artificial intelligence. Computers taking over, or something like that."

"You have been under a rock, haven't you?"

"You could say that. I'm out here to get away from all that."

"Welcome back to reality, hoss. In the past few months, it's become one of the biggest controversies in the country. As far as how passionate people are on either side, it's on the level of abortion or stem cell research. You can't get through one newspaper without reading about it."

"I haven't looked at a newspaper in two years, man. What's the deal with it? I did overhear someone the other day talking about some Singularity Summit they are having in Seattle."

"Exactly. The idea of the Singularity is that technology, which is moving at an admittedly *scary* rate, will lead to the creation of smarter-than-human intelligence and the ultimate end of the human race as we know it. And by 'smarter-than-human intelligence,' they're not talking about a computer who can beat a human at chess. They're talking about a *being*—using the term loosely, evolved from our own technology—that will be able to beat us at everything in life. They could take our jobs, our girlfriends, even our lives. They could be super humans, robots, or nothing that familiar. It's all very speculative at this point."

He crossed his arms and leaned toward me, getting closer to his point. Though the topic was rather interesting, I was getting no closer to signing up for whatever it was he was about to ask. "Theorists say this could happen soon, like twenty-or-thirty-years soon. They say that there will be a point in time—an *event horizon*—where everything changes. A point of no return. These people, some of the smartest in the world, say that no one could possibly predict how it will come about or what will be on the other side, but that it *will* happen. That event horizon *is* the Technological Singularity, or Singularity for short. The beginning of the unknown."

He ate a piece of Comté—a cheese that can always be found in my refrigerator—and enjoyed it before continuing. "One of the pioneers on the AI side, Ray Kurzweil, uses the analogy of the computer he used in college at MIT back in the seventies. It was the size of a room and only a few people in the world had access to such power. Now, more than a billion people have smart phones in their pockets that are many times more powerful than that computer at MIT."

He stuffed another piece of cheese in his mouth. "Man, that's good."

"I know."

"Anyway," he said, "Kurzweil says technology is not only getting faster, but it's getting faster *faster*. It wasn't that long ago that the Wright brothers flew the first airplane. Less than seventy years later—in the same lifetime for some—we put men on the moon. Where to next?"

"Who knows?" I stood and stepped up onto the stone rail, where I began to relieve myself into the grass. A coyote howled off in the distance. "As long as I can pee outside on my farm, I'll be happy."

"The little things in life, right? Those are what matter."

"That's right," I agreed, enjoying the view.

"Like the one in your hand."

I shook my head. "You're never going to grow up, are you? Don't make me—"

TURN OR BURN

I was enjoying my sweet relief when Ted came up from behind and pushed me, midstream as it were, knocking me into the grass. Some things never change.

A few minutes later, we were both back in our chairs and I pulled out some whiskey. We each took a shot and Ted picked up right where he'd left off.

"Imagine this, Harper," he said. "Seriously. In our lifetime, humans will have computers installed *in their brains*. Imagine a soldier who could access a computer just by thinking. He could see any map or speak any language without lifting a finger. Singularists say that these super humans will be the most creative artists and inventors and scientists, curing diseases that we never could, writing music that Mozart would drool over, solving environmental problems; that kind of thing. Even making ethical decisions."

I let him keep going. "But Artificial Intelligence is just part of it. You've got scientists in other fields doing similar work, like geneticists trying to reconstruct DNA to fix diseases and other human vulnerabilities, like mental or physical disabilities. Or nanotechnicians trying to repair the body with millions of nanobots that you can shoot into the bloodstream. Take that same soldier and add that he doesn't need to sleep or eat as much as a 'regular' human, and if he gets shot, you can fix him up with an injection and put him back in the field within minutes."

"I had no idea you were such the intellectual."

He shrugged. "I just know what I've been picking up the past couple weeks. I'm no expert, but that's what this is about. It affects everything. Think of the Olympics. We'll have to separate competitors into categories. I don't think it would be fair to make one of us compete against a super human, right? Someone tweaked to have quicker reaction time, stronger muscles, less sensitivity to pain or exhaustion. It's the steroids argument on steroids." He laughed at his own joke.

"I'm still listening."

Just as he'd done for so many of our missions together, Ted had laid out the backstory, and now he would dive into the specifics. And then I would say no and try to get a couple hours of sleep.

CHAPTER 3

My client is a guy named Dr. Wilhelm Sebastian. He is one of these guys that Singularists love. I guess he is one himself. Complete nut job, but smart as hell. He and his partner, a Dr. Nina Kramer, have a lab at UW funded mostly by DARPA, the Defense Advanced Research Projects Agency. They are supposedly on the cusp of doing exactly what I'm talking about. He says they've made it possible for a human to access the Internet via their brain using a neural implant."

I laughed. "How the hell do you do that?"

"They drill into the skull and attach this microscopic implant—it looks like a mini-hairbrush—to the brain, wiring it to thousands of neurons, using electronic circuits of some kind. Obviously it's way over my head." He went back for more cheese. "They haven't done it with a human yet, but they've done it with a chimp."

"That's impressive," I said, still knowing his words were useless. I didn't care if he was protecting the man who invented time travel. I wasn't going to be involved.

"Yeah. Can you imagine?"

"So you're protecting geeks now?"

"Well, think about it. We could spend all night listing the

people and organizations that are already fighting these kinds of technological developments with every resource they have. Hell, flip on the news. It won't take you ten seconds to find some hater out there bashing it. If these two doctors really are able to put a computer in a person's brain, this is the biggest step yet in uniting man and machine. This terrifies people. It means that we're not that far from creating super-than-human intelligence. People think this is the end of the world. Machines taking over. People are terrified."

"I don't doubt it."

"Dr. Sebastian told me that their next attempt is *mind uploading*. That's uploading a human's conscious mind into a computer, giving him the ability to live forever, or at least for a whole lot longer than we do now. It's far out, nearly unimaginable stuff, but they think they can do it. Then, they could even create virtual worlds where this new mind, free of its human body, could explore."

He turned his glass around in his hands and continued. "His family's been getting death threats. First one came six weeks ago. That's when I put a team together. But I lost one of my guys last night. His wife found out she has breast cancer, so he's out. And I need you."

"And there it is, ladies and gentlemen."

"The Singularity Summit starts in two days. It's at the Convention Center downtown. All these nerds from around the world—people from NASA, Microsoft, Google, Apple, et cetera—come to listen to scientists and visionaries and philosophers talk about how we might reach the Singularity and what life could be like after it occurs. They're expecting heavy protests. Guess who the headlining speaker is." Ted filled the glass and put his feet up on the table. "Yep…Dr. Sebastian. He and his partner will be demonstrating their work in public for the first time. He's got a wife and two little boys, Harper. I need your help. Need somebody like you on the team."

TURN OR BURN

"Right. I feel like we're back in the desert already. Tell me about the team."

"There will be four of us. Will Dervitz. I found him in Africa last year. He knows what he's doing. And then my cousin, Francesca Daly. You've met her, right?"

"No. Heard you talk about her, though. A woman...really?"

"Get over it. She can outshoot and outthink you all day long."

"Right. I've heard that before."

"It's good pay and I know you need the dough. What is it you told me one time? 'How do you make a small fortune in the wine business? Start with a large one.' You need me as much as I need you. A couple weeks at the most. I know you're ready to get back out there. Live a little."

"You don't know anything about me anymore. My head's still not right."

"I think you're better than you let on."

I stood, turned, and opened the door. "C'mon, Roman."

My savior got to his paws and slipped through the crack in the door.

"What do you say, partner?"

I looked at him. "Not a chance. I'm going to get some sleep. You're welcome to stay if you'd like. You know where everything is. Make yourself at home."

"I'll probably take you up on that."

"No problem. See you bright and early. I'm sorry you came all this way."

"I knew it would take some convincing."

"It would take more than that. Good night."

"Tofu," he said, stopping me. "You're not still taking the blame for what happened to Jay, are you?"

There it was...that elephant. I chewed on my lip for a second, staring at the ground, contemplating a response. I didn't have one. "Good night, Ted."

"You have to let it go," he said.

"Thanks, Ted. And now you're going to tell me it wasn't my fault. Fuck off." With that, I closed the door.

Upstairs, I brushed my teeth and climbed into bed so that I could get another terrible night's rest. Nothing like tossing and turning, spinning in useless thoughts, waiting for the demons to come. I was almost getting used to them. I'd certainly forgotten what sweet slumber meant.

***

Ted and I go way back. I was under his command my first few years in the Special Forces. We'd worked in Kosovo and Northern Africa together, and he'd done everything he could to help me advance. And when we returned from war zones, we'd spend time together in Seattle. His ex-wife used to take care of us. Let us sit on the porch and talk about the things no one understood. She'd let us be and show us love when we needed it. But he drove her off eventually. It was hard to avoid. The things we've seen can't be shared. No one can understand, and it separates us from the innocent. A great big dividing line most often too thick to break through.

We both left the Army at the same time and started doing private contract work. That's when I met his younger brother, Jay, for the first time. Jay was ex-Navy, a year younger than me, and he'd been contracting for a couple years by the time Ted and I got on board. In fact, he's the one who talked us into it. He's the one who got us our first jobs. Despite what happened, I still have some grand memories of those days. Back then, the three of us ruled the world together. There was nothing we couldn't do in a war zone. I pity the fool who tried to take us on.

The deal with contracting was that it paid better and we didn't have to follow rules. I love the Army and the Green Berets as much as I love our country, but I believed I had more to offer as a contractor than a tied-down military man. We could pick our

TURN OR BURN

battles and be more effective fighting them. The three of us were bouncing around Iraq long before Saddam and Blackwater were household names. Making six figures and a real difference.

This was before the government got greedy and started paying any numbskull with a gun to get a job done. It used to be only those of us who had served could get the gig. Only those of us who had real knowledge of how to win battles, how to work with allied forces, how to produce results, how to protect. But contractors came to be in such high demand that there just weren't enough of us, and they started taking anyone that knew how to pull a trigger. That's why Jay was killed, because he'd been surrounded by idiots. But I was set on taking the blame and guilt to my coffin. If his death was any one person's fault, it was *mine*.

Aside from the obvious, the devastating fact about that day was I couldn't really remember it. I could see bits and pieces but it wasn't a memory like most. And that broke my heart. I couldn't even give Jay the respect of remembrance. I wanted so badly to relive those hours, to analyze what we'd done wrong and how I could have changed things, but I couldn't. Once it got ugly, I blacked out.

So I hadn't taken a job in two years; decided I wasn't capable. I don't think anyone would have argued with me. And I'd closed myself off from the world. Being responsible for a man's death is too much for any man to handle, and the same men who had killed Jay had tortured me until I could taste death, and that didn't help things, either. That week in Afghanistan, I was shown the dark side—something that I can't shake. Even in my dreams. It took my soul and broke it down, like a fist crushing a cracker to crumbs.

Yeah, I felt like those crumbs. No doctor in his right mind would ever clear me for battle again.

I'd never be ready.

CHAPTER 4

"What are you doing up?" Ted asked me, coming into the kitchen with a bag in his hand. The sun hadn't quite come up yet. Roman went over to him.

"I got my catnap. That's all I can do these days."

"Nightmares?"

"Is that what they're called?"

"Got a call from my team," Ted said, not letting me wallow in my sorrows. "King 5 is reporting protesters already pouring into town. Sounds like Battle in Seattle all over again. Remember that WTO disaster back in the nineties?"

"Yep."

"Could really use you on this one." He poured himself a cup of coffee out of the press. "I know you're hurting inside. I know you think you're a liability, and maybe you are in the real world. But not when you've got a gun in your hand. It's like a pacifier in your mouth, and you know it. Nothing can fix you like returning to the swell."

I had to admit it. Ted had a point.

"I have a reputation to uphold," he continued. "I've never lost anyone on my watch. You know why? Because I pick the best. Even if I have to stop in hippie wine-land to get 'em. Now

TURN OR BURN

quit acting like a little girl and go pack your bags. It's Seattle for God's sake. A long way from any war. How bad could it get?"

"One week?"

"Two weeks, max."

I thought about it. I needed the money and the action. And Ted was right: it was a quick fix. And I could use it. Better than vodka or codeine or heroin.

Better than the barrel of a gun in my mouth.

"What the hell. Give me ten minutes. I'll follow you." So much for strength.

I leapt up the stairs two at a time and threw my things together. Nine minutes later, I tossed a bag in the back and climbed into my diesel and turned the key. She crunched to life. Roman jumped in and buried his head in my lap. I lightly pinched his ears. "Not this time, buddy. I need you to look after the place. Will you do that?"

I grabbed his muzzle and looked right into his eyes. He was everything to me. Everything. "Be back in a couple weeks." I let go of his muzzle, and he buried his head back into my lap. I pulled him away and said, "Go on." He looked mournfully at me one last time and jumped out of the truck. Chaco, my go-to guy for everything on the mountain, would take care of him on the farm while I was away.

I rolled down the windows and followed Ted's Toyota out of the driveway and onto Sunset Road, the main road that was home to all the Red Mountain vineyards and wineries. Roman was in my rearview mirror, running with everything he had, a trail of dust following him. I pushed down the gas. He ran harder.

As I reached the Stop sign at the end of Sunset, Roman came up next to the truck, panting. I said, "Go home, boy. Chaco will take care of you." He barked, put his head down, and turned back, slowly walking the mile back to the house.

As I pulled onto the highway a couple miles from the house, I called Chaco and told him I'd be out of town for a while and asked if he would take care of things. He said he'd be happy to look after Roman and my place, and I bid him good-bye.

I'd gotten to know Chaco through some mutual acquaintances about two years ago. Now I relied on him without fail. Chaco could grow or fix anything. His roots went back to Mexican cocaine cartel work back in Oaxaca. After turning in his machine gun, he swam the Rio Grande with nothing but jeans and a shirt and worked his way up through California and then into Washington State. Came up to work the cherry and grape harvests, and he proved himself. When I'd returned to Red Mountain to plant a vineyard, I'd forgotten a lot. It had been more than a decade since I'd worked with grapes. Chaco brought it all back for me, and he became a friend.

I didn't listen to anything on the drive. Just watched it all go by, trying to keep up with Ted. Truth was, I craved silence. I really had to be in the mood to listen to music, and I sure as hell didn't want to listen to some dipshit run his mouth on the radio.

The journey three hours west to Seattle was a geographic marvel. Not even I could complain about it, especially on a clear day. The snowcapped Mt. Adams lay ahead and rose higher up from the horizon with each mile. Sixty miles of vineyards and hops, all the way to Yakima. If you've ever had a Coors or Budweiser, you've tasted Eastern Washington hops. They grow more there than anywhere else on the planet.

We climbed the Manastash Pass toward Ellensburg. Came down the other side and started toward the Cascades. The temperature dropped. I started to see snow. The steep, broken cliffs and monstrous evergreens rose high overhead, and I put my hands at ten and two, negotiating the winding mountainous roads. It was a world away from my vineyard in the desert.

An hour later, the road flattened again and traffic picked up. We passed a billboard for the Singularity Summit. It was black with silver writing explaining the where and when, and on the upper right hand corner, there was a picture of this doctor who had hired us. The caption underneath said: *Headlining Speaker, Dr. Wilhelm Sebastian, lead scientist of the Fusion Project, will change the world.*

I dialed Ted, starting to get a bit more curious. "Okay, you've got me. What the hell is this doctor up to?"

"I don't know that I can explain it that well," he said.

"Give me your best."

"Okay. They've figured out a way their chimp, Rachael, can access the Internet using brain waves. The idea is that eventually none of us will need computers or cell phones…or at least we won't need to drag them around. They will be embedded into our brains.

"Sebastian said it's very crude and undesirable now. They had to drill a hole in Rachael's brain in order to connect the implant, but the hope is that they can figure out a less invasive way soon. They're still a year or more away from being able to try it with a human, but it works. He showed it to me. And it's a game changer. How do you give a student a test like the SAT to test his knowledge and ability if he has access to all the answers just by thinking his way onto the Internet?"

"How could they possibly prove this with a chimp?" I asked.

"This implant communicates directly with an Intranet built specifically for the project. The first website they used was very basic. A green square is on the right. A red one on the left. If Rachael can move the flashing cursor to the green, she gets a nip of peanut butter. If she moves it to the red, she gets a pretzel. Once she figured out the pattern, she never once went back to the red square. She's a peanut butter kind of girl."

"How did she know how to move the cursor?" I asked.

"Just by thinking it, really. If she thinks the color green, almost wishing the cursor to move there, it does. This is all part of the nanotechnology embedded in this tiny chip in her skull. I think that's where the genius of the technology comes in. That chip. It's a computer mouse that you place inside your mind. It's the same thing as your brain telling your hand to open or close.

Same neural communication. I'm telling you, Harper...it's mind-blowing."

"I'm sure. So you still have to have a way to see what you're doing? A way to see the screen? I would think you would be limited."

"Sebastian said they were very close to finishing a contact lens that could display that same screen. Then the next step would be figuring out a way in which you could see a screen in your mind just by closing your eyes. Or closing one eye. Or maybe not even closing an eye. Who knows?"

"I'll be damned."

"So they started building onto the Intranet from there, inventing new games and websites for Rachael. They got her to where she could navigate through as many websites as they felt like creating in order to find the green square. All using colors to lead the way. They were even able to teach her to scroll up and down. I saw all this with my own eyes in his lab last week."

"And this is what he's going to demonstrate at the Summit?"

"Exactly. Only a few people have seen it so far. He's introducing it to the world tomorrow."

"So what's the plan now?"

"The doctor's house," he said. "We're moving him now."

***

We crossed Lake Washington and started into Seattle, the city that I dreamed about growing up back on the other side. Even after the desensitization of my life and the passing of all those years, I still got the chills when I got close.

Oh, Seattle...the land of Pearl Jam and Nirvana and Soundgarden and Jimi Hendrix. Though I couldn't listen to music much anymore, it was music that seemed to define this place. A fog hid the skyline until we were right up on it. Like a burlesque dancer, the city slowly began to reveal itself as I hung a right onto

TURN OR BURN

I-5, first the Mariners' and Seahawks' stadiums and then the skyscrapers of downtown. I couldn't see the surrounding mountains today, but I knew they were out there, and they'd dropped my jaw more times than I could count. Seattle was a magic city, filled with darkness and mystery and life.

CHAPTER 5

Dr. Wilhelm Sebastian's house was located a few blocks from the water on the top of the hill in Magnolia, a peninsula neighborhood northwest of Seattle that they called the "Island," despite the facts. Tall bluffs lined the shore, dropping steeply down into the Puget Sound where the water bashed the cliffs on nasty days, splashing up toward the giant homes resting so close to the edge.

The house was full-on Art Deco—lots of glass and modern angles. The kind of place that "new money" (something Seattle has in spades) builds. I'm sure you could see the entire city and half the state from the front door when it was clear out. A cold May wind pushed its way inside the door as we entered the house. Hopefully it would warm up soon, but summer doesn't start until July in Seattle, so I wasn't holding my breath.

Our team was on high alert. The threatening phone calls were a big deal. They had the family scared out of their minds. Especially considering that the Summit was coming tomorrow. We had the phones tapped now. Not much we could do as far as being on the offensive. We had nothing to work with.

After I met the team, Ted sent me and his cousin, Francesca Daly, right back out into the gloom to walk the perimeter before we moved. Francesca Daly: not exactly what I'd expected. She looked nothing like Ted. I guess I was expecting some ultra-tall woman with a bald spot and fifteen-inch biceps. Not so. Francesca was classic Italian, borderline cliché. I could have guessed her name. Long brown hair with a bit of natural curl. Warm amber eyes. A little mole on her right cheek. She was medium height and in good shape and had the disciplined posture of a military-type.

We had barely even shaken hands when she decided to take a step way over onto my bad side.

I asked in the most courteous way, "Where are you from?" Looked her in the eyes, waiting on an answer.

She turned away from me. "Don't look at me that way." Her English came with a healthy Italian accent, and it sounded more British than American. "It's not going to get you anywhere." Yes, *those words* came out of her mouth. That took guts.

"Don't get ahead of yourself, lady," I said. This Italian transplant had gotten the wrong idea. I flung out my hand and pointed at her. "Women are the last thing on my mind."

"I bet."

"Look, you might be Ted's family. Hell, you could be his favorite person on earth, but that doesn't mean I have to treat you like your shit smells like tulips. I'm here to do a job. If you are insecure about your good looks, you can take it somewhere else. I barely noticed."

She wasn't even looking at me. "Please. I know your kind, and I'm just saying, don't bother."

"You know what? You need to tell yourself that exact thing. Don't bother, lady. In fact," I added, putting two fingers under my eyes, "look at me for a second."

She turned her head and put those brown eyes on me.

I continued. "Consider me married, unavailable, uninterested, gay, castrated, transgender, unisexual, and full of hate, all wrapped into one. You can even think of me as your grandma if you want. I wasn't looking at you like I wanted to get into bed with you. If I happened to look you in the eyes, it was a sign of respect. Something you clearly don't deserve. Now let's get past this and go to work."

She was floored. Mouth-dropped. Humbled. Saddened. Embarrassed. Like I'd flipped her skirt up on stage. I felt kind of bad about it.

After a few seconds, she said, "I'm sorry."

"It's all in the past. I've already forgotten."

Sure, she was good-looking. Any idiot knew that. So are several million other women across the world. Her casual jeans and running shoes weren't fooling anybody; she had one hell of a body, the kind you can't create in the gym. Something you're lucky enough to be born with, end of story. I didn't care, though. Hadn't cared about women in a long time. I'm just trying to take care of myself. That's why her comment set me off.

"You want to head north?" I asked. "I'll move down the hill. Meet you on the other side."

She nodded, and we parted.

It is in the element of high alert that I dwell most comfortably. I worked my way down the hill, eyeing every window, every stopped car. The neighborhood was quiet. It was noon on a weekday. A few slow drivers were headed out to do whatever it was they did. Parked cars were on every block, their emergency brakes surely on. I've heard that the inhabitants of Magnolia can't leave when it snows. They'd slide all the way down the hill. It was an expensive, safe neighborhood. We were making sure that we could move the doctor and his family to the armored Suburban without any problem. Once they were inside the vehicle, we were okay.

I turned back up the hill. Francesca was cutting the corner on the sidewalk. We looked like we lived somewhere around there, out for a leisurely stroll. But I kept looking up. I've been doing bodyguard work for years, and the problems generally come from

TURN OR BURN

up high. Windows, trees…any place where an enemy can get the advantage.

About six houses down on the opposite side, I picked up something. Saw a flash or reflection in the window. I didn't like it. Instead of engaging immediately, I kept moving. Walked casually until I'd passed another house and was out of sight. I spoke into the hidden mic in my shirt. "I don't like something over here. Want to help me out?"

Her voice came back through the wired earpiece wedged into my ear. "Are you still going down the hill?"

"Yep. Meet you at that Stop sign at the bottom."

Five minutes later, we were together and focused on what was going on. Focused on saving lives. Absolutely no concern for our previous friction. We were professionals.

I looked up the hill and said, "The green house on the right. I saw some kind of movement, maybe a reflection—binoculars or something—in the second window from the east. It's got an unobstructed view of the doctor's driveway. I think it's worth looking into." As I said it, I really hoped I wasn't crying wolf. My condition had made me slightly paranoid.

"Let's do it. Go knock on the door."

"Why don't you do it?"

She nodded. "Stay behind me."

"Yes, ma'am." She walked up the sidewalk and hung a right into the very short driveway. The driveway was empty. I cut through the neighbor's yard and settled behind a line of bushes with a good view of the front of the million-dollar house. Two stories, green with white trim. Well-kept. Trimmed bushes. No lights on.

She knocked on the door.

As I have touched on already, the best part about not working for the government anymore was that I didn't have to follow the rules. Of course, as a US civilian, I was subject to the legal system, but if I didn't get caught, then I wasn't subject to anything. All of us contractors take advantage of that freedom. That's why the government hires us; we will break the law if need be.

Francesca knocked a third time and rang the doorbell. No answer. I came out from behind the bushes and began looking in windows. Nothing out of the ordinary. A very clean home, like the housekeeper had been there recently. Almost like they were about to sell it. I wound around the side of the house, still looking inside. A window on the east side was open.

"I got a window open over here," I said into my microphone. It was wide enough for someone to scramble out. Or in. I surveyed the yard behind me, moving down the hill. Nothing.

I ran back around to the front of the house. Didn't see Francesca. I tensed up and said her name just above a whisper. "*Francesca.*" And again. "*Francesca.*"

CHAPTER 6

The door was slightly cracked. She must have gone inside. I hoped she had. I drew my gun. Pushed the door and it swung open.

"*Fran*," I said. I wasn't about to expend any more energy on all fifty syllables of her entire name. "Fran," a little louder. I stepped onto the shining oak hardwoods; there were dog scratches evident where the sun hit the floor just right. I hoped there weren't any pit bulls headed down the stairs. A huge painting of Pike Place Market in the snow hung above the fireplace.

I listened closely. The floor creaked above. I raised my gun. Moved silently to the bottom of the stairs, then came around fast.

Francesca was standing at the top. Her gun holstered. "All clear," she said.

We finished our circle around the block. I turned to another channel on the radio and reported to Ted that all was good and we were headed back.

When we returned, Dr. Wilhelm Sebastian was sitting on the couch next to his wife. He was a good-looking guy, but he did his best to hide it. He should have shot his tailor in the foot. His pants were hemmed six inches too high. Scrawny white shins were staring back at me. He had suspenders on, too. I didn't even know you could buy those anymore. He looked way younger than I thought he'd be. Not even forty. Curly brown hair, only a few grays sneaking out near the ears.

He stood. "Pleasure to meet you," he said, with a Dutch accent.

"All mine." He shook my hand with the presence and calm of a man who sits in a rocking chair, smokes a pipe, and listens to Coltrane every night after work. Wiser than his years. He looked at me like he knew that, too, like he could dance circles around my mind. Like I was just a little peon in his world.

He gestured toward his wife, and she stood and shook my hand. She was taller than him. Prim and proper, long skirt with a blouse. Hair in a bun. Angular face, very little makeup. She looked smart. I didn't think Dr. Sebastian would marry someone with a low IQ. I shook her hand and we locked eyes. Then she turned to her two four-year-old boys who were fighting over a toy fire truck. "Come introduce yourself to Mr. Knox, boys," she said.

Ignoring her, they kept pulling at the truck. That turned out to be a big mistake.

"Boys!" she snapped, and I think it startled all of us. This woman had a temper. Through clenched teeth, she said, "Leave the truck alone and get your butts over here! Introduce yourselves to Mr. Knox." They stopped in their tracks and headed my way.

I shook their hands. As they walked away, Luan said, "Go to your rooms," and popped them both on the side of the head in a not-so-nice way. Both boys immediately broke into cries as they started up the stairs, and I didn't blame them. The woman had a mean streak. Dr. Sebastian didn't appear to like it, but he didn't say anything.

The local news was on, covering the budding protests. Seeing the news on television really was like stepping back into reality. I'd avoided it all for so long.

We watched some of the protesters driving in. The media was

guessing two thousand people so far. They showed video of different groups, signs in their hands, shouting. From what I could tell, the majority was the religious type, and though they're not supposed to be violent, I couldn't help but wonder if there was real trouble in some of those eyes. In twenty-four hours, we'd be driving right through them and know for ourselves. I had the feeling we shouldn't let the doctor go, let alone speak, no matter how much he insisted.

Ted nodded at me, and I said to the doctor, "It's time. Let's move you guys."

We'd already loaded up their bags, and we led them out quickly to the open doors of the Suburban. I rode shotgun and Ted drove. Francesca and our other guy, Will Dervitz, followed us in the doctor's Porsche Cayenne. We rode south toward downtown. Very few words were spoken.

As we drove along Elliott Bay, I stared off to the right over the water. A cruise ship was leaving the port, probably on its way to Alaska. Further down, a ferry was creeping out of the haze, bringing people from one of the islands that I couldn't see today. Seattle is funny like that. Once you get a clear day, you can see the lush green of Bainbridge Island across the bay, and you can see the majestic Mt. Rainier—covered in snow—rising up into the clouds to the south like a bridge to the heavens, and you can see the sharp peaks of the Olympic Mountains not too far away in the northwest. And you know you are in one of the most beautiful cities on earth.

Makes even a man like me want to believe there's a higher power. But most of the time, it's all hidden by the thick fog and low-flying clouds that get trapped in between the mountains, and you just kind of know that it's all out there. It's like having insider's knowledge of how lucky you are to be there. You know you'll see it all again one day soon.

We moved left onto Denny Way, into the depths of the Emerald City. I scanned for trouble, searching through the sea of people that all seemed to dress in gray, the color that most captures what Seattle is all about. Seattle camo, they call it. As we came to a stoplight, I hit Ted's leg and pointed. "Two o'clock." He looked.

A group of protesters were walking along the sidewalk toward the Convention Center, their signs held high. One man, with a full beard and a long white robe, eyed me. He walked with a slight limp. Could have been Moses. Once he saw that he had my attention, he held his sign out in front of him, making sure I read it. In red block print, it read: *Turn or Burn. God Only Has So Much Patience.* The man pointed a long, bony finger at me. I stuck my hand out the window and gave him a thumbs-up.

Seeing plenty more protesters on the way, we finally reached the Pan Pacific Hotel in South Lake Union. SLU, they call it. SLUT, if you're referring to the uppity trolley that runs up Westlake Avenue shuffling around the employees of Amazon and whatever other high-tech, super geek havens that were popping up around there. The soldiers of the corporate world—laptop in one hand, red eye coffee in the other—off to make the shareholders happy.

We pulled into the circle and moved the family into the lobby quickly, without drawing attention. The top floors of the hotel were apartments, not hotel rooms, so we already had keys and didn't have to check in.

We cleared the apartment and then led the family in. They weren't going to leave for the rest of the day, so we had some time to catch up and plan. Ted left Dervitz to guard the door, and the three of us went to check in to our rooms on a lower floor. We agreed to meet in the downstairs restaurant in an hour.

***

"Hey, sweetie," I said, taking a seat next to Ted in the restaurant.

"It sure is good to have you on board, Tofu. I knew you'd cave."

TURN OR BURN

"What the hell is the doctor thinking?" I asked, not taking his bait. "This doesn't feel good. He'd be smarter to leave it alone. Why even consider putting his family at risk?"

Ted adjusted in his seat. "I've had this conversation with him several times. He believes in this stuff."

"Enough to die for it?"

"Apparently."

The waiter brought over some pizzas, and we dove in. Ted had ordered a cheese one for me. I've gotten a hard time about being a vegetarian my whole military life. Hence my call sign: *Tofu*. But Ted had long ago given up trying to change me, and he didn't even attempt to make fun of me any longer.

"Hey," Ted said, "even if someone is stupid enough to try something, we'll get them. We always do."

"I hope that doesn't change. If it was my call, I wouldn't agree to this. I'd protect him, but I'd get him out of town. I wouldn't let him go tomorrow. I certainly wouldn't let him speak. It's not like security in there is that tight."

"It's tighter than you think, especially since the protests picked up. An army of cops will be there. This is invitation-only. Hard searches as you walk in. I think we're okay. Besides, part of the contract was escorting him tomorrow. If I had said no, he would have found someone else. If anyone's qualified to do it, we are. Hell, Dervitz has walked a couple presidents into situations like this. It's all about planning."

"How about his partner? This Dr. Kramer. Someone guarding her?"

"No. I offered to put together a team for her and she declined. She hasn't received any threats, so she isn't that worried about it. I actually rode up to her place in Green Lake to make the proposal, and she shot me down pretty quickly and headed out the door for her nightly jog around the lake."

I raised my eyebrows. "Sounds like she's being hard-headed."

"I'd say so, but it's not my business anymore."

"Where's Francesca?"

"There you go, Tofu," Ted said. "I had a feeling you'd like her."

"Hardly. A fiery Italian woman is the last thing I need in my life. She reminds me too much of my mother. How the hell did you end up with an Italian cousin?"

"My dad's brother flew in the Navy and was based in Rome for most of his career. Met an Italian bird. Had a daughter."

"Gotcha. Well, she's a damn handful. You should have warned me."

"You sure it's not you that's the handful?"

"I'm—"

"Heads up," he interrupted. "She's walking in the door." I didn't bother turning.

CHAPTER 7

Francesca sat down and immediately went for a slice. I said to her, "I hope you didn't clean up on my account. I told you what I thought, right?"

She finished chewing, then said, "You're a waste of space, *bambino*. No one thinks you're funny."

"I'm just establishing our relationship from the beginning. I don't want you thinking I'm like every guy with a shoulder holster."

"You've got some anger deep down, huh? I should take you outside and knock you around a little bit."

I shook my head. "Knock *me* around a little bit? Funny."

Ted laughed. "You'd be surprised. You wouldn't be the first."

"I'm all good," I said, looking at her. "I'd hate to embarrass you."

"You wouldn't come close."

"Damn, you're something. Mama must have told you every day growing up how pretty you were. Am I right? Her special little princess. You're such a cliché."

"*Sei un coglione!*" She took her glass of water and flung it at me. I jumped back in my chair and leapt up, trying to stay somewhat dry. She threw the glass at my chest, but I caught it. Then she looked at Ted. "I don't know why you brought this guy in."

With that, she walked out the door. I glanced over at the waiter, who was clearly enjoying the show. "That funny, big guy? Can I get some towels…please?" I sat back down. Ted was drying himself off. "Did I say something wrong?" I asked. "This is *exactly* why I hate working with women."

"You're real good with them," Ted said. "Real smooth. No wonder you haven't gotten laid since you were fifteen."

"Right. Funny how these warrior girls are all good with killing people, but then you pick on them a little and they girl up on you."

"Just let it go, Harp. Take a breather."

He was right, but I wasn't going to tell him so. I wish I was better at giving people the benefit of the doubt, but I'm really not. I dislike you until you change my mind.

And I guess this is the part where I try to analyze what clearly is a deep-seeded issue with women. I was a momma's boy growing up, believe it or not. She and I were really close, and losing her certainly broke me for a long time. So was it my mother dying an early death, leaving me and Pops to fend for ourselves? I know you can't blame someone for getting cancer, but the subconscious doesn't always work with common sense. I don't know what else it could have been. Never really had my heart broken. Hell, I hadn't given a woman a fighting chance to get into my life since high school, and we all know that doesn't really count. At least I recognized that I had some sort of issue. Isn't that the first step? Oh, to be normal again.

"Why don't you take a couple slices up to Dervitz?" Ted said. "He's probably a bit bored and hungry. Go bug him for a while. I'm already tired of looking at you."

I stood and patted Ted on the back. "Don't worry, Ted. She'll be okay by tomorrow."

"She better be."

TURN OR BURN

"Don't forget...you talked me into this. I told you I wasn't ready."

He shook his head. "You're better than this."

I walked out the door and took a breath, looking around. The Pan Pacific Hotel was part of a three building development. The other two were high-end condominiums. At the bottom of all three were stores and a couple restaurants. A Starbucks (shocker). Scraps Dog Bakery. Be Luminous Yoga, and that's Baptiste style, not Bikram. A salon. A chiropractor. A boutique where you can buy twenty-thousand-dollar coffee tables made of a fossilized tree trunk. Everything you need to be a yuppie. And there were yuppies everywhere. All walking around with their little recyclable grocery bags filled with beeswax candles and Omega-3 and twenty-dollars-a-pound organic blueberries from the Whole Foods just down the steps. All dabbling with becoming vegetarian or vegan. So trendy. Made me want to start eating meat again.

Back in the hotel, I stepped out of the elevator on the fifteenth floor. Will Dervitz wore his jet-black hair combed to the right, and he had a dimpled chin and a pointy nose. If he sharpened it some, he wouldn't need a knife to protect himself. "You getting bored up here?" I asked him.

He was sitting in a chair by the door. "You get bored doing this, people die."

"No doubt." The guy was not a comedian. I handed him the pizza. "Why don't you take a break? I'll take over."

"That's all right. Daly is coming up shortly."

"I got it. I'll wait for her. You haven't even gotten a chance to check in yet."

He took off, and I sat in the lobby section of the top floor. Twiddled my thumbs for a while. Though I don't like to admit when I'm wrong, I will do my best to make up for it. That's why I wanted to wait on her. A couple elevator dings got me excited, but it wasn't her. Yes, *excited* is the word. For some reason, I was starting to like her. I felt like not being mean to her anymore.

Fifteen minutes later, she came out of the elevator. She almost went right back in once she saw me. I raised my hand and did a half wave. "C'mon…" I said, standing up. "Can't we all just get along?"

"I thought Dervitz was up here," she said.

"I sent him back. Wanted a chance to talk to you. Pull up a chair. I'll entertain you for a while. Not much going on up here anyway."

"You don't get it, do you?" Her accent grew stronger with her temper. "I'll work with you, but we're not friends. You're a jerk."

"That's a nice way of putting it. Probably sounds more complimentary in Italian."

She sat and I sat down in a red chair opposite her. "I'm not a jerk. I come off that way, maybe, but I'm not. You have to give me a chance. No, I take that back. Give me a few chances. I'm not a jerk…I just don't make the best first impressions."

"Truer words have never been spoken. I have news for you. I don't need any more friends. You're good right where you are. Let's just take care of this family and do our job."

"Suits me." I didn't say anything else. We sat in silence for a moment, and then I started humming an old Irish number, filling the void.

"You're dismissed," she said.

I stopped humming but didn't move.

She pointed me toward the elevator. "Please go."

"All right, then." I rode back down to my room, wishing I had treated her differently from the outset.

I spent most of the night hating myself, wondering why I didn't always treat people the way they should be treated, wondering why I was such a prick, why I was so bad with other humans. I wanted to fix it, but as I had learned, change doesn't come easily.

CHAPTER 8

I was in the gym in the building across the circle from the hotel at 5 a.m. the next day. I did five miles on the treadmill. Turned around and hopped off, thinking I was the only one in there so early. I'd been in my own world and hadn't heard her come in, but she was on the other side of the gym, lying on the bench throwing some iron around.

I went her way. She wore very little other than some beads of sweat and some tight black material covering up the goodies. "Good morning, Ms. Daly. They let you off duty?"

"Hi," she said flatly, pushing up another set.

I reached over and grabbed two dumbbells. "Want to arm wrestle? I feel like we have some things we have to get past. We could settle it right here."

"Can we do this later? I'm really not in the mood for you. Another few days and we'll never have to see each other again."

"I guess that means no arm wrestle." I went over to the other bench and began to do some bicep curls. I looked up at the news and saw they were talking about the Singularity Summit. I turned on the sound and we listened to a Channel 7 newscaster telling people to steer clear of downtown, that estimates of people expected for the protests were in the thousands. Then they showed this woman preacher named Wendy Harrill jabbering about how evil these Singularists were, how they were trying to play God. I'd seen her on the tube a couple times over the years but had never given her words much of a chance. Harrill had been getting her fair share of fame over the past few days, though. That was for sure.

I turned to Francesca. "I don't think today is a good idea. I really don't. It's risks like this that lead to problems."

She didn't say anything. Finished her reps and stood from the bench. She grabbed some heavier weights and started on some squats.

I stood and watched her. "That's where you get those thighs. I was wondering." I smiled.

She put down the weights. "You want to get off my back, Knox? Let me get a workout in without having to listen to you. Please."

Francesca threw her leg up against the wall and started stretching. I did *not* notice the perfect form of her thighs all the way down to her muscular calves. And I didn't notice how hard she worked on her body. Know what I mean?

She switched legs. Threw the other one up against the wall. Again, I did not notice how agile her body seemed. I did not wonder what fun we could have together.

"Let's just start over," I said. "You had a chip on your shoulder coming into this thing, and I think if you'll just take a deep breath and think about it, you'll know everything is okay. You are not a target here."

"A target? You really are something, aren't you? What you don't realize is, I don't care."

"Oh, I think you do. But let's not let that get in the way of us."

That did it. Put her over the edge. "You're an asshole." And she left me there on the bench. She hopped onto the treadmill and pushed some buttons. In seconds, she was jogging her way to nowhere.

I'd had enough myself. Why couldn't I keep my mouth shut? *She's a lady! Treat her like one, Harper.* I went back to the locker room, stripped down to a towel, and went into the dry sauna for a while. Then I threw on a robe and headed out of the men's room.

Nearly ran into her in the hall. "Excuse me," I said.

She blew out a breath of air like she was extinguishing a burning car and kept moving toward the women's locker room. I bid her adieu and returned to my room. It was getting light outside. Beyond the fog and the clouds, somewhere out there above the sky of the Pacific Northwest, the sun was doing a little tiny something to tell us it was daytime.

***

At fifteen minutes before ten, we met in the doctor's suite. He was dressed in another pair of pants that barely covered his calves. He wore a pressed white shirt and glasses and looked very much like he could prove Fermat's Last Theorem in less time than it takes me to sharpen a pencil. Still, despite the geek in him, I noticed how well he carried himself. How confident he was. Like the way he dressed was a calculated decision in order to bring about a certain result. I bet he was a lady's man back in med school.

Even though she wasn't coming along, Luan Sebastian was well-dressed. I guess she was the type that didn't like people to see her any other way than clean, done up, and appropriate.

Dr. Sebastian was administering shots to the boys, something Ted had told me about. The entire family took shots on a daily basis and the contents were some kind of special concoction of minerals, vitamins, nutrients, and so on to boost their health. This doctor was quite hard-core. Frankly, I didn't see why anybody would want to add years to his life.

Ted was talking about who we should be looking for and the

doctor interjected. "You know," he started in his thick Dutch accent, "it is not just Bible thumpers that could be gunning for me." He spoke slowly and deliberately, with pauses. "Certainly anyone exploring possibilities apropos life extension is possibly upsetting the religious set. And that's who you'll see most out there today. But there are others that disapprove as well.

"You can start with the arguments against stem cell research—a similarly disturbing topic for some. A moral dilemma exists that has nothing to do with religion. They think toying with nature is a bad idea. Bioluddites. Eco-fascists. Anarcho-primitivists. Think Ted Kaczynski, the Unabomber. He was a Neo-Luddite." He raised his voice. "Some of these birdbrains think we should stop using electricity!" He lifted his hands in the air. "Pull the plug! Now there's a novel idea. They live in fantasyland! What these people don't comprehend is that *technology is coming.* It's a step in the evolutionary process. My friend William Gibson says, 'In the future we'll look back at the past and laugh at the so-called distinction between the real and virtual world.' I think he's right. And it's simply a matter of who gets there first. I hope it is us, as opposed to, say...China."

I liked what he had to say. Everything about this guy was smart, almost like he was more evolved in his own right. You couldn't help but feel like an inferior being around him.

After we discussed the game plan, the doctor kissed the boys good-bye and then went to his wife. "I love you, darling."

She nodded but didn't say anything.

He removed his glasses and looked her in the eyes. "I wouldn't dare let anything come between you and me watching our children grow. I'm in good hands. Nothing will go wrong. These measures are simply precautionary. I'll see you this evening."

He kissed her on the cheek, but she didn't seem very receptive. Talk about a fireball. This woman was making my mother look like a pushover, and that, my friends, she was not.

TURN OR BURN

"Okay, then," he said. "I'll see you tonight."

Ted and I escorted the doctor out of the building. It was the first time he'd left since we checked him in the afternoon before. We moved down the empty hall, two of us in front and one behind the doctor. We boarded the elevator. It stopped on the fifth floor. A woman with a briefcase stood waiting. She had on dark slacks and high heels and looked like she was on her way to her 10 a.m. Would probably grab a cup of burnt coffee on the way. I waved my hand and said, "Ma'am, you're going to have to wait until the next one. Sorry." She didn't argue.

We reached the bottom floor and moved with purpose towards the exit. Ted and I scanned the lobby, analyzing each person, noticing eyes, hands, movements, and gestures. Nothing seemed out of the ordinary. The bellman opened the doors for us. Francesca had pulled the Suburban up to the front. She was standing with the back door open. She'd cleaned up since the gym. Looked sexy in her simple attire. No heels. Women can't wear them in this business. You never know how far you might have to walk or run. I could see a little bulge in her suit jacket from her handgun.

The doctor stepped inside first, and I went in after him. Ted rode shotgun. Francesca drove us around the circle of the lot, weaving past a couple taxis, and then we were off. We'd analyzed the entire run the night before. Only a half mile to cover. Nothing, in the scheme of things. Everything sometimes.

CHAPTER 9

The clouds had finally parted. We'd only gone a few blocks in the armored SUV when we started to see signs of the madness. I did not like being in that car. Eyes were on us and I was in my head. Was I ready for this? Would I ever be? I'd been thinking that getting back into the action would help, but it didn't feel that way right then. Seeing the scene around me, and Ted and Francesca sitting up front focused on protection, I realized I didn't feel like one of them anymore. I felt like a foreigner and part of me wanted to say, *Stop! I have to get out. You need to go on without me.* But I wasn't going to do that. I had bought a ticket, and now I needed to take the ride.

There were all kinds of people, and they seemed to be everywhere. Some were chanting, others screaming through megaphones and waving signs and marching, all for their different reasons. As we suspected, and as I could tell by their signs and banners and shirts, most of them were motivated by religion. But I saw someone waddling through the crowd in a space suit. Another not far away wore a robot costume. It seemed others were there for the fun of it, almost like they were attending the newest Comic-Con.

On the corner of Seventh and Olive, outside of Blueacre Seafood, a group of people in neon orange T-shirts were standing together in a circle, holding hands. Their eyes were closed, and it looked like they were praying. These kinds of people covered the sidewalks and spilled into the coffee shops and fast food joints and out into the street, angrily shaking their fists and making noise.

I couldn't stand protesters. I wanted to grab them all by their necks and scream, "Go get a job, you pricks!" Or, "Occupy *this*!"

From what the doctor had told us earlier, the Singularity Summit had grown greatly over the past few years, turning into one of the hottest tickets in the country. What began as a get-together of a couple hundred had turned into an international affair with a growing list of VIPs. And now, this...

We moved as quickly as we could south on Seventh Avenue. I read some of the signs and banners. *Make the Wrong Choice and He'll Abandon You. Jesus Did Not Have a Computer. Don't Choose the Highway to Hell.* And then there were some that didn't have the religious message, like: *Hubris kills. Pull the plug.* That kind of thing.

The closer we got, the denser the mob became. The cops were in force, too, all wearing neon vests with *Seattle Police* on the back. Some were on horseback, weaving their way through the crowd. From what we'd seen yesterday, a block in every direction leading to the Convention Center was locked down.

Up ahead, I could see the barricade where they had blocked off the street. A thick line of SWAT stood with shields and sticks, ready for the crowd to try to penetrate. We just had to get inside. Looking left, I watched two men get thrown to the ground and cuffed by police. Others were circling around the scene, screaming and throwing things at the cops. Another traffic light stopped us. We were the third car back. Two blocks to go...

A loud boom.

We all whipped our heads back. A giant of a man was trying

to see inside our vehicle. I touched my gun, ensuring it was there. He started beating on the windows with both fists. I didn't think he could break the strong glass, but it wasn't worth the risk.

Francesca was driving, and she didn't need me to tell her to move. She held down the horn and started working her way to the wrong side of the road. Two cars had to stop and move onto the sidewalk to avoid hitting us. But she didn't stop, like we'd all been trained to do. When you're driving in that kind of situation, you must drive offensively. Don't give other drivers the time to make decisions. Make the choice for them. Make them get out of the way or stop. She didn't let up until we'd gone another block, and we passed through the last light before the barricade. Several other cars were in line to get in. We pulled up behind the last one and waited.

I shut down for a minute. That had really put me on edge. This voice in my head kept telling me I wasn't ready, but I pushed it away. I couldn't let Ted down.

I turned around and stared at the astounding sea of people and the great quantity of signs bobbing up and down over the mass. I cracked the window. A group was chanting, "Don't play God! Don't play God!"

The guards finally let us in after checking each of our IDs and running a dog around the car and a mirror under it. It was a good feeling to be out of that mess. If someone had been gunning for the doctor, it would have been easy to strike with some sort of bomb. We were okay, though. For now.

"There it is," Francesca said. The Convention Center came into view. Massive silver block letters along the front read: *The Seattle Convention & Trade Center.* The walls were made mostly of glass. A sky bridge reached out from the fourth floor and rose over the street to an adjacent building. The Convention Center covered two full blocks. Plenty of exposure. If I was the one trying to cause problems during the Summit, I could have had my way quite easily.

TURN OR BURN

Simply put, I had a terrible feeling about what was to come.

We rode down into the parking garage and wound our way to a spot three levels down. Lots of people that could have been clones of the doctor were working their way to the entrance. The real geek squad. All of them had probably memorized the periodic table before they could walk. The ones that everybody picked on during grade school who were now married to all the good-looking, smart women.

We followed the crowd, flanking the doctor, not relaxing for a single second. Ted walked several feet behind us, and Francesca and I took either side. We rode to the first floor, and each of us worked our way through a security line, much like you'd find at an airport. As we got up to the front, we handed the officer our guns and papers. He let us pass without dealing with the detectors.

On the other side, we were handed an off-white pamphlet. There was a quote on the cover by Raymond Kurzweil, who would be speaking later that day. It read:

The Singularity denotes an event that will take place in the material world, the inevitable next step in the evolutionary process that started with biological evolution and has extended through human-directed technological evolution.

Inside the pamphlet, there was a list of events and speakers, including biographies and descriptions relative to each talk. On the third page, there was a picture of Dr. Sebastian, and below him, a picture of his second in charge, Dr. Nina Kramer, who had straight blonde hair and fair skin—like she had some Viking blood running through her. She looked about ten years younger than Sebastian and was clearly in good shape. Ted had mentioned that she was a runner. She was standing next to their chimpanzee, Rachael. Kramer would be showing up later in the afternoon with the chimp. Their presentation, the one everyone was psyched about, would take place at four.

We proceeded to the escalators and rode up to the open third-floor atrium where everyone had gathered. The ceilings were multiple stories high. There would have been lots of light coming in through the giant walls of glass had the sun been shining, but of course it wasn't, so artificial light lit the mood.

As we reached the top, swarms of people moved toward Dr. Sebastian, like paparazzi after a movie star. Sebastian turned to Ted. "I will need my freedom. I don't want this to be a big deal. These are my colleagues and fans."

Ted nodded and the three of us dissolved into the crowd. The doctor immediately jumped into a lively conversation with a group of pocket protector types. It would have to be one crafty assassin to fit in with these yahoos.

I walked over to Francesca. With my eyes working the crowd, I said, "Good workout?"

She mumbled something in Italian I didn't understand.

In my best Italian restaurateur voice and with wonderfully exaggerated hand movements, I replied, "Okay, *bella*! Fettuccine! Lasagna! Parmigiana!"

She shook her head. The people near us who heard my rant looked at me like I was crazy. If only they knew. I guess I'd dug my own hole with Francesca. She'd started it and I couldn't let it go. But now I was getting on my own nerves. *Can't you keep your mouth shut?* My mother would have smacked me in the head if she heard that.

That didn't stay on my mind long, though. I had a job to do, and any of these people could have been the person we were looking out for. I hadn't worked in a while and my tools had dulled. I could usually pick an enemy out of the crowd with ease, but it wasn't so anymore. I'd lost some of my precision and confidence.

There was no excuse. I couldn't screw up.

***

TURN OR BURN

As the day progressed, conference attendees, Dr. Sebastian among them, followed their schedules and chose which speakers or panels they wanted to participate in. While protecting the doctor's life, I couldn't help but soak in the theories and beliefs coming out of the mouths of some of the great minds of our day. CEOs, inventors, doctors, scientists.

Not that my opinion mattered, but I was sold on what could be happening in the coming years. A period of time really could be coming soon, where the technological achievements would surpass anything we could imagine. One of the most interesting talks I heard was from Ray Kurzweil himself. Ted had mentioned him back on the vineyard. Kurzweil began his work decades ago by creating a computer that could compose music on its own. His belief was that this period of time, this event horizon, could happen as early as 2045, and that specific year was based on his thoughts regarding exponential technological growth similar to what Ted had already described to me. It was actually so simple that even I could understand it.

Yeah, I didn't doubt the Singularity, and oddly enough, I didn't dread it, either. Nor did the people who I heard talk that day.

CHAPTER 10

The last meeting before lunch was on the sixth floor, and it had collected quite the crowd. Many people had been forced to stand in the back and along the sides. Were they about to show the new *Star Wars*?

The media section in the back right was overflowing with reps from local and national outlets. The room comfortably held about two hundred people, but at least fifty more were squeezed in there. Each row was elevated above the one before and looked down at the table centered on the small stage. Five panelists sat there behind their name tags, looking back up at the crowd. Above the stage, a projector displayed the title of the panel: *How Living Well Past 100 Will Change Everything, From Health Care to Finance to Relationships to Faith.*

I was just blown away by the fact that people really wanted to live that long. It was easy to imagine that the human race could figure it out, just not *why* they would want to. Give me seventy, and I'm pulling the cord. Life ain't that good.

Dr. Sebastian had chosen a seat about halfway up, and he was waiting excitedly with his small Apple laptop resting on the countertop in front of him. Ted sat next to him, doing his best not to attract attention. I was at the top of one set of stairs near

TURN OR BURN

the door, Francesca at the other.

The moderator finished introducing the speakers, and people clapped with admiration. As one member of the panel began to address the first question, I noticed a thirty-something woman with dirty blonde hair looking around the room. She sat two seats away from the doctor. She didn't appear to be paying attention like the others, and I watched her for a few moments. She redirected her attention to the panelist currently speaking. A general rule of thumb in this situation is that you don't need to worry as much about women. It's mostly men who kill people. She was slightly questionable, but nothing to sweat about.

I reminded myself that the last thing I needed was to let my PTSD get the best of me. Make a move on this girl, and I'd be in the spotlight. I knew I could easily fall into the trap of pulling a few false alarms and getting scrutinized for it. Then I'd be scared to speak up when something went wrong. And someone might die. It was a balance I had to find, and a little confidence would go a long way.

I kept looking around as I half-listened to some philosopher type go on about how followers of certain faiths would have to reexamine and reinterpret their beliefs, just like they'd done when evolution became more accepted. My mind was attempting to wrap around that one when my eyes went back to the woman. She sure was fidgety. But she was trying not to be. Like she was trying to keep herself together. She was holding her shaking leg, attempting to keep it from moving. I didn't like it.

I took a few steps forward, passing a couple of the latecomers. I tried not to get in their way as I got a closer look. Now the woman had her right hand in her lap under the counter, and she was digging her middle fingernail into the cuticle of her thumb in an extremely aggressive, painful-looking manner. Those were the signs we looked for.

Was she just an anxious person? Had something happened to her earlier to provoke such a response? Or was she there to cause problems? Only one way to find out, and that was to get her up and out of there. Ask her a couple questions.

I felt the heat, though. I'd already appeared paranoid in the doctor's neighborhood when I thought I'd seen something in that window. Really didn't want to do that again. I'd been doing this for more than a decade, though, and I felt something inside of me. Some sort of agitation. Something was wrong.

I had to go with it.

I looked up at Francesca who was eyeing me from her position at the exit door on the other side. I nodded down at the woman and then made my way. Reaching the row where Ted, Dr. Sebastian, and this young lady were sitting, I slipped past the backs of two people and reached out for her. Her leg was now moving like it had a motor in it, bouncing up and down on the ball of her foot. The philosopher type was still waxing on, saying that new religions would surface as a result of the Singularity.

The woman had on a khaki jacket cinched tight by a large belt at the waist. Her hair was pulled back in a ponytail, and I noticed she'd been quite liberal with her makeup that morning. I tapped her on the shoulder, and it scared the hell out of her. She jerked back like I'd shot a gun next to her ear.

I said in a whisper, "Can I borrow you for a minute, ma'am? Real quick."

Her reaction wasn't comforting. Behind her bluish-green eyes, I could see her mind racing to make decisions. The muscles in her arms and hands and neck tensed.

I stuck my hand out again and motioned with two fingers for her to come.

The battle in her mind subsided, and she nodded and began to stand.

I knelt in the aisle so as not to be in anyone's way and waited for her to collect her things. Watched her carefully.

Then she jerked at the belt holding her jacket too quickly, and I started for her. A couple screams erupted as I threw my hands

TURN OR BURN

at her, grabbing her shoulders. By then, I really hoped I wasn't overreacting. My shattered ego couldn't have taken it.

I caught a glimpse of steel as the jacket pulled away from her body. She had a gun. I pulled her backwards and she fell into the seat. Her hand came up holding a little Smith & Wesson, and it was coming toward me. I grabbed her arm and blocked any further motion, and she fired the gun into the ceiling.

The room turned to chaos.

I slid my right hand up her arm to the gun and ripped it from her grip, then stepped over the back of a seat to get into her row. I tumbled on top of her and fought her swinging hands and kicking feet. My hand went instinctively to her throat with my free hand, the other one still gripping the gun. The woman's shirt had pulled up from her waist, and I noticed some kind of strange mark, like a branding, on the right part of her stomach. Funny, the things you notice in the frighteningly quick seconds of battle.

As I choked her into submission, a shot rang out, and blood splattered onto both of us. I whipped around as Ted collapsed to the ground.

"*Ted!*" I yelled. At that point, I had no idea how bad he was hit, but it looked like a headshot. Things were moving to quickly to be sure.

What I am sure about is that my hopes of ever being the warrior I used to be were obliterated in those few seconds. A paralyzing sensation overcame my body, and my mind went to mush.

In a haze, I looked up. Another woman was there, holding a smoking handgun. She'd shot Ted and was now aiming her gun at the doctor. Fighting with everything that I had, using what I'd learned over the past year, I found some control. No one else was going to die.

The woman didn't have time to pull the trigger again. I placed a bullet at center mass and her chest exploded. Her gun flew into the air as she dropped back against the table and slid to the ground.

"Stay down!" I yelled to the doctor, who was only a few feet away from me, lying on his stomach.

"Francesca! Where the hell are you?"

"Coming!"

Still holding the first attacker by the throat, I raised my head and looked around. Francesca was working her way through the last of the crowd as everyone fought to get out the door.

"Clear the room!" I yelled to her.

"On it." She began to move from row to row, ensuring there was no one else waiting for the right time to take a shot.

That's when I felt something wet dripping onto my arm, and the woman I was holding went limp. I looked down. She was drooling white foam. I felt for a pulse in her neck. There wasn't one. She was dead.

"Ted," I said, "you with me?"

He didn't answer.

"Ted, you okay?" Keeping my eyes peeled for more trouble, I moved on my knees toward him.

Half his face was missing. *No, he wasn't with me, and he wasn't okay.* One of my oldest and dearest friends was lying flat on his back, unrecognizable, blood flowing out of his dead body. I'd seen his brother the *exact* same way, and I could have prevented both of them from dying. *I could have fucking stopped it!*

A waterfall of rage and confusion and delirium dumped on top of me, and it was almost too hard to handle. My hearing and vision went first. Then the muscles in my shoulders turned to rocks, and my fingers locked into the shape of claws. God help anyone or anything that was close by, because I wanted to break and throw and kick and punch and destroy it all.

I finally let out a yell that shook the building. That release led me to black out.

When I came to seconds later, I was rocking back and forth.

TURN OR BURN

No, I told myself. *No, no, no. You get your act together. You are a soldier, Knox.*

Finding strength, I dug deep down and brought myself back. *The body obeys the mind. The body obeys the mind.* And it did.

I took Ted's hand and put my face up to what was left of his. "Say hello to your brother for me," I uttered. "I'm sorry. I'm so damn sorry."

CHAPTER 11

I returned to reality with sharpened focus. A soldier's focus. We had to get the doctor out of there. That's all that mattered at the moment. That was the mission. Ted was gone, and there was no bringing him back.

As cops poured into the room, the three of us worked our way out the door. Holding Dr. Sebastian's arm, I screamed, "Private security! Two female shooters down. There may be more. They're after the doctor here. I have to get him out."

Dr. Sebastian was in terrible shock, as anyone not accustomed to violence would have been. We had Ted's blood splattered all over our bodies. But once we were out of the room and working our way toward an exit, he said, "My family...please make sure they are okay."

"I'll call them," Francesca said, walking next to us. She dug the phone out of her pocket and dialed. "Dervitz, evacuate the family. Someone went after Sebastian. We will reconnect soon." She hung up.

We found a set of stairs on the other side of the floor and were able to disappear before too many cops got involved. We knew it was only a matter of time before someone stopped us and kept us from leaving. I couldn't have that.

TURN OR BURN

We weren't going to lose anyone else.

Breaking out the door into the parking garage, we found more chaos. A line of cars was trying to work its way to the exit as people ran by them, desperately searching for safety.

Francesca and Dr. Sebastian piled into the car. I checked underneath and made one circle around just to make sure we didn't have any surprises waiting on us. I was at about 60 percent of my old self, but my survival instincts were helping fight the PTSD. We had to get out of there.

I hopped into the driver's seat and got us moving. The cars were backed up trying to make their way out. I took a left and drove under the sign that said *Wrong Way*, and it worked. I noticed some other cars following me as I began to circle around the ramp.

"I need you to take care of my family," Dr. Sebastian said again from the backseat.

Francesca turned around to face him. "They're okay," she said. "Will is moving them, and we'll have you guys together very soon." He thanked her.

Francesca turned back around. In times like these, you don't notice the beauty. You notice the strength. No tears. No wailing. No confusion. No shock. A strong woman paid to protect. Francesca Daly was one hell of a woman, and I needed to put a little effort into respecting her. She was a soldier, and she was on my side, and I was thankful for it.

"What do you think?" I asked her, inching further into the traffic. "Probably need to get out of town."

"Assuming they're after the doctor, which we really can't be sure about, I agree with you. Where do you want to meet the others?"

"Get them on I-5 North. We'll figure it out from there."

We finally made it out of the garage and onto the main street. It appeared that most of the protesters had no idea what had happened. They were still everywhere, marching and shouting and holding up their signs. Truthfully, I wanted to shoot them all. A bunch of damn clueless, clock-punching commoners. They were no different than the two women back there. Ted was dead because of *them*.

Ten blocks away, we finally reached clear streets, and I steered toward I-5. My mind went to what had happened. Two female shooters. Were they after the doctor? Had to be. How had they gotten weapons into the building? And more importantly, why? This would be an FBI profiler's wet dream. Two young white females teaming up on an organized assassination.

***

Dr. Sebastian's children came barreling out of the other SUV as we pulled into the lot of a Safeway grocery store off an exit twenty minutes north of Seattle.

"Daddy, daddy!" they said, running toward our SUV. Luan Sebastian and Dervitz were right behind them.

At that point, I decided to call the FBI and ask them to take over. The taxpayers would foot the bill now. Not our job anymore. The Sebastians would pay us for services rendered, and the contract would be terminated. Free of the deep ties Francesca and I shared with Ted, Dervitz hit the road, off to work his next gig. *Bon voyage*, dude. We don't need you anyway.

I wasn't going anywhere.

CHAPTER 12

"I'm sorry about your cousin," I offered, as we got onto the highway headed back toward the Convention Center. I knew the lead detective wanted us back there immediately.

"He was your friend, too," Francesca said. I could hear the pain in her voice.

"Yes, he was. More than that. I owe him way more than that."

"You were the one who said it from the moment you showed up. We shouldn't have let the doctor go in there."

I nodded. "We shouldn't have let him."

"Probably. But we took the risk. Ted knew what he was signing up for. We all did. Casualties are always a possibility. I want to know what happened, though. I feel like we owe it to Ted to find out."

I was half-listening, lost in my own thoughts, thinking about my friend. When you're out on the battlefield, you're there for a reason. Something leads you there. Some people fight for their country, their honor, or their pride. Some fight because they find happiness in chaos; they need war. That one probably fit me best. That's why I'd signed up. Didn't have anywhere else to turn. Some are in it for the money, or sometimes it's just the only thing one knows. But once the weapons are firing and you're watching people die in front of you, only one thought is on your mind.

Survival.

If you're a good warrior, I believe it's not just your survival, but that of your comrades, too. That's all that matters. You and your team making it out alive. There's a connection beyond family. It's the comrades you're sharing a foxhole with that remind you that you're human, that you're not alone going through the darkness, the nightmare. That's a connection so much deeper than anyone else could ever know.

I remember times—countless times—when Ted and I worked reconnaissance missions in the desert, getting dropped behind enemy lines in the middle of the night and racing to dig hide sites seven-feet deep in the sand before the sun came up. The hide sites could barely hold two or three of us, and we'd build a canopy and let the wind cover it with sand, making us virtually undetectable, save the little air hole we'd cover up with a branch or whatever we could find. We'd spend three or four days together trapped in there in one hundred-plus heat, not showering, shitting into bags, collecting information on the enemy, and hoping they wouldn't discover us. You learn a lot about people when you go through that kind of hardship. Bonds develop.

Yeah, when Francesca Daly was telling me that Ted meant a great deal to her, I did know exactly what she meant. I was going to have to face his mother and father and tell them for the second time in my life that their son was dead. So I wanted to know what happened to him, too. How had two women gotten weapons past security and, more importantly, why? Why did they come into that building on a suicide mission to kill Dr. Sebastian? Why were they so against the Singularity or the doctor's research? Were there others involved? If so, I wanted them to pay. Ted would have done the same for me. He would have felt the same guilt that I did.

TURN OR BURN

Why did Ted have to die today?

We parked a few blocks away this time and began to weave through the dispersing crowd. The protesters had lost their momentum and many of them were headed home. As we'd heard on the radio, they'd already cancelled the entire Singularity Summit. The streets were littered with signs and handouts and other waste. The police were doing their best to bring an end to the day's disaster before anyone else was hurt.

***

"Why the hell did you leave the scene?"

"I had a man to protect," I said. "What would you have done?"

"Don't test me." Detective Coleman Jacobs did not frequent the gym unless the steam room was his only stop, and he proved that with a belly that had to be contained by a belt I felt sorry for. I'd never sympathized with leather until that day. A black man with freckles up high on his cheeks, he wasn't that tall, probably five-ten. His pants were cut extremely wide, all the way to his ankles, to the point where they nearly covered up the toes of his shoes. And his tucked-in shirt showed the perfect curvature of his stomach. He was standing there, his hands planted on his hips, on the fourth floor of the Convention Center, very near the room where everything had gone down. Where Ted had been murdered.

Detective Jacobs and I had to establish ourselves right out of the gate because I think we both had the feeling we'd see each other more than we wanted to over the next few days.

"Test you?" I replied. "I was acting in the best interest of the doctor, who *I* was paid to protect." I looked at Francesca, remembering my manners. "Who *we* were paid to protect, who was most likely the intended target. We had no idea what else to expect, so we made the decision to evacuate the doctor."

"All right, all right. I'll let it slide. I don't have time to play

Whose Dick is Bigger? right now, Mr. Knox. Though I'd probably win." He winked at Francesca. "I'm going to need you both to go sit with my guys over there and answer some questions. I'll be back with you in a little while."

"Sure," I said, deciding to warm up to him. He wasn't as much of an idiot as I'd thought. Maybe a jackass, but not an idiot. "Sorry for the hostility. It's been a long day."

"Well, I'm sorry about your friend."

"Where is he?"

"In a van on the way to the morgue."

I nodded. "With the two women?"

"Yep."

"How'd the other one die? Do you know?"

"Looks like she ate a pill of some sort, cyanide maybe, but we're not sure yet. She wasn't shot."

"No, she wasn't. How'd they get the guns in here?"

"Look, I've got a lot of work to do. Let me worry about the details on my own." He waved over one of his cronies, and he began to walk away. "And Mr. Knox," he said. "Ms. Daly."

"Yeah?"

"You two don't go playing cowboy and cowgirl. I know about you both. I know who you are."

"Don't worry about us. Just find out why this happened to our friend...please."

"That's why they pay me."

The uniformed cops separated us. I took a seat at a wooden table in the main lobby next to a younger cop dressed in a crisp blue uniform. He should have just worn a sign that said *Impressionable*. I was about to eat this poor boy up.

"Your name's Harper Knox?" he asked me.

"Yes."

"Jacobs said you're a Green Beret?"

"I was," I replied.

TURN OR BURN

"Hats off to you, sir. I had a dream of heading in that direction, but it never panned out."

I looked him in the eyes. "Any idea what happened in there? Who they were?"

"Oh, I'm not really supposed to talk about it."

"C'mon, now. I'm just curious. Ted Simpson was a good friend. And the finest soldier I've ever known."

"I believe you, but…"

"So I'm asking you to give me a few details to tell his parents over on Bainbridge Island when I go see them later today. I was there when his brother was killed, too. The information will not go beyond that. What happened in there?"

"I really don't know much," he replied.

I leaned in closer. "Anything will help. They will want to know."

"Don't get me in trouble."

"I will not."

He sighed, giving in. "I don't know their names. But I saw the bodies. The medical examiner found the same branding on both of them. Not sure what it was. No one is."

I had a quick flashback of seeing that mark on the woman's stomach. "Yeah," I said. "I saw it on one of them. You got a picture of it you could send me?"

"No, sir."

"Don't call me 'sir.' "

"Okay. One of them had a piece of paper in her pocket, too. You didn't hear it from me, but it said *Forgive me*."

"Whose pocket did they find that in?"

"No idea."

"How'd they get the guns in there?"

"C'mon. I can't tell you this stuff."

"Just tell me how they got the guns in there. I want to know how my friend died. If you can't trust a Special Forces soldier, then we should all give up now. Give me a break. Your leader over there will never know."

The officer looked around, making sure his superiors weren't nearby. "One of the guys working the security line helped them out. I don't know the details…they're holding him now. But it sounds like someone took his family hostage and forced him to get a bag to the two girls. That's really all I know. We just got word about this a few minutes ago."

That caught me off guard.

"That's all I can tell you," he finished. "Now, I really need for you to tell me what happened."

I spent the next ten minutes giving the young officer the details. Francesca was waiting for me when we finished, and we found Detective Jacobs on the way out. "We're going to take off," I told him.

"All right. Don't go too far. I may want to talk to you again."

"We'll be in town. In the state, at least. Has anyone gotten ahold of Ted Simpson's family yet?"

"Not yet."

"We're going to see them now. We'll take care of it. Please keep his name out of the news for the rest of the afternoon."

"10-4."

CHAPTER 13

We barely made the 5 p.m. ferry to Bainbridge Island. I drove the SUV on board, pulled the emergency brake, cut the engine, and rolled down the windows. The air was chilly. We were near the front of the boat on the starboard side, and we both watched the water and mountains beyond as the ferry pulled away from downtown. The sun was resting just above the sharp peaks of the Olympics that rose from the horizon like jagged walls protecting the Puget Sound.

But I didn't feel protected. Out of nowhere, the realization of Ted Simpson's death hit me like a club to the face. Any feelings of loss I had experienced before that moment were completely superficial. What started to come over me was horrifying. My stomach and chest cinched up, like someone had their hands inside of me, squeezing and twisting. I couldn't even take a breath. Images of his dead body permeated my visual cortex. With what little air I had, I said, "I'll be right back," and got out of the car.

Bent over, my hand gripping my chest, I made my way down the length of cars. I was light-headed and dizzy, and the cars around me began to spin. I started to fall, but I caught myself, placing my hand on a car hood.

The driver poked his head out the window. "Hey, man. You all right?"

I focused long enough to say, "Yes. Just feeling a little seasick." Then I kept moving, making sure I was far enough from the SUV. Once I knew Francesca wouldn't be able to see me, I went to the rail, nearly collapsing. It didn't matter if my eyes were open or closed. All I could see were the dead faces of Ted and his brother, Jay, morphing into one another. Even in death, they looked so much alike. And I'd been there to see them both take their last breaths.

As the Bay breeze cooled me down, I began to get a grip. I emptied my mind and let all my thoughts and all those images drop into the cold water below. *Let go. Let go. Let go.*

The tightness in my body disappeared. Wiping the sweat from my face, I put my hands on the rail and looked out toward Mt. Rainier for a while. More than anything, I felt shame. I know I should have felt overwhelming regret or sadness, and I did, but more than those, I felt shame. Nothing worse than feeling like you've lost what makes you a man.

I finally returned to the car. So much for all that healing. Sure, I could handle a helicopter flying over the vineyard, but I couldn't handle being back in the war. I needed Roman next to me, stat.

Francesca asked me if everything was okay, and I nodded. Then an awkward silence came between us, but I had no desire to fill it. My recovery had just hit a brick wall.

***

Pulling it together, I borrowed a pen and paper from a neighboring car and began to sketch the mark I'd seen on the woman with the dirty blonde hair, recalling it easily. It would have fit in a circle with a three-inch diameter. Three legs came out of a center point, all spiraling in the same direction, starting out thicker and growing thinner all the way to their curly tips.

TURN OR BURN

When I finished, I showed Francesca what I'd seen and what the cop had told me. "I've got someone who might be able to tell us more about it," she said. She took a picture of my sketch with her phone and forwarded it.

I turned on the radio. "Let's see if they've released the names yet."

Several stations were discussing the murder at the conference. According to the newscaster, the protesters were continuing to disperse but arrests were still being made. They referred to the deceased as the two female shooters and the male victim.

My brain wanted to toss out theories, but it was too early. I didn't want to fall into the trap of making assumptions. So, in an effort to distract my mind, I said, "I'm going to ask you a question, and this time, I don't want you to get the wrong idea."

"Go ahead."

"Where are you from?"

Francesca took a deep breath and turned the radio down. "Look, I'm sorry for reacting the way I did yesterday. In this line of work..."

"You don't need to explain," I said, appreciating our first real conversation. "I get it. And I'm over it. Where are you from? Tell me something about yourself."

"Rome."

"Georgia?"

"No. Italy."

Then she noticed the little grin I had put on, and she shook her head. With that accent, only a child wouldn't guess she was from Italy.

"My father was a fighter pilot and was stationed in Rome, Italy, until I was thirteen. He met my mother over there."

"Then where'd you go?"

"Back to where my dad grew up. Los Angeles."

"You're an L.A. girl? Uprooted at thirteen years old and dropped into L.A. That explains everything."

She rolled her eyes. "I was an L.A. girl for a *second*. I moved back to Rome to go to University and have lived there ever since. My parents moved back there once my dad retired."

"So I should say you speak good English, not good Italian."

"Of course. My father never let me speak Italian in the house. He wanted to make sure my English was impeccable."

"You're still an L.A. girl, though," I said. "You were there for the impressionable years."

"This is true."

"Are they proud of you?"

"Are my parents proud of me? Sure, I guess so. They'd probably rather I was a teacher. How about yours?" she asked.

"They would be, I think. Lost them years ago."

"Now, that explains everything."

"*Touché.*"

"Just kidding. That was rude," she apologized.

"I asked for it."

Francesca sat up in her seat some. "You're Army, right?"

"Barely. Beelined it to the Special Forces but got out after four years. Been contracting ever since."

"Aren't Special Forces types—especially Green Berets—supposed to be masters of working with people?" she asked. "Training allied forces and whatnot. Doesn't seem to fit your style."

"I'm not the first cynical Green Beret. I can turn on my likeable leader button if I have to."

"Is that right?" she laughed. "I think that button is no longer operational."

"You could say that." *At least I'm not diving in the dirt anymore*, I thought again.

She put a hand on my arm. First time a woman had touched me in a long time. "I'm just kidding."

The ferry captain came on the loud speaker and asked all passengers to return to their cars. We were almost there.

"Where are *you* from?" she asked. We were both enjoying the lighter conversation. "Tell me how they raised such a specimen of imperfection?"

I smiled. "The glorious mecca of Benton City, Washington. A little place called Red Mountain. Now famous for wine. I come from a family of farmers. Three generations of dirt diggers. I was raised driving a tractor."

"Was your dad in the Army?"

"No. Granddad."

"And how'd you turn into such an asshole?"

"Thanks for the compliment, Francesca. You really know how to make a guy feel good, don't you? I'm not that bad."

"Are you kidding me? You are unequivocally, undeniably, a monumental asshole. They made the word for people like you."

"Now, you're really flattering me. I'm going to blush."

"Oh, c'mon. You pegged me. I'm the little princess. Mommy told me how beautiful I was growing up. That's not too far from the truth. What happened to you?"

"I see…you want the sob story."

"Exactly what I want. Give it to me."

"Well, I was a real good kid growing up. Innocent, almost nerdy. Straight A's all the way through. Never got in trouble. Got a full ride to the University of Georgia to study veterinary medicine. The summer before I moved down South, my mom got sick." I paused, feeling the painful memory settling in my throat. It had been many years, and it wasn't getting any easier to broach the subject.

"Ovarian cancer," I said, trudging on. "She got bad quickly, so I postponed school. She died that October. My dad broke down, too, so I decided to forget about school entirely and stick it out with him. Help him heal. But three years later, I buried him. That's when I decided to join the Army. I left our cherry trees to die and enlisted. Then left the battlefield and returned to Red Mountain two years ago. Ripped out the orchard and planted grapevines."

"That's a very nice story, Harper. Not to be glib, but you have seriously damaged my initial judgment of you."

The ferry docked, and I put the SUV in Drive and followed the car ahead of us down the ramp toward Bainbridge Island. "Don't go changing your opinion of me yet."

That's when I realized she'd gotten me to talk way more than I generally like to.

***

The Puget Sound was dotted with lush and hilly islands all the way up the coast to Canada. Bainbridge was the closest one to Seattle and home to many people who work in the city but don't desire the fast-paced lifestyle. Of course, some move out there and never ride that ferry back. Like all the islands up and down the coast, there was a much more laid-back, bohemian style way of life ever-present there. The Japanese and the Filipinos used to farm berries on Bainbridge Island, but now it was an island of artists, writers, naturalists, marijuana enthusiasts, and the like.

I had not been to Ted's parent's house in two years. The last time had been right after Jay had been killed. I'd just returned to the States on my way to plant the vineyard and wanted—needed—to see them, to tell them how much it hurt me, too. Now, I had both brothers' blood on my hands.

I'd spent many evenings at their parent's home over the years. They were good, simple people and fantastic cooks. They'd always cater to my vegetarian lifestyle by tossing a rib eye on the grill for me, just in case I suddenly decided to up and change the way I'd been eating for two decades. They knew when to talk about the wars and when to leave them alone, and I liked that about them.

They owned a few acres of stunning hillside property overlooking Elliott Bay back toward the mainland. We drove up the gravel driveway and stepped out of the car. Those islands get even more rain than Seattle and the all the green, from the trees to the grass, showed it. I noticed Mrs. Simpson still tended to her garden on the side of the house. Llamas and horses were walking around in the neighbor's yard.

Ted's father heard us and came out of his tool shed with a red-handled shovel in his hand. Ted had told me that his folks worked in the yard more than anything else these days. Before that, he was a Boeing guy. He started walking over to us.

"What a surprise," he said with excitement. "I didn't know you two knew each other."

I didn't say anything. As he got closer, he saw it in our eyes. It's a look all parents of soldiers are always dreading. He'd already seen it once in his life.

The shovel fell from his hands into the grass, and he dropped to his knees and began to weep.

The fragility of life is nearly too much to bear sometimes.

II

"The central problem of an intelligent species is the problem of sanity."

- Freeman J. Dyson

CHAPTER 14

The cops finally released the names of the two women: Erica Conway and Lucy Reyes.

Once we got back to the mainland, we got onto I-5 and headed toward the home of Ms. Conway's parents. Her last-known address was not difficult to obtain. Francesca and I had built up a lifetime's worth of contacts in the business. She put in a call and had the address in minutes. Lucy Reyes's last-known was in Billings, Montana, so we thought the Conway's house would be a good place to start.

They lived in Tacoma, the city that shares an airport with Seattle and lies a little over thirty minutes south. A smaller version of Seattle, and a better or worse caricature, depending on who's talking. We found their home in the middle of a cookie-cutter suburban neighborhood just outside of the city. Twenty or so cars lined the street with several more in the driveway. Obviously, their friends and loved ones were there, comforting them.

No cop cars, which was good news. They'd probably already gone by. It had been several hours since the shooting. If Detective Jacobs was any good, he had to be way ahead of us by now. I did feel quite confident, however, that we'd beat him to the finish line, wherever that was. Incompetence runs thick through our justice system. That's why I make my own justice.

"I'll go in and feel things out," Francesca said. "I think this needs a woman's touch."

"Suit yourself. Let's see what you're made of."

"Watch and learn, soldier." She winked and closed the door. I watched her walk away, wondering how such a beautiful woman could be in this line of work. She seemed too innocent and too kind. Maybe that's why she was good at it.

I welcomed being alone for a little while. As I watched people come and go, I replayed the decisions and events leading up to Ted's death and found so many ways that I could have saved him. Even up to the last minute. Bottom line: I should have seen the other shooter. Two good men's deaths were on me now, and I was reminded once again that my life was cursed. Spend enough time with Harper Knox, get close enough, and die. My worth on this planet was negligible.

Forcing the thoughts away, finding strength in vindictiveness, I powered up my computer and read some news sites talking about the day's event. I found no new information.

Finally, saving me from myself, Francesca came out of the house and made her way back to the car. "How'd it go?" I asked.

"I got into a chat with one of her high school friends. He said the family hadn't seen Erica in two years. They'd had an intervention and Erica stormed out. Drinking and drugs. Not sure what specifically. He didn't know. But he said her best friend kept in touch with her a little. He pointed her out, but I didn't want to approach her yet. She was with Erica's mom. So I want to wait until she leaves and follow her. She was saying her good-byes."

Francesca turned the key and rolled down her window. And we waited. Exchanged a few war stories. In some act of defiance against growing up, she joined the Marina Militare, which was the Italian Navy, and after a few years someone at Blackwater recruited her and she started working the Middle East. She'd been working with Ted two years.

"We nearly crossed paths," I said. "You must have replaced me on his roster."

"Something like that. An upgrade is what he called it, if I remember right."

"Oh, I'm sure."

We watched people come and go for forty-five minutes. The air moved crisply through the open windows. Finally, Francesca pointed the woman out. Jamey Rush. She got into a BMW X-5, and I followed her out of the neighborhood. In a few minutes, we were back on the highway.

We followed her taillights all the way to Bellevue, a city near Microsoft. Money floated through the sewage over there. People pissed gold coins and I hoped it hurt. Jamey pulled into a high-end apartment complex with an array of cars that mommy and daddy gave their little precious ones, so that they could fit in with high society and marry who they needed to marry. I'm not judging. That's just human nature. Survival of the fittest. Keep climbing that ladder until you're looking down at everyone.

I parked and said, "I guess it's my turn."

"Go for it."

I waited until the woman was near the building, underneath the lights. "Jamey?"

She turned to look at me but didn't stop walking.

"Hi, Jamey," I said. "Could I please have a moment of your time?"

"Who are you?"

"My name's Harper Knox. We both lost friends today. I need your help figuring out why."

"I don't know you. Please leave me alone."

"Just five minutes. I need to ask you a couple questions. My best friend died five feet from Erica today. Just a couple questions. I'm a good guy."

She stopped and I caught up with her. Stuck out my hand and we shook. She was a big girl; not overweight, just big-boned. At least that's what her mother probably told her. Very warm eyes, like she might be the leader of her Young Life division.

"I'm trying to figure out what happened," I continued. "I believe Erica was a good person deep down, though I know she got into some bad stuff."

"She was a good person. You're right."

I looked at her for a minute, then said in almost a whisper, "What happened to her?"

"I don't know."

"You can trust me, Jamey."

She crossed her arms and looked around. "She comes from a really good family. I've known them a long time and never saw it coming. None of us did. She just changed one day. Started hanging around with some people I didn't like toward the end of college. This was back in Tacoma. She wouldn't even return my calls. I kind of had a feeling she was doing drugs…even tried to confront her a couple times. But that pushed us further apart."

"What kind of drugs, would you say?"

"I don't know everything, but she eventually told me meth. I don't even know how you do it."

I nodded. "Me either."

"And… and…never mind." She looked away and then down.

"What?"

"I don't know you."

"Please, Jamey. I don't want anyone to hurt anymore than they already are. I just need to know why my friend died. And I don't want anyone else to die."

"Isn't that the cops' job?"

"I've been doing this since you were in middle school. I want to help the cops. That's all. Sometimes they need it. Tell me what you were going to say."

"I think she might have even been selling herself."

"Why?"

"Comments she'd make. I tried to revive our friendship a few times. Tried to reach out to the part of her that was still real. And she would open up to me...sort of. I was able to have a conversation with the Erica I knew. She'd tell me I didn't want to know the truth. But I'd go over to her house and see bruises on her. The things she was wearing became more and more revealing. She'd hit the bottom and couldn't hide it from me. She stopped returning my calls. I gave up after a few months. She snapped at me the last time we talked and told me to quit trying to be her friend. So I did.

"Two years went by. She'd gotten in a pretty bad fight with her parents, and I think her dad basically disowned her. I heard nothing about her for a long time. Almost like she didn't exist anymore. Then out of the blue, I came home from work one day and she was here. Standing right where we are."

"When was this?"

"Oh, must have been six months ago. Around Christmas time. I know the holidays are sometimes hard for people who are lonely. That's what it seemed like. She started crying when she saw me. I asked her to come inside but she wouldn't. She was acting so paranoid, like someone was watching her or chasing her. It was weird, though. She looked better. Like she'd put some weight back on. Her skin looked better. I asked her what was wrong and she wouldn't tell me. I asked her how I could help, and she said I couldn't. She gave me a hug and told me she loved me. Asked me not to tell anyone I'd seen her and she walked away. I tried to follow her and she waved me away and started running. I ran after her for a while, telling her we all cared about her, and that we'd been looking for her. But she outran me."

"Did you tell the cops?"

"I told her parents but I think they'd given up."

"How about today? I'm assuming you told the cops all this."

"Yes. I told them everything. Of course I did."

I don't carry cards, but I wrote my number down on a piece of paper and handed it to her. "If anything else comes to mind, let me know. I'm going to figure out what happened to your friend."

"Thank you. Please let me know."

I climbed back into the car with Francesca. "Seems to be someone behind all this. Erica came to see Jamey six months ago. Made it seem like she was running from someone. Or that someone else was in control."

"What do you mean, 'someone else was in control?' "

"That's what we're going to find out."

CHAPTER 15

Anybody who has been in the Pacific Northwest long enough knows that if you are looking for tweaked hookers, you have a 100 percent chance of finding plenty of them in Seattle and Portland. Not that we were looking for Erica Conway—who would be on a slab at the coroner's office by now—but we were looking for her kind. I guess you could find those types just about anywhere, but if you were a prostitute and you wanted to make the best cash, Seattle—Pioneer Square in particular—would be the place. At least, it was a good spot to start.

Hunger got the best of me as we drove the bridge crossing over Lake Washington, so I swung by Via Tribunali in Capitol Hill. As I folded a slice and crammed it into my mouth, Francesca said, "No meat? Ever?"

"Not in a long time."

She shook her head. "I feel bad for you."

"It's the veggies that keep me looking young. I'm older than I look."

"Right."

"How old are *you*, Frannie?" I asked, knowing I'd get some kind of Italian fire thrown back at me.

"*Che palle!* Don't call me that. And don't ask a woman how

old she is. Didn't your mom teach you anything?"

"I love how you women soldiers have something swinging between your legs one minute and then turn into prom queens the next. Drives me crazy."

She rolled those big brown eyes. "Here he goes again. God, you're awful sometimes."

"You're a real peach yourself."

"I'm getting used to it, though. You're a little off in the head, but I don't think you're *all* asshole."

"Through and through, lady. Trust me. One hundred percent, certified, grade-A asshole."

"Nah...you just need to talk it out. Not with me, but someone qualified. Highly qualified. In fact, you might need a team of doctors. A highly-qualified team of doctors. All Harvard grads."

"Are you done?"

"You'll need to find the best in the world."

"Keep going," I said, taking another bite.

"NASA scientists."

"Really?"

"It may require military funding."

"I mean, really?"

"Actually, we might be going in the wrong direction. I'd say a team of engineers is all it would take, someone who could figure out how to pull the Washington monument out of your *culo*."

I shook my head.

"I'm done," she said, stifling her smile, enjoying herself way too much.

We found a Kinko's and made copies of the mark found on the bodies, plus some photographs of Erica Conway and Lucy Reyes that we'd pulled off the Internet. Then we drove downtown and parked in a garage off Third Avenue. By the time we were on foot, it was 11 p.m. The whacks were starting to come out of the alleys.

A few cops were strolling, but they were mostly there to curb the violence. They wouldn't know where to begin if they started going after misdemeanors. I watched one group of gentlemen passing around a crack pipe not twenty feet from two cops, and not a thing would be done. Then there were the homeless. Some on drugs. Some who appeared to be but might be clean as a whistle. The ones who were really out there were having long conversations with themselves as they limped up and down the street with no idea of what was going on around them, smelling of excrement and bourbon and sweat and onions.

Francesca and I walked side by side as we passed these types. "We'll kill them with kindness first," I said, "and see if we can get some answers. If that doesn't do it, we'll get aggressive."

"Thanks, Commander Harper."

On the corner up ahead, right outside of a smoke shop, a group of girls stood in a circle laughing. Very questionable motives. Lots of tights and skimpy garments. Heels that elevated them above the rest of the crowd so they could scope out their prey. Too much makeup, covering up the scars of a life doing what they knew was wrong. Profiling 101. *Go get 'em, Harper.* I turned to Francesca. "Watch this."

Francesca instinctively pulled away, a little grin on her face. As I approached the women, one of them looked me up and down and said, "You need something?" They all turned.

"I do, yeah." I pulled out the pictures of the girls and held them up in front of my face. "I'm looking for a couple friends. You ladies recognize them? I could really use the help."

A sassy one with blue lipstick took the lead. "Who are you? Get outta here. Why would we know?"

"Well...I think they were in your line of work."

She got a little closer. "'Our line of work?' And what is that, exactly?"

"I'm just looking for a couple friends. Trying to help them out. Do any of you know them?" The girls were kind of half-looking, but they were clearly scared of pissing off the sassy one.

"Get outta here," she said.

"Please."

"Go, or you're going to get yourself into trouble."

"Thanks for your time. You're a real asset to society. A pillar!" I raised my hand to the rest of them. "Ladies, have a good evening."

No one said anything as I stepped away in defeat. Francesca had a smile that might have upset me had she been a man, but her twisty little grin made me smile myself. Despite my best attempt at not softening, I couldn't help it. We had our first real laugh together.

"Nice work," she said. "Now I know why Ted brought you on."

"Why's that?"

"You're a charity case."

"God, you're a riot, Frannie. Roman comedy at its finest."

"You lack a woman's grace. That's all."

"Please. I'm sure there's soooo much I could learn from you."

"Oh, you're right. You are actually good to go. The perfect man. God's son."

We went a block south, and it was still more of the same. Gangsters, punks, trannies, hippies, hookers, trannie hooks, homeless, druggies, and then who I guess you'd call the normal people walking around checking it all out, like they were at the freak show at the circus.

Francesca spotted a couple of questionable women and said, "I'll be right back." She went over to them and started up a conversation. They seemed to welcome her. When she returned a couple minutes later, she had her smile going again. I was starting to see what the boys meant about every soldier under the president falling for her. I'd be damned if it was going to happen to me, though. *Shit. Shit. Shit.*

She came back my way. I did not welcome how she made me

TURN OR BURN

feel at that moment, with her victorious smile and her confident strut—this little game helping both of us forget about Ted being gunned down earlier that day. *Don't get all human on me, Harper. Don't do that. You're not like that anymore.*

I suppressed the smile before she could see it. Enough of that for the day. "What did you find?"

"Nothing." She pushed me. Quite aggressively. I caught myself from falling backwards. "But they talked to me," she continued. "Said they've never seen either one."

"Well done."

"I can teach you if you'll let me."

"That's okay. I'm good. They didn't recognize the mark, either?"

"No."

So it went like that for a while. After one or two more screamers, I started getting the hang of it. You get more bees with honey. That's what Francesca kept telling me. A little honey and some lies here and there. I got into one method that seemed to work really well. I started telling them that I was looking for the two women in the photos because one was the love of my life, and I had to find her. I wanted to marry her. The ones that bought it obviously hadn't seen the news yet. I was pretty sure by the next day that they'd all find out one way or another.

Francesca and I kept working our way south, all the way through the International District, near where the Mariners and the Seahawks play.

***

It was well past midnight when we finally got a hit. Of course, Francesca got it. Not me. I'd hear about that the rest of my life, I was sure. I knew she'd gotten lucky because she'd been talking to the same girl for a long time before she finally waved me over. We all sat at a picnic table. A bearded man slept happily on top of a broken down cardboard box not too far away.

The woman's name was Lana. I shook her hand, making a mental note to soak my hands in gasoline later. A streetlight not too far away lit up the scene around us just enough to make out her face. Her eyes were heavy with mascara, and her skin told exhausting tales of unhealthy living. She was one of the ones who kept Virginia Slims in business. Her hair was matted at the ends. I wanted to ask her when she had last taken a shower, but instead, I said, "Pleasure to meet you."

Francesca was on my side, sitting close to me. She said, "I told Lana we'd give her fifty bucks if she'd help us out. She says she knew them both. They used to work this area."

"They didn't go by those names," Lana said, "but it was them. They was my street gals."

I perked up. "Street gals…nice. What names did they go by?"

"Cher and Dolly. This one was Dolly," she said, pointing to Erica Conway. "I haven't seen them in a while…but they was good gals. Real good gals."

"What happened to them?" I asked. "Where'd they go?"

"Who knows? Maybe they took jobs with Merrill Lynch. Or ran for office."

I smiled. "I mean, where do you go in this line of work? Why would they quit?"

"Maybe they cleaned up. Maybe they run down south where it's a little warmer."

"So you stopped bumping into them both at the same time?"

"I think so. Wasn't paying attention that much. But they was chummy for a long time and then they was gone."

"How long had you known them?"

"Dolly, I knew for almost a year. I only knew Cher a couple months."

I slid a picture of the mark on both women's bodies and used my phone to illuminate it. "Both of them had a mark like this. Ever seen it before?"

"Only marks I saw on them were track marks." She grinned and we got a glimpse of teeth that weren't fit for a mummy.

"Anything else you can tell us, Lana?" Francesca asked her, taking over.

"Not much to say, really."

"What were their habits? Help me get to know them."

"They did what we all did. Tried to get men to pay for sex. Hope that you get lucky enough to spend the night in some nice hotel room."

"Did they get lucky often?"

"Dolly, probably more than most. Look at her. She's a little bit of a step up from the rest of us. She saw plenty of clean sheets."

"What about Lucy? Cher, I mean."

"Dolly had that child under her wing. They worked together sometimes, you know. Dolly would get the job and then make a deal to get Cher in on the action for a little bit more money. It's safer for the girls that way, if they're together. And more bang for the boys and their bucks."

"How often did they do a deal like that?"

"I wasn't their babysitter. I don't know. Maybe I saw 'em get in the same car together ten times. Hey, I'd say you got your fifty dollars worth. Hand it over." She stuck out her hand.

"Just a couple more," I said, noticing her filthy, greedy hand. "Did you ever recognize the same people or cars that were picking them up?"

"No."

"Okay, well we might come bug you again, if that's all right. There'll be more money in it for you." I handed her the cash and a slip of paper with my number. "If you happen to talk to anybody else who knows anything or if your memory digs anything else up, call me. Again, more money."

"I will." She was looking around, making sure her pimp

wasn't eyeing her.

With that, Francesca and I got back in the car. "Why don't we head back to the hotel and call it a night?" I asked. "It's going to be another long day tomorrow."

Truthfully, I needed more time alone to deal with my broken pieces. Once I got back to my room I sat at the desk for two hours, my head in my hands, working through it all, every muscle in my body tensed to the point of tearing.

CHAPTER 16

An angry Detective Coleman relieved me from a miserable sleep with a phone call at about 6 a.m.

"Domino's Pizza," I said, trying to will myself into having a better day.

"Harper Knox."

"That's me."

"Who the hell do you think you are? I'm talking to a woman down in the International District who has your phone number in her pocket. I don't suppose you know anything about that, do you?"

"Nope. I'm up here in Banff right now at the spa getting a facial." I rubbed my jaw, trying to relieve the pain from clenching my teeth all night.

"Smart-ass," he replied.

"I'm serious. Now, who are you talking about? Who is this girl?"

"I'm not going to listen to your bullshit. Stop now. I'm warning you. Don't get in my way." He started losing his cool. "If you continue to get in the way of my investigation, I will put you in jail. I don't care if you shoot Purple Hearts out your ass."

"In fact, Detective, I do. And let me tell you: those pins on the back, if they're not closed, hurt sometimes."

"This is your last warning."

"Can I ask you one question?"

"What is it now?"

"Did you ever figure out what that mark means?" I had to know.

"You have to be kidding me. I hear your name again, Harper, and my next stop will be visiting you in a cell. Good-bye."

In a robotic tone, I said, "Good-bye, public servant."

Then I lay in my bed for a few minutes thinking. The police obviously knew about Erica Conway's sketchy past. And I'm sure they knew about Lucy's, too, whatever that might have been. Some savvy reporter would have her story on the AP line soon enough. It had only taken Francesca and me a couple hours to learn quite a bit about Erica, so it really wasn't rocket science. But still...why? Why did they decide to break into the Singularity Summit and pull guns on the doctor? Still assuming it was the doctor they were after. Or was it Ted? If it was Ted, then mission accomplished.

And the other questions would most likely have answers soon. How did they know each other? Were they working with anyone else? Wasn't it strange that the two women, who you could have easily argued were morally absent, had some kind of serious problem with the Singularity? Or was there some other reason to go after Dr. Sebastian?

I spent ten minutes cross-legged on the floor meditating and then flipped on the tube. Maybe there were some overnight revelations. It took me just a few minutes to find CNN. No, I didn't care about some twenty-year-old celeb skipping out on her community service in Hollywood. A few tick-tocks later, they brought up the Summit. The journalists had been just as quick as the rest of us. First thing they showed were pictures of Erica and Lucy. And guess what? They were both prostitutes. They showed an interview with one of Lucy's old friends confirming the rumors that Lucy had been known to sell her body. Then they discussed Erica Conway. Meth, cocaine, and prostitution were her hobbies.

So there it was. Two hookers—two drug addicts—break into a high security conference and attempt to kill a leader in the field of Artificial Intelligence. Why did they care? Was it something much more personal? Had Dr. Sebastian known these two women? Had he done something to them? Or with them? Was he a client? I had a real hard time imagining the cute little doctor with his high trousers swinging by and picking up hookers after spending all day in the lab working on his Fusion Project. Although he did have some lady's man in him, prostitutes didn't seem like his bag. Or was it all as obvious as it seemed: that they were after him for what he was doing in the lab?

I needed to speak to Dr. Sebastian's wife again. We needed to talk more about that threatening phone call, and also learn more about his enemies. And it wouldn't hurt if I knew a little more about the Singularity.

Francesca knocked on my door. She was showered and ready to go. "*Buongiorno.*"

"*Bongo cheerio.* Come on in."

"You're still in bed?" she asked. "I thought you said you didn't sleep."

"Not much. I dozed off around four. Just woke a bit ago. Let me grab a shower really quick. Don't go anywhere."

I popped into the shower and began to scrub. Francesca came into the bathroom and started talking to me, and it was only weird for a second. *C'mon in*, I was thinking. But she started chatting with me like we were two guys in a locker room. "So I know what that mark was all about."

Lathering shampoo into my hair, I said, "Talk to me."

"It's called a *triskelion*, and it's been around since the Neolithic Age. Depending on the era and culture—the Celts, Neo-Pagans, Christians, Buddhists, et cetera—it can mean a lot of different things. The cyclical motion can signify motion or man's progress. The three legs can represent the cycles of life—you know, birth, death, and rebirth. Or it can refer to the phases of the moon. Or spirit, mind, body, or past, present, future, or even the Christian Holy Trinity: the Father, the Son, and the Holy Spirit."

"That really narrows it down. I wish it could have been something a bit more specific. Maybe a swastika or something."

"Well, who knows? This could just be something between the two of them. Like a tattoo that two friends get."

"Having it burned into your skin is a bit more aggressive than getting a tattoo. That had to hurt."

"No doubt about it. But I'd say everything about these two women is aggressive."

"I'm thinking this is some sort of gang work."

"Maybe so," Francesca said, walking out of the bathroom.

I finished up and met her back in the bedroom. Sat down on the bed shirtless. Francesca was at the table now, watching CNN. She muted it. "I'm sure you saw this. We spent all last night trying to find out more about them when we could have just sat around and waited until these guys had it."

"Yeah, well it's good to stay ahead. At least we made a friend, even though the cops got to her as well." I told her about my call with Detective Jacobs.

"We're going to have to be more careful," she replied.

"Dr. Sebastian has a lot of enemies, but what did hookers have to do with it? I can't seem to come up with any kind of logical explanation."

"Maybe someone paid them to do it," Francesca offered.

"But they had to know they weren't going to get out of there. Why would they do something so risky?"

"They might have been lied to. They could have been told there was an escape plan. I can't imagine those two girls were the smartest on the planet," she said.

"Francesca, that's awfully mean of you."

"Do you disagree?"

"Of course not," I said. "They were giving blow jobs to fat, dirty baby boomers that couldn't get any without paying for it. I'm not going to associate that with intelligence. Just saying it sounds like I'm rubbing off on you."

"Enough," she said. "Or maybe they thought they could handle some jail time. Could have been paid for it. Jail couldn't be worse than what they were doing."

"That's subjective," I said. "Don't know about you, but they were getting more than I was."

"Classy, Harper. Nobody screwing assholes these days? Shocker."

"Not this one." I stood and got my phone. "I've got an idea." I dialed a number I knew by heart. A guy I went to high school with. "Jason, it's Harper. How are you?"

"Oh, geez. Haven't you run out of favors yet?"

I pulled a shirt over my head. "I was just calling to see if you wanted to join my bowling team."

"Right. You know, saving my life more than a decade ago doesn't mean I owe you forever."

"You don't owe me anything. This is more…just friends helping friends."

"I'm going to lose my pension because of you."

"No chance. A friend of mine was killed yesterday during the Singularity Summit. And I'm trying to figure out why."

"Of course you are. I'm sorry to hear about your friend."

"Thanks. A Detective Jacobs is running the show."

"Yep, I know him."

"I'd love anything you can get me on him. But more importantly, I need to know what they have right now. What do they know that they're not telling the press?"

"Uhhh…okay."

"One more thing. I need a list of everyone that was arrested during the protests. Names and addresses. It would help me a great deal."

"What do I get out of this?"

"You still owe me, Jase. This is the last time—"

"I thought you said I *didn't* owe you."

"Please do this for me."

"Jesus. All right."

"Let's meet at that Imperial Lanes Bowling Alley on Twenty-Second. At ten."

Jason sighed. "Fine," he said. "See you there."

CHAPTER 17

First, we needed to go see Luan Sebastian. We left the hotel and drove across town in the rain, the kind just light enough that you can leave your rain jacket at home. In all the madness, I hadn't even thought about what was going on back at the vineyard. So on the way to the Sebastian's home in Magnolia, I checked in with Chaco. Roman was happy, but there were some problems with the tractor, and Chaco said he couldn't keep fixing it forever. Said I needed to buy a new one soon. I told him a new grape press was in line before a tractor. Ted had been right. Making wine eats cash. It might have been healing me, but now both my wallet and I had severe cases of PTSD. And I certainly wasn't going to get paid for what I was doing now.

Two FBI men in an unmarked sedan stopped us as we walked up to the Sebastian's house. I told them who we were, and they called Luan.

"Go right up," he said after speaking with her.

Luan answered the door of her home with an apron on. An ironed apron. Even in cooking mode, she was all nice and neat. Her hair was still in a bun. Perfectly applied makeup. "Good morning," she said. "I never got a chance to thank you for yesterday."

"Our pleasure. I'm glad we could help," I said.

"I'm sorry to hear about your friend."

"Thank you. We wanted to have a few words. We're trying to get to the bottom of all this."

"It's the least I could do."

"Thanks," I replied. "How's your husband?"

"He's fine. Back to work already, of course."

"How about your boys?"

"They're great. Playing upstairs. You guys come inside."

"We won't be long," I said as Francesca and I entered. "Just a few questions."

We followed Luan inside and took a seat in the living room. Something about "modern" always means uncomfortable. I was going to need a masseuse after a few minutes of sitting in their chair/contraption with a circular ottoman.

"Tell us about the threats," I started. "I know you've already spoken about them many times." And I'd heard about them several times from Ted, but hearing things straight from the source can often open new doors.

"Well, for the first one, we were all here. I was in the kitchen cooking dinner. The phone rang. No one else picked up so I got it after a few rings. I said hello. A man's voice I'd never heard before answered. He said, 'Those that interfere with God's greater plan must suffer in hell's eternal flames.' Then he hung up. That was it. That's when my husband contacted you guys."

"How about the others?"

"There were three calls before we changed our number. The first two were from the same guy. The second time...he quoted something from the Bible, but I was so shaken up I honestly can't remember what he said. It was similar, though; about flames and hell. My husband picked up the last one. He didn't say anything but stayed on the line for a long time. That was it."

I ran a hand over my beard. "Does he have any specific enemies? I mean, outside of the medical world. Anything not having to do with his profession?"

"I didn't realize he had a life outside of his profession."

She said it awkwardly, but I let it go with a little forced smirk. "Neighbors; the guy at the grocery store. Anything?"

"Not that I can think of."

"How did you two meet?" Francesca asked. She was on the couch with Luan.

"At MIT. We were in a lot of the same classes."

"This was grad school?"

"Yes, of course."

"What were you studying?"

"We were both studying chemical engineering at the time. He switched over to the biology department after a year."

"And you chose not to finish? I think I remember you saying that."

"I got pregnant. We did, I mean. So I took some time off."

"Were you ever going to go back?"

"Sure…that was the intention. I never found the time, though. Raising two boys was about all I could fit onto my plate."

Francesca said, "Can I ask you something a little more personal, Luan?"

"I suppose."

"Have you and your husband ever had problems with your marriage? Did you ever split? That kind of thing?"

"No, of course not. Sure, we've had our ups and downs, but we never split."

"Has he ever cheated on you?"

"No. That's absurd. He doesn't have time to."

"Nothing with his partner, Dr. Kramer?" I asked, just throwing out anything that could get a rise, thinking that there had to be some jealousy over the fact that Luan's husband worked so many long hours with Dr. Nina Kramer, this young Scandinavian blonde. From my experience—though I can see the women of the world shaking their fists at me—all women have a bit of insecurity when it comes to other attractive women. So it was a good way to stir the pot.

"Of course not," she said in a snappy tone. She didn't like that question. You see…as I had suspected, ladies.

"Luan," my Italian partner interjected, "Please, don't get upset. These are just standard questions."

"How about the chimp?" I asked. "Any possibility there?"

Francesca brushed me away. "Harper, please shut up."

"You ask me this because of the prostitutes?" Luan asked. "You think he knew them?"

"We have no idea," I said, jumping back in. "It just makes sense to pursue any possibility." She was a bright one, that Luan Sebastian. And oddly more outgoing than she had been in our past encounters. Perhaps nearly losing her husband had softened her some.

"I can assure you he has never had a prostitute in his life. They disgust him. Not to mention he is OCD about cleanliness. Despite what all these religious yahoos are saying—that Wendy Harrill woman on TV especially—he's a really good man. I wouldn't say he believes in God and Jesus Christ, but he is as spiritual as anyone I know. Whoever those women were, he did not know them." A little defensive, but I tended to agree with her.

"I hear you, Luan," I said. "I don't doubt your husband's character."

"Why don't you just ask *him* these questions?" she asked.

"As you can imagine, our questions are not welcome by the authorities. He's a little hard to get to at the moment without drawing some attention. I *am* going to find Dr. Kramer soon, though. You don't happen to have her address?"

She gave me the address in Green Lake and told me how to get there, which I wrote down on my trusty notepad.

TURN OR BURN

Then I said, "I know there are plenty of reasons, but I want to hear this from you. Why don't people like what your husband is doing? What's wrong with it?"

"Because of what it leads to, Mr. Knox. Once this technology goes into the first human brain, how far are we from putting whole computers inside the brain? Inserting terabytes of memory? How far are we from copying one's entire brain onto a hard drive? How far are we from mind uploading? Being able to take one's entire mind—the memories, the thoughts, the experiences, the knowledge, the individuality—and upload it all onto a hard drive. That's when it gets scary. One day, they're going to be able to hook you up to a computer and make an exact copy of everything that makes you *you*. Then, when your body dies, you will not." She looked at me and raised her eyebrows.

"So it's more like making an exact copy, as opposed to actually sucking out the mind from the body?"

"Right. From what Wilhelm told me, there would be two of the same thing, the exact same thing. And the new brain would grow just like the old one had."

"It doesn't sound like it would be the same person."

"There are arguments both ways. We've talked a great deal about it. Think of a Word document. If you save a copy onto a disc and open it on another computer and continue to modify that one after deleting the original, then is that the real document?"

"Perhaps."

"It is. It really is. You can see why this would upset people. If you were a believer in the afterlife, suddenly you must make a choice that we never had. *Do you want to die?* Or go to—" she raised her fingers in quotes, "'Heaven?' And if we choose to live on, would we do so in some kind of created software world, or would we create robot bodies that could be our vessel? *Then* what happens when we grow to such a population that we outgrow earth? Could we transfer everyone, via satellites, to some other planet? You can really get out there with your thoughts."

It occurred to me that they had spent much of their marriage discussing the Singularity. She was well equipped to discuss the topic at length, and showed much more than a passing interest.

"What if *heaven* was a virtual world that we create?" she continued. "Then it would be true, that you create your own heaven."

Was this really possible? Well, if I were living two hundred years ago, and someone told me about Skype, I would not have thought it possible. Look at military warfare. Men used to throw stones at each other. Not two hundred years ago, armies used to face each other in lines and fire their guns back and forth. Now, we fly unmanned drones and engage enemies with joysticks thousands of miles away from the battlefield. So, yes: I was a believer.

"I've been thinking a lot about who would go after my husband specifically," Luan said, "and I don't think he was targeted because of his work with Rachael. I think it was because he was the keynote speaker of the Summit. Because he represents this movement. Anyone involved in these kinds of technologies is breaking down what we grew up believing. There's a chance that fifty years from now, the only thing certain in life will be taxes. Death might just be a choice…carried out by hitting the delete button."

A chill ran up my spine.

CHAPTER 18

We arrived at the Imperial Lanes Bowling Alley just in time to meet Officer Jason Hartman, who I knew from my days growing up in Benton City. The year I went to Fort Bragg, he went to the Police Academy. Now, he was a cop in Kent, Washington, not too far down the highway.

About ten years ago, after not seeing him for years, I had run into Jason when I went out to run an errand while staying in Benton City at my parent's farm. I was driving over to the hardware store to grab some zip ties and came around a corner to find two cars had slammed into each other. One was on fire. I ended up dragging Jason out and saving his life. Complete coincidence. But I had been squeezing him dry of favors ever since.

I sat down in the shotgun seat of his little Honda. Jason was a stubby, short fellow. He was one of those people that you could never tell if he was in shape or not. He had a pudgy nose to go with it.

"You know," he started, "sometimes I wish you'd never pulled me out of that car."

"Sometimes I wish I'd climbed in there with you. So it goes, ol' buddy. What you got for me?"

"Detective Jacobs. He's good at what he does. Solved that raincoat murder last year. That guy with the axe."

I knew the one and nodded in acknowledgement.

"He's got a good record. I imagine he will beat you to finding out what's going on. Why don't you let him?"

"I serve my own kind of justice. Certainly don't trust someone else to do it. Besides, I've made promises to people."

He nodded. "I understand."

"So what'd you hear?"

"They obviously know both women were prostitutes. One you killed, the other died of cyanide poisoning. They know that at least two other men are involved, the two who held the security guy's family hostage. Jacobs is trying to find out more about them. They wore masks but we know they're white. Didn't hurt anyone. As far as Jacobs's next steps, he's looking deeper into both women's lives. That's all I could get for you…except this."

He reached under his seat and handed me a thick stack of papers. I looked through it. It had names, mug shots, arrest histories, and last-known addresses of everyone associated with the Summit the day before.

"There are 308 people on there," Jason said. "I don't know what you expect to do with it—not that I care, as long as my name doesn't come up. They'd have my job, no doubt about it."

"Have I ever done you wrong?"

"Other than stealing Debbie Hammond from me?"

"Man, you still haven't let that go, have you?"

"I never will."

We said good-bye, and Francesca and I went back downtown and found a coffee shop where we could look through the pages of the arrests. It was going to be a long day. It had been twenty-four hours since Ted was shot, and we hadn't gotten very far.

We sat at a small bistro table in the semi-crowded shop with cups of single origin, fair trade hipster java steaming in front of us and began thumbing through the pages. Three hundred and eight arrests. Most of them were out or getting out today. How the hell could we sift through this information and get anything useful? I began to read through my half of the stack carefully. I was particularly interested in those with longer rap sheets. Someone in this pile had to know something. Not that they would be willing to share what they knew, but perhaps we could get it out of them. These people were the most vocal against Singularity. They were the ones willing to spend time in jail over their beliefs. Perhaps even willing to kill for their cause.

After a while, I said, "I'm not seeing anything that immediately jumps out at me. How about you?"

"Not yet. Maybe we'll have to visit every single one of these people. Ask them questions."

"We don't have the time. There has to be a pattern."

"Then let's find it."

I nodded. "I'm really backing off the idea that this had something personal to do with Dr. Sebastian. Let's face it. He wasn't sleeping with these girls. It has to do with Singularity. Why else would they try to get him during the Summit? It's too risky—unless they're making a statement. And Luan is probably right. Sebastian was the target because of what he represented, not because of what he was doing. This is a group motivated to fight Singularity. It has to be."

"Right. This isn't two prostitutes and their two pimps getting even for some unpaid debt."

"Exactly what I'm trying to say. I think we have to assume we are looking for an enemy to Singularity."

"So, we've got an answer right in front of us."

"Yeah, someone here has to know something."

"Still," Francesca said, "it doesn't explain why Lucy and Erica are involved. What? Did they find God all of a sudden?"

"That or they were paid to do it. What other motivation could there be?"

"I can't think of any."

A homeless man pushed his way through the door, and I watched him for a moment. He must have finally collected enough change to get his caffeine fix. The man had a terribly hunched back and brought with him a tremendous stench that floated through the air like fresh cookies from the oven in an opposite world. When he saw me, he began to head my way.

He reached our table and said, "I was told to give this to you." He handed me a piece of paper.

I took it and he turned to leave. "Hey, wait a minute," I said.

The man didn't turn around. I unfolded the piece of paper and read the short note.

"Hey," I said, louder, unintentionally grabbing everyone's attention in the coffee shop. The man stopped. I got out of my chair and went up to him. "Who gave you this?" I asked, lowering my voice.

"Just some guy outside. He gave me twenty bucks. I didn't read it, man."

"What did he look like?"

"I don't know." The homeless man's breath was quite unpleasant.

Francesca came up next to us. "What's going on?"

I ignored her and said again, "What did he look like?"

The man shrugged his shoulders.

"Black? White? Red?"

"A white guy. Maybe forty years old."

"What color shirt?"

"Green, I think. I don't know, man."

I looked at Francesca. She was holding the files and ready to go.

"White guy, green shirt. He's probably watching us. Find him. Head south. Put his face in the dirt." With that, I calmly exited the coffee shop and stepped onto the sidewalk to take a look around.

TURN OR BURN

People that play these little adolescent games aren't used to playing them with someone like me. Whoever it was thought they could get some homeless guy to hand me a note, and I'd be so flustered that I wouldn't think to go after them. Or wouldn't think it was worth it. More often than not, in this kind of situation, the person responsible thinks they are safe in the background. Sometimes, they even hang around to watch what happens, perhaps to make sure I got the note or just to enjoy the show.

We were up on Fifth Avenue. Almost lunch time and the streets were packed. But I scanned the crowd. In the movies, you always see someone look around and then give up. In real life, you don't give up until you know they're gone. You at least put a little extra effort in. It should be common sense, but it isn't.

In the spirit of breaking laws, I jaywalked and started jogging, guessing a direction. It was almost like being a keeper in a soccer game guarding the goal during a penalty kick. The keeper has to make a guess as to which way the ball is going. Otherwise, his reaction time won't be fast enough. Sometimes it works. Other times, not so much. Certainly better than doing nothing.

Once I crossed the street, I moved right, still scanning the crowd, looking for a green shirt or anything out of the ordinary. Like any eyes on me. Taking another gamble, I hung a left and went down Spring Street. The hill dipped down to the water and I moved quickly. I was starting to lose hope but I kept going. *This guy is only human*, I kept saying to myself. He didn't fly away. The person who wrote that note had to be within a few hundred yards.

After a few more minutes, I dialed Francesca, hoping that she had the guy hog-tied on Fourth Avenue. No such luck. Oh well, it was worth a shot.

"What did the note say?" she asked.

"I'll show it to you. Meet me back at the coffee shop."

She was there before I was. I handed her the note. She read it out loud. "*Go back home, Harper. The two of you will leave this alone or die. Your friend's death was an accident. Consider this a peace offering.*"

"Doesn't sound like Detective Jacobs to me."

"Uh, no. It sounds to me like we're on the right track."

"That's what I was thinking."

Out of nowhere, a haziness came over me. The world around me began to spin. That all-too familiar feeling. The one I couldn't run from. I closed my eyes.

"You okay, Harper?"

I shook my head, barely hearing her question.

"Harper?"

I peeled my eyes open after a few more seconds. My vision came back. "Yeah, just...I don't know. I'm fine."

Gaining control, I looked around. Out there somewhere, someone was watching us. I could feel it. Behind some corner, someone had their sights on us.

"Let's head back," she said, certainly noticing I was off in some way—and oh, how embarrassing that was. I tried to keep the thought from festering.

We walked up the street. After a few steps, I got my balance back. My truck came into view around the next block, parked at an angle on a severe uphill slant.

The second we turned the corner, the truck exploded into flames. A thunderous boom shook the street. I instinctively jumped to my right, covering Francesca and slamming her against the concrete. As we hit the ground, I scrambled to get on top of her, protecting her from any falling debris. "Keep your head down!" I yelled. People everywhere were screaming in terror.

Once the worst was done, I slowly moved off Francesca. My truck was lit up from bumper to bumper; the flames reached twenty feet in the air. The windows were all blown out and the chemical smell of burnt rubber assaulted my sinuses.

I looked back at Francesca and touched her cheek. "Are you okay?"

TURN OR BURN

She nodded. "Yeah, I'm fine. Thanks for that."

I stood and helped her up. Then I jogged up the hill towards the truck. Francesca followed me. I looked for anyone that might have been hurt. The windows of a barbershop only twenty feet away had been shattered. The brick walls were black. I walked that way and looked inside. Several people were on the floor. "You guys okay?"

"Yep, everybody's fine," a man said as he pushed himself up off the ground.

Sirens began to sound in the distance. People on both ends of the block were staring at the scene. It was almost a miracle that no one had been hurt.

Unless that was by design.

"Jacobs isn't going to be happy about this," I said, staring at the truck, watching it burn, feeling the heat. "But I couldn't care less," I added.

"That's exactly how I feel," Francesca said. "Do we tell him about the note?"

"I don't think so," I said. "What do you think?"

"Definitely not."

CHAPTER 19

"So you and Francesca Daly were returning from having a cup of coffee when all of a sudden your truck blew up? Out of the blue…no reason at all."

"Exactly."

"You're so full of shit, Harper."

I was back at the hotel and had just explained to Chaco that we would not be buying a new tractor or grape press until I had a new truck when Jacobs called. After speaking with the cops and helping them fill out their little reports for the second time in two days, Francesca and I had walked back to regroup.

Jacobs screamed at me for a while, proving to have quite the temper. Then he said, "My threat still stands. I find you investigating this case, you will be arrested."

"Detective Jacobs. Sir. I have no interest in this case. The man I was protecting is still alive. Ted's death upsets me, but she who pulled that trigger is also cold and stiff. I'm good."

"That better be the case."

I hung up the phone and grabbed a shower, and then went down to Francesca's room one floor below. She'd done the same; her hair was still wet. She wore jeans, no shoes, and a tight white T-shirt. Very, very tight. *Hmm*. Some things you can't help but notice. She had a way of wearing men's attire and making it looking utterly feminine.

I raised the stack of papers with the arrests on it. "Back to work?

"Yep."

Her room was just like mine. A king bed in the middle. A table with two chairs by the window that looked out over the stores below. I closed the blinds. "No need to make it easy on them."

I gave her half the stack again. She sat on the bed and I sat at the table this time. "I really don't know what we're looking for," I said, "but we don't have time to talk to every single one of them. There's got to be an easier way."

We analyzed the sheets for a while. Most of the people had been arrested before. No violent crimes, save one. I wrote the offender's name down.

"Harper," she interrupted.

"Yeah?"

"I just wanted to say thanks again. *Grazie*. You can say all day that you were just reacting, but you still were looking out for me today. Thank you."

"That's what we do, isn't it?"

She nodded.

"Had you been a male soldier, I would not have done that."

"What?"

"You heard me."

"What are you talking about?"

"I can stand to see a man hurt but not a woman. My first objective was to protect you. Because you are a woman. It's something so deep inside of me I can't shake it, no matter what. Just like any man. No matter what other lives are at stake. It doesn't matter that I know you can take care of yourself. That's why I don't think women should fight. In the field, we have to worry about you hot ones getting hurt…raped. It clouds judgment."

"You're so full of shit. Don't lay your mommy issues on this. We add just as much value as any man. And we sign up for it. Don't forget that. We know what we're getting into."

"Well, you can't fight like men, either." I smiled at that one. Yes, I was getting under her skin, and that was really why I was saying it. I was being a jerk. There was something appealing about seeing her get upset. Maybe this was my way of flirting, though I still wasn't sure if I wanted to get involved. Not that she had any intentions of opening up her doors to me.

"You don't think I can fight?" she asked. She stood from the bed and came toward me. I didn't know how to react.

"What?" I held up my hands.

That's when it came. Full brute force. She punched me with everything she had. A full-on right to the cheek. No holding back. I dropped from the chair onto the carpet. It was a hell of a punch, actually. Then she kicked me several times in the stomach and ribs. Full throttle.

"What are you doing?" I asked, trying to catch her leg.

She stopped for a second. "You don't think women can fight? I'll kick your *culo* right now."

"You joking? I'm not going to fight you."

She kicked me in the stomach again and I lost my breath. "Then this is going to be fun. I'm going to hurt you."

"No, you're not." I pushed up to my knees and tried to grab her leg. Had it for a second but as I began to twist it, she slipped away. "I'm not going to fight you," I said again.

She came down low and punched me in the jaw. Blood hit the carpet.

"All right!" I said, raising my voice. "You're pissing me off. You don't want me to hurt you."

"I want you to try." Another punch. That's when I finally took control, caught her arm, and pulled her down. She landed a little harder than I'd wanted, but she didn't seem to mind. Holding her arms pressed down above her head, I got on top of her. We were both breathing heavily, and the climate suddenly changed. I was a foot above her, looking into her eyes.

"We done here?" I asked. "Can I let you go?"

She nodded ever so slightly and I released her arms. Her hand went up and I flinched, expecting another punch.

Instead, she grabbed me by the back of the neck and pulled me toward her. She pulled me down, pressing her lips to meet mine. Still over-the-top aggressive, we began to kiss. I felt the warmth and moisture of her full lips caressing my face. I could still taste the blood from her punches in my mouth. I have never experienced such a random juxtaposition of emotions. Desiring once again the vulnerability with a woman, and at the same time feeling the need to protect myself. I went with my primal instinct and pressed myself against her, closing in on her scent.

"I like fighting you," I said. There is nothing like kissing a woman who has just punched you. In fact, I'd never been punched by a woman before, so this was an entirely new experience for me. Not that I was thinking of any of that at the moment. I was completely present, in the state that the men in orange are always trying for but never attain. How can you truly reach some sort of thoughtless Nirvana without a woman like Francesca all over you, touching you, teasing you, pulling and pushing you into some netherworld?

"Jesus, lady. You know how to turn a guy on."

"Stop talking," Francesca ordered, like some commander in her own sexual revolution. She pushed me over, switching positions, taking control and forcefully slipping her tongue inside my mouth. Sitting up, she ripped off my shirt. My blood was running south. She kissed my chest as my pelvis throbbed and pulsated to the beat of her drum.

I noticed a comforting smile on her face as she started to slow down for a little while, taking in what had happened so far.

Where was this going to go? I hadn't been here in a long time...a very long time. I hadn't been with a woman in probably more than three years. I'm telling you, my mind had checked out. At the risk of sharing too much, I hadn't even masturbated in more than a year. Uh, yeah, I was bad off.

But this felt necessary—not that she (nor my anatomy) was giving me a choice. Wanting her badly was the understatement of the season. What was going on between us seemed very right.

I reached down and began to pull her shirt up and over her head. She pushed my hands away and did it for me, arching her back up and away from me, just long enough to get the shirt off and toss it across the room. This woman, Francesca Daly, was in the mood. And I liked it.

I wanted to get in past that white bra so badly I could have ripped it right off her body. I pushed it up off her large breasts, and they released into my hands. Dark, swollen nipples in between my fingers. I touched and kissed them, throbbing with a thirst for her. Helping me with my rustiness, she unclasped the bra and it fell.

She got aggressive again, kissing me like I'd been away at war and we hadn't seen each other since our wedding day. Well, the first part was true. I had been away at war. For a long, long time.

My mind—amazingly—began to wander. I started thinking about what this was all about. I felt too free and vulnerable for this to be real. *Francesca Daly, who are you to wake me from my nightmares?*

I could have kissed her for days, rolling around, exploring our sexual frustrations, wearing each other out. But the pants stayed on...and maybe for the best. I felt like I'd just been laid by the Rockettes, but our zippers hadn't even come down. I was breathing like I'd just won a marathon. At last, we collapsed next to each other on the carpet.

So there we were, two soldiers, having broken down, letting our human emotions control us. Something we're trained not to let happen. But I wouldn't have changed it. Our friction, all that fire building up between us, had led to this moment. Looking back on it, that moment had been coming a long time. It had been written into our lives from the moment she'd started up her attitude with me at the doctor's house in Magnolia two days earlier.

It was awkward trying to figure out what to do next. I felt like puppeteers had grabbed us both for a few minutes and had some fun, and now they'd abandoned us.

***

"I wasn't expecting that," I said, still breathing heavily. Francesca was on her back, her front exposed. Simply gorgeous. She leaned her head over and beamed her punishing, even torturing, brown eyes at me. The kind of eyes that seem like they might not really be human. Especially when you're the one lying on the carpet, looking deep into them from only six inches away; melting into them, being soaked up by them.

"What were you expecting?"

"I'm not sure. I don't think I was. Don't get me wrong, though. You just put a smile on my face."

"Oh, I did? I don't see it."

"Well, I'm smiling somewhere. Trust me. You are a game-changer," I said.

"Now don't start getting all attached. That was just a result of too much sexual tension in the midst of the loss of a friend. That won't happen again."

"Wow…when I finally wouldn't mind a little of the girl in you, you turn into a hardened veteran again. What am I supposed to do with that?"

"You're supposed to get up and get your eyes back on that paper. That was fun…now let's get on with it."

"Suit yourself." I stood and tossed her shirt and bra to her. "Put your clothes on, soldier. This isn't a brothel."

Francesca shook her head with a tiny little smile as she caught the clothes. While she put herself back together, I pulled my shirt on and started flipping through pages back at the table. Not that I could really concentrate. What the hell had just happened?

My phone rang shortly after. "Harper, here."

"Hi, it's Lana. From the park last night."

"Sure. Lana from last night." I looked at Francesca. She was sitting back on the bed, thumbing through the documents, acting like *that* hadn't just happened.

"So I talked to some people," Lana said.

"Yeah, I heard. Got a call from the cops this morning. They said you gave them my number."

"Sorry, honey. That's the way the street works. I'm not looking for trouble. What I *am* looking for is cash. Can we meet? I got something I didn't tell the cops."

"Sure...how about right now?" Anything to get me out of that hotel room. "You know where those hot dog stands are next to the Seahawks stadium?"

"Yeah."

"See you there in twenty."

"Bring cash."

I hung up, stood, and walked over to Francesca. "Want to come? She's got some info for us."

"Let's go."

An idea suddenly occurred to me, though, and I had to express myself. "If there's really not going to be another of what just happened," I said, "can we at least have a quick encore? I'd like to revisit a few things. I may have missed something."

"It's already in the history books. Forget about it."

"Did I mention I'm fascinated with history? Quite the historian, actually. Especially Roman architecture."

She rolled her eyes.

CHAPTER 20

Lana, the madam from Third Avenue, was waiting for us, almost with her thumb out. There were three hot dog stands with people gathered around, wishing there was a football game inside the massive stadium hovering above us. It was still raining but not enough to worry about a jacket. It was funny to think that back home, the vines were catching some nice ripening rays and seeing some ninety-plus temperatures. It was going to be a hell of a good vintage for me if I could get back to the vineyard in time to make sure nothing went wrong. And I'd almost gotten laid. My kind of year.

Francesca parked. We'd taken her Range Rover since my truck got obliterated. And I must say, she looked good driving it. I was trying real hard to ignore that fact that we'd been rolling around on the carpet earlier. As she said, it was over. Done-zo. Time to flip the page. I didn't like it, but after spending a couple days with her, I'd gotten to know how hard-headed she could be. Let me tell you, our relationship was terminated. Her hard head was as tough as my luck.

As we were getting out of the car, she grabbed my arm and said, "I can tell you're still thinking about it. Don't bother. We have a job to do. Don't make me regret that."

"Regret what?"

"Right."

I had a hard time believing she'd moved on so quickly. I hadn't loved in a long time, but in my youth, I did have a few educational lovers that had brought me up to speed with what women want. So, in other words, I'd like to think that I did know what I was doing, and I wasn't that easy to forget.

Oddly enough, Lana was wearing the same outfit she had on earlier: a short skirt with a tight shirt that showed the outline of ample breasts. She was chomping on some gum, and it was clear no one had ever taught her to keep her mouth shut while she chewed.

"Follow me," she said. "The girl I found is over there."

We went back toward Pioneer Square and turned into an alley. On the other side of a dumpster, there was a girl—and I mean *girl*—maybe sixteen years old, all whacked-out on something, sitting cross-legged on the ground and eating out of an Asian takeout box. She looked up as we approached.

"This is them, sweetie," Lana said to her.

We both said hello and introduced ourselves, speaking in some kind of super-compassionate way, almost like we couldn't hide how bad we felt for this one. She didn't have much meat on her bones. A wool hat covered up her eyes, and she was shy about looking up. Barely made any eye contact.

"Can we sit down?" Francesca asked.

The girl extended her hand holding the fork, inviting us into her personal space. A half a serving of sweet-and-sour chicken was in the box. The three of us squatted on the concrete facing her. The smell of her Asian food mixed with the unpleasant perfume of the garbage bin not fifteen feet away.

Francesca took this ball. Repressed, destroyed young women were not my specialty. "What's your name?"

"Jess."

"Lana said you might know our friends, Lucy and Erica."

TURN OR BURN

"Yeah, I know 'em."

"Are you aware they were killed?"

She nodded yes.

"We're just trying to figure out why. As you probably know, they were good people. When did you see them last?"

"How much cash you going to give me?"

"It depends on what you have to say."

"Why don't we start with something?"

Francesca handed over two twenties. Jess grabbed them like she was drowning and Francesca was handing over an oxygen tank.

"I'm going to need more."

I held up my hand. "Why don't you talk first?"

"It's all right," Francesca said, waving me off. Francesca handed her another two twenties. "There's more where that came from if you have something we can use."

"All right." Jess set down her box of takeout. "I used to see them a lot. We all knew each other pretty well. They were good girls, especially Erica. Lucy was kind of quiet, but Erica was real nice to me." She stuck a forkful of food in her mouth.

She continued. "They was always working up on the corner of Spring and Fifth, working that route, and they had a few regulars. I recognized the same cars. Then one day, they didn't come back. I figured they'd gotten a longer job. Sometimes guys take us for a week or more. That's what I figured, but I never saw them again. I always kept an eye on 'em because they were getting more work than most of us. I was jealous, I guess. Even us street girls lose biz in a bad economy. I guess men go back to screwing their wives, even though they know we'll take care of 'em better."

I pictured the worst. And I made the decision right there that this girl was done doing tricks. I was going to help her out, whether she liked it or not. Whether that meant tracking down her parents or putting her in jail, either way, I was going to get her out of all this. It just wasn't right.

She looked at me, and I got a good look at those blown-out, lost eyes. "Don't judge me. I can see you doing it. I'd rock your world, baby. You don't even understand. God gave me a gift."

"I don't doubt it."

"Don't even bother with him," Francesca warned. "You wouldn't enjoy it."

Jess smiled and I looked at Francesca, thinking, *what the hell does that mean?*

Francesca ignored me and said to Jess, "So did you see who took them that last time? Do you remember anything?"

"Yeah. I saw his face. Big, thick glasses. White beard."

"What was he driving?" I asked.

She blew air out, frustrated, like I'd asked her to give me a bite of her food. "Do I look like a car girl?"

"Call girl or car girl?"

"Please don't listen to him," Francesca said, dismissing me with a hand. "Do you remember what color? Was it an SUV, a truck?"

Shaking her head, she said, "It was a little car. Like a two-door something. It was green, I think."

We waited for more, encouraging her to talk with our silence, but she kept quiet and started looking around. Like someone was watching us. I turned too, wondering what was up. I didn't see anything out of the norm.

"What's up?" I asked. "You see something?"

She shuddered a little but shook her head no. In a much quieter tone, she said, "I think that's all I want to say. I want you to leave."

"Five more minutes," Francesca said. "I'll give you another eighty. We just want to know more about what he looked like."

She started getting up, leaving her food on the concrete. "I want you to leave me alone. I don't know anything else."

"Please, Jess."

"Leave me alone!"

"All right, all right," I said, standing up, too.

Then her head ripped back and her body fell hard. I never heard the shot. Her blood painted the brick wall behind her. I turned toward Francesca. She was pulling her gun. I did the same. Lana was running away, screaming.

Then, an overwhelming case of tunnel vision hit me. Too much for me to control. I completely lost all balance and thought. Started falling.

Next thing I knew, I felt Francesca pulling me behind the dumpster. I shook my head, trying to wake myself from this dumb stupor. Through squinted eyes, I saw Jess's body lying there. Her blood was following a stream down into a rut in the concrete.

The next few minutes were hazy. I found out later Francesca thought I was shot. I guess that's how I was acting. She felt for a wound but never found one. She slapped me hard, trying to bring me back. The shooter was trying to get us. Couldn't hear the shots, only the impact of the bullets against the steel of the dumpster and the cracked concrete below. I could feel my body wanting to go to the fetal position, but I fought it, trying to get a grip.

Francesca slapped me again. I started to come back. "*Get with it, Harper!*" she was shouting. "Get with it!"

"Yeah, yeah, yeah. I'm with it."

Another bullet hit the ground near us, but the shooter had no direct line. I saw Lana disappearing down the other end of the alley. I moved to a squat.

"He's just around the corner there. I think we wait him out. No sense running and giving him a shot."

Reality was coming back. I didn't know what had hit me. Like Ted had said, I had been under the impression that my PTSD would diminish if I got back into a war zone, but that wasn't the case. Stress seemed to be invoking some sort of involuntary reaction. I didn't know what the hell was going on, but I needed to get a grip.

"I'm trying not to fire," she said. "We don't need to leave any signs that we were here. They'll have a hard time finding evidence in the rain, but they could find a bullet."

"Okay."

"Hopefully Lana will keep her mouth shut, but we can't count on it."

We both tucked up against the dumpster, the dead girl near our feet. I fought some thoughts off about how maybe she was better off this way. That certainly wasn't my decision. But I knew we'd pretty much killed her.

We waited right up until we heard the police cars coming. Then we made a run for it. The shooter had taken off, too. You can't last long walking around downtown with a rifle during the day.

CHAPTER 21

Both of us had Jess's blood on us, enough to cause a couple people to take notice as we made our way back to Francesca's Range Rover.

"What the hell was that back there?" Francesca asked in an accusatory tone.

"What?"

"Don't waste my time, Harper. I've seen this before. What the hell happened to you? You could have gotten killed. You could have gotten *me* killed."

Not something I wanted to talk about. That was for sure. I let some time pass before I said anything. "There's a reason I don't work much anymore. The last few tours messed me up."

She shook her head, avoiding some kind of nurturer role. "What the hell are you back in the business for?"

"That's a good question. I missed it. I thought it might help. You pick the excuse. Right now, I'm wondering the same thing."

More silence.

"Well, I'd say we're onto something," she finally said, letting me off the hook for a minute. "We know what the man looks like. Sort of."

Trying to avoid the scars of what just happened, I said, "Yeah,

I wonder how far Detective Jacobs is from the same info."

"He'll be standing over Jess's body within twenty minutes."

"No doubt about it. A green car. White beard. Thick glasses. Not a lot to go on. It's something, though. There have to be more people like her out there."

"Right, but I don't want to end up on the wrong end of a murder trial. We're a little too close to the action right now...and you're falling apart on me."

"I'm fine."

She pulled into a self-service car wash on Elliot. I pushed in some coins and started spraying the car. Then, inconspicuously, I began to clean the blood off me. She did the same.

Back in the Range Rover, both in wet clothes, she said, "I think we keep beating the piñata. There's a reason Lucy and Erica didn't come back that night. And didn't come back, ever. Didn't show up until yesterday. Someone picked them up and..."

"And what?" I asked, agreeing with her thoughts.

"And paid for something long-term."

"I think that's a good possibility. But how does that turn them into murderers?" I started answering my own question. "Only two ways I see it. Just like we were talking about earlier. They were paid to do it. Somehow fooled into thinking they would escape or that their time in prison would be worth it. Or," I said, raising a hand, "considering the marks on their skin and the cyanide, maybe we're dealing with some kind of gang...or even a cult. A Charles Manson déjà vu. Maybe Erica and Lucy were brainwashed. Seems far-fetched, but how else do you explain the triskelion? I think we're looking at some kind of cult twist. Either way, this group is extremely dangerous."

"And we will hear from them again."

"I'm sure of it." I wiped away a bead of water rolling down my face. "Where do we go now?"

"A thrift store. I can make myself look like a hooker in ten minutes. I'm going to work the street tonight. See what I can find. Maybe I'll see or hear something. I'll try to find out more about this guy."

"I like your style, Daly. That's not the worst idea in the world."

***

I'll tell you one thing that was easy to find in Seattle: a thrift store. Especially in Capitol Hill. Like any city, Seattle is made up of neighborhoods and each one of them is different. Ballard was for the slightly more normal people who don't care too much about being close to downtown. South Lake Union was for the yuppies. Belltown and Downtown were for the socially aggressive. Green Lake and East Lake were for the well-to-do, and Fremont was for the laid-back creatives. And so on.

Well, Capitol Hill was for those that don't want to be judged. The ones that want to be free of any sociological divide. Let me tell you...you could be who you want to be. With that type of population comes a cutting edge vibe that I dig. Great cocktail bars, great vegetarian food, great people watching, and great thrift stores.

We found one quickly. Francesca worked her way through the racks and then disappeared into the dressing room. She took her time but eventually walked out. I turned and then did a double take.

"How do I look?" she asked.

I nodded, trying not to give too much away. "Not bad," I said. "That should work." In truth, she was stunning. Even in those rags. I suddenly wanted to cancel everything and go back to the hotel.

I drove this time. We crossed over I-5 back to downtown and pulled up near Fifth and Pine, the homerun of people watching. As she opened her car door, I said, "Keep in touch with me, Francesca."

"Okay, Papa. I'll be a good girl."

"I'm serious."

"Are you worried about me?"

"A little."

She reached over and pinched my cheek. "I'll be fine, *bambino*."

"Ted would want me to watch out for you."

"Ted would want me to watch out for *you*." With that, she disappeared into the light rain and coming darkness.

I was starving and decided to pop into this little vegan place back on Capitol Hill called Plum Bistro. Man, I was in the mood to eat some plants. After one heck of a good meal and a glass of the House of Independent Producers Merlot, I decided to go by Dr. Kramer's house. Maybe she'd have something new to add. From what Ted had told me earlier, she'd turned down protection, so she might be easy to get to.

I drove up the west side of Lake Union. Dr. Nina Kramer lived in a turn of the century home right across the street from Green Lake. I got close and started looking at street signs. It was dark by then. Right about the time I found her house, I saw the police cars. Something told me it wasn't a coincidence, and I was right. I parked nearby and walked over to the scene. Three police cars and an ambulance were on-site. Another three black and whites were pulling up. All the lights on top of the vehicles lit up the night. An officer was just finishing up marking the scene with yellow tape. I tried to get by and he stopped me.

I stood with the tape pressing against my waist and watched as they lifted a body out of the water. A crowd was collecting behind me. I saw the blonde hair and knew it was Kramer. I watched for a couple more minutes. Looked like she was wearing running shoes. They zipped the body up in a body bag and lifted it up into the ambulance.

I turned, shaking my head, thinking I was right...she was easy to get to.

***

TURN OR BURN

I went back to the hotel. Sure was a lot of death for one day. But I tried not to think about Francesca being in danger. She could take care of herself.

Sitting on the floor, I tried closing my eyes and locking into some mindful meditation, just like I'd learned from Thich Nhat Hanh's book, but it was pointless. Even he, the powerful Buddhist monk, might have had trouble at that moment if he'd been in my shoes. My mind was in overdrive and no amount of slow breathing and images of pebbles floating to the bottom of a river was going to slow it down.

I gave up and started going back through the arrest records. Each page had a mug shot on the top left corner along with name, last-known address, work history, and then the arrest history. What else could I be missing? Someone on those pages knew something.

I stared at each picture. At the arrests. Looked for patterns and reasons. Saw a few things that were certainly worth looking into. Wrote down some names. Then something smacked me in the face. I'd been so shaken up by the blood and death of late that I hadn't listened to what the young prostitute, Jess, had said. *Thick glasses. A white beard.* I was looking at the guy. One Jameson Taylor. He had a thick white beard and a cauliflower nose. He wasn't wearing glasses, but sometimes they make you take them off for the mug shot. I could see little marks on his nose that could be from glasses. *Could be something.*

Jameson Taylor. Born in Wichita, Kansas. Never arrested before. Released the morning after the protest on bail. "Are you my guy?" I asked out loud. "I think you have to be."

I thought about Detective Jacobs and wondered if he'd come to these same conclusions.

I had the last-known and it wasn't too far away. I needed to go pay this guy a visit. Should I wait on Francesca? No, I think not.

CHAPTER 22

"Hey, my name is Rich Donaldson. I'm so sorry it's late, but I saw your light on. I'm looking for Jameson Taylor."

The lady staring back at me from the front door of his last-known address looked at me with confusion. I was in Renton, WA, a little blip on the radar south of Seattle, standing outside one of the many circa-1972 brick ramblers I'd passed along the way.

"He doesn't live here anymore," she replied. She had to be pushing sixty and wore pajamas and slippers that were way too big. *Were they his?*

"And are you Mrs. Taylor?"

"Are you a cop?"

I smiled. "Absolutely not. I'm trying to find out some answers about an old friend...not Jameson...but someone he knows. I think." I tried to be as nonchalant as possible. "You're Mrs. Taylor?"

"I was. *Am*, maybe. We were married for a long time. Haven't signed any papers making the big *D* final, but we haven't seen each other in months."

"I'm sorry about that. I only need a few moments of your time. I'm trying to help a close friend. Like I said, Jameson is no

TURN OR BURN

way in any trouble, but he just might know him. That's all."

She had very warm, calming eyes. The eyes of someone who'd been through a lot but still knew what love was. The eyes I might have had once. "I can *try* to help you," she said. "Not sure that I can, though. Come on in."

I thanked her and followed her inside. She had cute, cottage-style taste. Five panel doors. Hand-painted white furniture. Lots of wood all over the place. Well-made stuff. I took a seat on a nice comfy chair by the window, which looked out toward the shed out back. She sat in the matching one. "That was where he spent most of his time," she said, looking out at the shed. "Carving, cutting, nailing wood. He can build anything."

I tossed out my best smile, showing teeth, like I had just stepped off a photo shoot for Colgate.

"So what's he done now?" she asked.

She really hadn't listened to me, had she? I thought I better get on her page and open up.

"Honestly, I'm not sure. Other than the fact that he was arrested yesterday."

She hung her head and sighed. "I shouldn't be surprised."

"Why's that?"

" 'Cause he's rewritten the book on the midlife crisis. What'd he do?"

"I'm not exactly sure, but he was part of the police round-up surrounding the Singularity Summit yesterday."

"Yeah, I've been following it. Doesn't surprise me a darn bit."

"When's the last time you saw him?" I asked.

"Let me think." She looked up into the air. "It's been months. He came by to get some things."

"So why would he have been at the Summit yesterday? Please tell me a little about him. What's this midlife crisis all about? Believe me, I'm not out to get him in trouble. Only trying to find some answers to what happened to a friend of mine yesterday."

"You seem like a nice person."

"I am, ma'am." *At least someone thinks so.*

"Then I'm going to trust you."

"Thank you. You can. Please help me."

"Why the midlife crisis?" she said, pondering the question with her eyes closed. "Why the separation?"

She opened her eyes. I gave her another Colgate moment, but just a quickie. "That would be a great place to start."

"Well, to be frank, I think he's lost his mind. I couldn't stand being around him anymore. You know that saying, 'a little knowledge can be dangerous?'"

"Sure."

"That's what I think of with him. Nothing against Jesus *at all*. I'm Christian through and through. But he started getting into things a little too much." As the words poured out of her mouth, it became pretty clear I was on the right path. "He started acting like I wasn't even worthy, quoting passages and such, telling me how to live my life. He started going to some new church and I didn't want to go. It sounded a little too aggressive for my taste. Three-hour services! Like I said, I'm fully religious, but I have things to do. I can't sit in a pew for three hours. I'd go crazy. My back couldn't take it anyway."

"Where was the church?"

"Somewhere in town, I think. In Renton or nearby. I honestly don't know. I think he said something about Hillside something or 'nother. Evangelical. Something like that. We were already having problems, so I think it was his way of escaping from home." She looked at me with a smile. "Would you like some mint tea? I should have offered."

"No, thank you. I just need a little more of your time. I'm sure you have things to do."

"Not really. But go ahead."

"How could I find him? Other than trying to find this church. Do you think he's still involved over there?"

"Oh, I don't know. He changes churches like I change shoes."

"Any other way I could track him down? Family or anything?"

"There's not much family to speak of. None that he keeps in touch with. He's not exactly loved by all." She tapped her fingers against the armrest. "There might be one way. If I was looking for him, I tell you what I'd do. I told you he loves working with wood. Building furniture and even carving smaller pieces. Like religious pieces. For as long as I've known him, he's been going up to this store called Jake's Woodworks up in the U District. I bet they could help you."

"Perfect." I stood and she did, too. We shook hands and she escorted me out.

Back in the car, I sent a text to Francesca, just to check in. It was ten o'clock. She'd be right in the thick of it by now. It was obviously too late to go by the woodshop or the church—I'd have to do that in the morning—so I decided to call it a night.

As the wheels of my mind turned, I glanced in my rearview. The oh-so familiar sight of police lights flashing. Damn it. This could get in the way.

CHAPTER 23

They had me locked in a cell within the hour. No explanation. No nothing. The cop had come to the driver side window. Asked me to get out. Slammed me up against the side, cuffed me, and tossed me into the back of his car, leaving the Range Rover on the side of the road.

Then he took me downtown to Virginia and Eighth, two blocks from the Pan Pacific. I had no explanation, but I did have a pretty good idea of what was going on. That's why I wasn't surprised when someone came to get me, set me up in an interrogation room, and Detective Jacobs came strolling in. He had way too much confidence. I didn't like it.

"Mr. Knox," he started, plopping down in the seat on the other side of the table. A fluorescent light beamed down from above and highlighted Jacob's fat cheeks and double chin. "Harper Knox. Ex-Green Beret. Born in Benton City, Washington. Now a contractor and a farmer. A winemaker! A wannabe Renaissance man. He thinks his shit don't stink." He looked me in the eyes. "You think you're so smooth that you can outmaneuver my team. Stay a few steps ahead. Oh, I don't think so. What you've done is caused a whole lot of trouble for all of us. Remember what I told you? Stay out of it or the next time we met would be at the jailhouse. You remember those words?"

"Is that a rhetorical question?"

"Why didn't you listen to me? Did you think I was joking?"

"You're going to have to slow down if you want me to answer all these questions. I can't keep up."

He raised his voice. "Your friend is dead, Mr. Knox. Isn't that enough to shut your fucking sarcasm up for one goddamn second?"

I didn't say anything, but I sure as hell didn't like him bringing Ted into this.

"This is your fault. You're the reason she's dead."

"She? What are you talking about?" My heart stopped.

"Francesca Daly. We just found her dressed like a hooker with her throat slit on Third. Probably where you sent her."

I glared at him. "You're fucking lying."

He squinted his eyebrows and lowered his voice. "I'm not lying. I thought they'd already told you."

I gritted my teeth. "What happened? Where is she?"

"At the morgue. She was dead long before we got there."

"You have to let me out of here. Right now!" I tried to stand and pulled at the cuffs that were locked to a ring on the table.

"Don't get so excited. You're not going anywhere right now. I don't need you trying to solve any more murders. Don't worry...we're on it."

I sat, trying to slow my pulse down so that I could think. "Who did it?"

"We don't know. Look, I'm not trying to be a dick. But I can't have you out there right now. I got an assassination attempt and three dead at the Summit, a car exploding downtown, a dead hooker shot with a sniper rifle, and a dead doctor. Now, a dead private contractor. I don't need some rogue Green Beret running around clouding up the water any more than you already have. I hope you understand."

Silence. The tunnel vision was coming back.

"I need you to tell me what you know. I need your help, and the sooner you start talking, the sooner you'll walk out the front door."

"You can't keep me in here."

"Watch me."

"I'll be out of here by the end of the day, and I'm going to have your ass outside of Nordstrom shining shoes. *If* I let you live."

"Nice, Mr. Knox. I can see you're coming around. I'm asking for your help. You don't need me to tell you that you have two dead friends that haven't even begun to decompose. I can't imagine you have that many more friends to lose, but if you want to keep more people from dying, then talk to me. If you want to sit in here for a few days, then do it. Fucking do it. Be a prick."

I looked at him like I was going to rip his throat out with my eyes.

He stood and said, "I'm going to give you a few minutes. Then I'll be back. I suggest you calm yourself down and get ready to help me out. I don't know what you have or know, but from looking into who you are, it wouldn't surprise me if you are getting somewhere. But now it's my turn. This is my investigation. So get ready to start coughing it up."

He walked out and I stayed cuffed to the table. Wanting to kill him. The door shut and I was stuck in the white room. I turned to my right and tried to look through the one-way mirror. Then put my head down and closed my eyes.

Francesca. Dead.

Francesca Daly. Dead.

I could still taste her. I could still feel her touch.

How had this happened? It was *exactly* why I couldn't fight alongside a woman. A man dies and it hurts. The closer you are to him, the more it hurts. But a woman...the hurt isn't the same. It reaches right into your heart, even those of us who barely have one. Like it's someone's sweet little daughter. You can almost see them in pigtails tied with pink ribbon, even when they're firing their RPK in the field. And if that woman happens to be someone you've exchanged some touches with, it gets even more complicated. Not that I could really zip it all up like that. It wasn't that easy. All I knew was that I'd just lost someone who I'd grown really close to in an extremely short amount of time. Maybe even fallen in—*no, don't say it, Harp. Not now.*

Being with her the past few days had felt really nice. Like, maybe we had something. She was a good kid. A good woman. In a life like mine, covered with blankets and blankets of darkness, she'd been a little warmth and light. Now, she was gone. As quick as she came. Come to think of it, just like any light in my life.

You get close to me, you die. I wanted so badly to wake my dead friends up and tell them how sorry I was.

My desire to find out who was behind this reached a new level of meaning. He who put a knife to her throat, whoever took her life, would pay with his own. In a very painful, slow way. Advice to those who've just met me: never, ever get on the other end of my appetite for revenge.

I stood and pulled at the cuffs bound to the table, yanking them back and forth. With fury, I screamed for Jacobs to let me out of there.

Nothing.

I sat back down and took some deep breaths. If my tear ducts had not dried up years ago, I might have cried. I couldn't even remember what that was like. There's something so powerful about all the pain and emotion of your life culminating in a burst of tears, each drop a concentrated bead of infinite release. How nice would it be to be able to shed a few?

And who the hell did Jacobs think he was, coming in there and slinging her death off his tongue like a jab against me? Like some sort of slight. He would pay for that, too.

***

I had my head on the table, trying to make some sense of life, when Jacobs finally came back in. It must have been thirty minutes. "You ready to talk?"

"Why'd they kill her?" I asked.

"I don't know. I'm hoping you can help me answer that. I'm guessing whoever it was didn't like her on their trail." He seemed less cocky and more sensitive now.

After a few moments, I said, "We found someone who knew them. Well, a couple people. Both prostitutes. We found one last night, named Lana. Then she introduced us to Jess. The one that was shot."

"Were you there?"

"Yeah. Yes, I was."

"Thanks for telling me. I know you had nothing to do with this whole shitstorm, and I'm sure I'd be doing the same as you if I was in your shoes, but...you know, I have a job to do and you aren't helping it. Believe me. I am capable and I want this. It's what I do. So did she say anything? Did you get anywhere?"

"Not much. Lana took us to Jess. We introduced ourselves. She told us that Erica and Lucy sold themselves as a package sometimes. And then she ate a bullet."

"That's it?"

"I'm telling you everything," I lied, hoping they hadn't also been following me when I went to Jameson's house. "That's all I know. She knew something but didn't have time to get it out. Now I need out of here. I need to see Francesca. I want to see her body."

"You'll get out soon enough. I need your word. You will not continue this running-around cowboy shit."

"You have it."

He stood. I was wondering how they had found me. Had there been an APB out on me and some random uniformed cop saw Francesca's plates? Or had they been watching Jameson's wife?

TURN OR BURN

As he reached the door, Jacobs said, "I'm going to need to keep you long enough to get what you know about Jess's murder. I'll send someone in."

I nodded.

"By the way," he said, "she's not dead."

I looked up at him. "What'd you say?"

"Your friend is fine. I don't know where she is but she's fine. We were onto her and tried to arrest her. She got away. Sorry I lied to you. I needed some answers. That's all."

"*That's all?*" I stood again. "You're telling me she's alive? *And you lied about it?*"

"Francesca Daly is out there somewhere, quite alive. Tell her that I'm letting you both slide this time. I will not, however, the next time. If I see either one of you again, I will do whatever I can to make your lives miserable. And you can see...I don't play nice. Don't kid yourself into thinking you're better at police work than I am. Don't waste your time. Have a good day. I hope I got your attention."

With that, he shut the door.

CHAPTER 24

She's alive. That mattered more than anything. Still, I didn't believe it until the knock on my door at 2 a.m. I smiled through and through. Man, I was turning into a softie.

When I'd gotten back to the hotel earlier, it hadn't taken me much time on the computer to find the woodshop Mrs. Taylor had mentioned, and not much longer to find the church. Riverside Church of the Woods. Not Hillside, like she had said. But it had to be the same place. Guess who the preacher was...the woman, Wendy Harrill, who I'd been seeing all over the tube preaching against the Singularity. How had I missed that? But I was certainly onto something.

Deciding I'd visit both places in the morning, I had crawled into bed and waited, passing the time watching the latest developments on the local news. They had barely mentioned Jess. All anyone was talking about was Dr. Kramer's murder. Prostitutes didn't rank as high as doctors on the sympathy scale. No details had been released regarding how, but the sheriff's office had confirmed that Kramer had been murdered. They had absolutely no suspects, which wasn't surprising at all. Of course, we all knew that whoever had been responsible for the chaos at the Summit was behind this as well.

TURN OR BURN

Finally, Francesca arrived.

I looked through the peephole first. She was still dressed like she sold herself for a living.

And she was holding up her middle finger. I twisted the knob and let her in. A big smile on her face. Of course, she hadn't been the one fooled into thinking their partner was dead. She had no idea what I'd just been through, and truthfully, I was embarrassed to tell her. Probably because I had some feelings for her that I wasn't comfortable with expressing. I resisted the urge to put my arms around her.

"Come in," I said. "Glad you're okay." Very matter-of-fact.

"What's that supposed to mean? Are you sleeping?"

"Not yet."

"You look like hell."

"It's been a long day. I think I got something. One of the men from the arrest sheets. You know the description Jess gave us? White beard, glasses. He was arrested yesterday."

"Nice work, Harper. I'm impressed."

"I went by his home. That is, his last-known. His wife said she hadn't seen him in months. Guy's name is Jameson Taylor. She put me onto a couple places where we can find him. We'll throw it on the agenda for tomorrow." I told her more details.

"You sound completely done."

"I'm okay. Did you have any luck?"

As she started speaking, I felt so thankful to hear her voice again. I could have listened to that Italian accent for hours. "Not a whole lot." She opened up the minibar. "I'm going to order some room service. You want some?"

"Sure. A veggie burger and fries, please."

"How did you make it through boot camp eating vegetables?"

"Not easily."

Shaking her head, she dialed room service. After ordering, she sat down at the table. "I heard they almost got you," I said.

"How'd you hear?"

"They picked me up. I just got out of a holding cell. Walked here. Your Range Rover is locked up somewhere. Detective Jacobs was all over me. He told me you were dead."

"What?"

I nodded. "Said they found you downtown with your throat slit."

She was silent for a while. Then, "That's not playing fair."

"I didn't think so."

"He wanted to know what we knew?" she guessed.

"Exactly."

"What a jerk," she said.

I sat on the bed. "Did you find anything on your trek through the underworld?"

"Not really. I met a couple girls who knew Erica and Lucy, but they didn't have much to say. Seems their death is the hot gossip on the street. Everybody is wondering what happened and nobody knows. Mouths are staying shut."

"Well, we've got a couple leads. A place to start."

"That's right." Francesca got up from the table and approached me. "You thought I was dead?"

"That's what he told me."

"How'd that make you feel?"

"How do you think?"

"Poor Harper." She sat next to me on the bed and opened her arms. "Do you need a hug? You're so cute."

"Cute?" I mumbled. "Give me a break."

She pushed me back against the bed. "I'm right here, *piccolino*. Alive and well. I'm flattered that you were worried about me."

"I never said I was."

"You did with your eyes. Don't get all tough on me now. Cute, innocent boy one minute; fearless Visigoth the second. I can play your games, too."

"Look what I've started."

TURN OR BURN

"I guess that means you get one more chance with me. Do you want that?"

"It might help some." How could I say no?

"That's not very convincing." She reached between my legs and took hold of me, and I grew in her hand. "I think he'd like some."

"We both wouldn't mind a little."

"Then take me."

I think that meant *green light*. I flipped her onto her back—hard and fast—and pressed against her body, moving up and down, and our tongues touched and danced around one another. She pulled at the collar of my shirt until the first button popped. Then she pulled the shirt over my head. I reached down, touching the soft bare skin above her waist, and then stripped off her clothes. The sight of her see-through black underwear ripped right through me.

There she was again, this Italian goddess, lying on her back, looking at me with big amber eyes, writhing like some gorgeous animal, asking something from me.

Then she was on top. She undid my jeans and reached inside. A woman hadn't touched me like that in a long time, and at first I shivered, right up through my spine. She rolled over on top of me and pulled my jeans and boxers off at the same time. Then she touched me more, and kissed me, starting at my shins and going all the way up.

When she reached my neck, I was on top of the world, barely able to control myself. Straddling me, she sat straight up and removed her bra. She brought her breasts up over my face and I kissed them, tasting her body. She wriggled out of her panties and got back on top of me. I slipped inside of her and she worked me like some sort of sorceress. She moaned loudly and pushed my limits, working her thighs in some kind of organic rhythm.

I didn't last as long as I wanted to, but who could have? She didn't make me feel self-conscious about it either. She took my hand and led me between her legs, and I worked my fingers in circles until she climaxed as well.

We laid there in silence, and she stroked my chest and whispered sweet Italian nothings into the air.

"What would you say if I told you I wanted to go about finding these people on my own?" I asked.

"I'd say you're confusing me with your girlfriend."

"I just—"

She put her finger to my lips. "What? You just don't want me to get hurt. I don't want to hear it. I am not your girlfriend. I am a soldier."

"I've never made love to a soldier before," I said.

"Was it everything you hoped?"

"Not bad for a first go at it."

"Not bad…right."

"It will get better."

"You don't get it, do you? We will get to the bottom of who killed Ted, and I'm not leaving until we do, but *that* will not happen again."

"That's what you said earlier. That promise lasted what…eight hours?"

"I needed to finish what I started. I'd say we got it out of our system. Now we can go back to work without any sexual tension burning up around us."

"Suit yourself, but I could go one more round in the morning. Just for the hell of it."

"Well, I know you couldn't go another right now." She took hold of the limp me. "This guy's not going to get up until a good night's sleep. Mr. One Hit Wonder."

I couldn't help but laugh. "That's probably true. But he could surprise you in the morning. You might see some things you've never seen before. Sleep here tonight. That will give you time to think about it."

"I could do that. A warm body would be nice."

TURN OR BURN

"A warm body…yep. That would be nice."
Then a knock. Veggie burger…better than a post-sex smoke.

CHAPTER 25

My eyes peeled open just before 6 a.m. Three hours of sleep. Francesca woke as I started to get out of bed. "Where you think you're going?" she asked.

"It's time to get up."

"Then get your butt back in here. I'll get you up, soldier."

She pulled me to her and turned my world upside down. Her hands knew just what to do, where to go. I'd felt more alive that morning, and over the past two days, than I had in a long time. She had a touch that reached deep down inside my soul.

Afterwards, I held her close and kissed her on the forehead. It felt nice. "I like you," I said. *And there it was!* I, Harper Knox, had just opened up to a woman—hell, to anyone—for the first time I could remember.

"Stop," she said. "Don't do that."

"Don't do what? Tell you the truth?"

"Just stop." She was quiet for a minute. She pulled away and propped her head up on her elbow. "I need to tell you something."

"Oh, wow. The mysterious woman wants to reveal herself?"

"I just want you to know for some reason."

"Fire away. I'm ready."

TURN OR BURN

"I'm engaged."

And with that, she fired one right to the bow of the *USS Harper Knox* that shook me to the bone. *Captain, we're hit! And we're taking on water!*

"No kidding?" I said, acting like she'd done nothing but mention what the breakfast special was downstairs. *They have a curry tofu scramble...I'm engaged...*

"Yeah," she continued, "it's complicated, but I'm supposed to be getting married."

"When?"

"Next June."

I laughed out loud, though I didn't think it was funny at all.

"Like I said, it's complicated."

"Uh, yeah, I'd say so."

"But I don't want you to think that I'm a cheater. I'm not a bad person."

I grinned a little and shook my head, ashamed at my stupidity, realizing that I'd been seduced.

"Where's your ring?"

"In my room."

"When's the last time you wore it?"

"On the plane on the way here."

"Interesting."

"Not really."

"I feel kind of used."

She kissed me. "I didn't use you. I was not planning on telling you about my engagement, believe me, but I didn't use you. It happened and I let it. And I enjoyed it."

"So tell me more. Might as well get it all out. Purge the demon."

"I told you not to take us seriously."

"No, I'm not. I'm just going with the flow. So what's the story?"

She sat up against the headboard, making no effort to cover

herself. "He's a Count in Palermo, Sicily. Well, his father is. He's in line to be. I think I told you…my father was a Navy pilot. He was stationed in Palermo at one point working with the Italian Air Force, and he became really good friends with this guy, the Count. His name's Nicolo Paraducci. Counts don't mean as much as they used to, but there's still a great heritage and respect bestowed upon them. He has a *palazzo* in Palermo that has been passed down through his family for hundreds of years. And his son, my fiancé, Salvador Paraducci, is in line to become the Count eventually. Through our father's relationship, we got to know each other and became very close. I was still in Rome, but we spent a lot of time together, going back and forth."

"This isn't exactly what I was expecting, but keep it coming. I feel like someone's reading me a Danielle Steele novel."

"Whatever. Then we went to University together in Rome and started dating officially. It was a big deal to his family and mine. His, because of the royalty and politics and everything. They, of course, loved me."

"Of course."

"It was a big deal to my family, too. My father was honored. He and Salvi's father—"

"*Salvi*? You're shitting me."

"Yes, Salvi. He and Salvi's father are best of friends and it meant so much to him. But my mother; oh, God. My mother grew up poor in Rome, and the idea of her daughter becoming a countess was a godsend for her. She's proud beyond belief. And if you know any Italian women, especially mothers, then you know what I mean when I say *proud*. This is not something to take lightly. So in a way, I was betrothed long before Salvi gave me a ring. This marriage was written in the books years ago. But I slowed things down when I joined the Marina Militare, and Salvi and I didn't see each other for a few years. It broke my mother's heart. She wouldn't even speak to me."

Francesca shook her head and looked off over my shoulder.

TURN OR BURN

"*O mio Dio*. My. Italian. Mother. I left the Marina Militare to get into doing contract work, and that's when Salvi and I ran into each other. Somehow I let myself start seeing him again, even though I knew I still hadn't gotten freedom out of my system. His family welcomed me back, and my mother and father were once again happy. The wheels began to turn, and it was hard stopping them. That's when he put a ring on my finger, and I didn't say no. *Couldn't* is more like it. This was six months ago. I moved back to Rome to live near my mother, and preparations were made. As you can imagine, a wedding in Italy is a monumental event, and when it is into a royal family, it's even bigger."

"But I don't love him," she continued. "Of course I love him as a friend. But I don't want to marry him. Sometimes I do, but I think it's all to make everyone happy. Everyone but me. I want to call it off but I can't. My mother would die. When I say that, I mean it. It would kill her. If I called it off, it would be in the papers. My mother would be ashamed of me. It would break my dad's heart too."

"So you're going to marry a man you don't want to marry?"

"That's the plan."

I sat up. "Not that I'm an expert on the subject, but marriage is between you and one man. It has nothing to do with what your parents think...or the media. We don't live in the Middle Ages anymore. Marriages aren't planned by mom and dad." I felt like I was pleading a bit and decided to back off some.

"Sure, it's that way here. You marry who you love. But it's still done differently back in Italy. Sometimes I think making my mother happy is more important than making me happy."

I nodded slowly.

"It's impossible for you to understand. You'd have to be Italian...it's true. So that's where I am. I've never cheated on him before, but something came over me. I was weak."

"How does Salvi feel about it?"

"He loves me. I'm sure of it. The idea of breaking his heart hurts, too. It would hurt a lot of people."

"If you're asking for my advice, you've heard it. But you're right, I'm not Italian."

A long silence followed. To think I'd let myself open up to her. This was exactly why I'd shied away from a relationship for so long. Who needed this? I didn't have a chance with this girl. I certainly didn't need any more complication.

I watched her naked backside move toward her clothes on the floor. Watched those legs, the muscles in her calves as they tightened, her hips sway, her breasts dip as she reached for her shirt. I thought to myself how we'd never be intimate again.

"So that's it, huh?" I asked. "Between you and me, I mean."

"That's it."

"Well, it was fun. Do you take a check?"

She glared at me. "Not funny." Then she pulled the shirt over her head. "Now, what's the plan today? I don't suppose you want to heed Detective Jacobs's warning and stay away, do you?"

"Not at all. I want it now more than ever."

"Then clean yourself up and meet me in the lobby in twenty. *Arrivederci.*"

***

I stood in front of the mirror for a while. That's what I get for trying to become human again. I wasn't right for it.

I shook my head, then lathered up and ran a razor over my face. My thoughts went to Ted. He had to know his dangerous little cousin would cause some problems. I couldn't believe he didn't tell me about her marriage. He had to have known.

I missed that bastard. Teddy. We'd had some fine times together, whether it was buried in a trench or pushed up to a bar in some no-name country drinking the local lagers and banging

TURN OR BURN

down enough shots of liquor to make your hair fall out. Literally. We were invincible, watching people die all around us. It could never be you, until it is. Now, Francesca's story reminded me even more that there was nothing bulletproof about me. We're all easy to hurt. We're all so vulnerable.

CHAPTER 26

Still in a towel, I walked up to the blinds and opened them part way. If someone had been waiting to snipe me all night, he had his chance now.

It was the first day of June, and you wouldn't have known it. I could see the trees getting blown around down below. The yuppies were in their North Face Gor-Tex jackets and Patagonia beanies, so I knew it was cold. The rain had stopped, and a bit—a wee, wee bit—of blue sky was trying to emerge, but it was still dismal outside.

I looked at the Space Needle, the tower built for the 1962 World's Fair and the defining characteristic of the Seattle skyline. An exquisite piece of Northwest architecture and one that conjures up great memories of my childhood. Up until my mother was sick, we'd eaten up there at the top of the Needle every year for probably twenty years, on my father's birthday. Like I mentioned, we were simple folk and this was one of the highlights growing up.

The restaurant is at the top of a long elevator ride, and it revolves. It takes about forty-five minutes to go all the way around, so by the time you finish dinner—assuming it's one of those few clear days you hope for—you can see a good chunk of Washington State. It was jaw-dropping and extra special for a kid growing up on a farm.

Thinking *better safe than sorry*, I closed the blinds and put some clothes on. My standard jeans, button-up, and a black corduroy blazer to cover up my shoulder holster, and some leather shoes that were long past needing to see the cobbler.

The elevator stopped at Francesca's floor, and there she was, ready for the day. "Good timing," I said.

I got the bellhop to hail a cab and we were off. Thirty minutes later, we were in her Rover on our way to Jake's Woodworks in the U District, meaning the University District, the home of the UW Huskies. It's not ten minutes from downtown but has a character all it's own, something that the young and ambitious bring. The Huskies stadium was right on the water, just a few blocks down. On game day, people tie their boats up at the marina and walk right in.

We found a metered spot on Forty-Fifth, in the heart of the U District. The summer students were crossing the streets with their backpacks and eager minds. We weaved past them for two blocks until we reached the address. *Jake's Woodworks* was etched on the glass door. The place looked like it had been there longer than the University. Being the true gentleman that I was, I opened the door for my lady and followed her in. Pipe smoke hit my nostrils. Two men were behind a long counter, tugging on tobacco. A customer was examining some knives behind the glass.

"Can we help you?" one of them said. He was wearing overalls and flannel.

Pipe-smoking woodworkers were my cup of tea. "I think so," I said. "I'm looking for a guy named Jameson Taylor. He's an old friend of mine and his wife—well, his almost-ex—told me you guys could help me. You know him?"

They looked at each other and Overalls said, "Yeah, I know him. He's been coming here a long time. But I don't know where he is."

I nodded, looking around the store. Hobbies are a funny thing, I thought. You find something you like to do and immerse yourself in it, like it gives you something to live for. Something to do while you're waiting to die. Maybe I needed to find something.

"How does one get into woodwork?" I asked.

Overalls stood up. "Well, depends on what you're looking to do. We got people who build furniture, art, shelves, instruments, you name it. Who wants to know?"

"My name's Phil Darry. I knew Jameson was always good at this stuff."

"I wouldn't know. Never seen his work. Not sure what he does."

I got a little closer to the counter. "You don't happen to keep records of your customers, do you? I sure would love to find him."

"Ah, we tried that for a little while. I might have a few left over. I guess it's worth checking." Overalls moved over to the computer and started fiddling around. The other one sat there tugging on his pipe and staring off into the store. It was the kind of place where people hang around even if they're not getting paid. There was a door to an office in the back, and I could hear someone back there, moving things around. I didn't think much of it.

Finally, he said, "I don't see it. Sorry about that. Come to think of it, we haven't seen him in a while. You want to leave a card or something? I can leave it here on the counter and next time we see him, we could let him know you're looking for him. I don't know when he'll be coming back but it might be worth a shot."

"Sure… I guess so. You got a pen?"

He found a slip of paper and a pen, and I wrote my number down.

"How'd you say you knew him, again?"

TURN OR BURN

"I don't think I did, but we went to the same church a while back. Became pretty good friends. Then he stopped going and we lost touch. I guess I'm just at that point in life when you have some strange desire to track down your old buddies. Some kind of midlife crisis."

"Yeah, I can understand that."

"Well, thank you."

Back on the sidewalk near our car, Francesca said, "That place was weird, right?"

"I thought so. Maybe that's how woodworkers are. I don't know any."

"I almost felt like they knew more than they led on."

"Me, too."

As we were getting back in, I noticed Overalls coming back down the street. He was waving a piece of paper. "Hold up!" he yelled.

I walked toward him. He was out of breath.

"Found it. Not me but my co-worker in the back there. We had another file of addresses I didn't know about." He handed me a sheet. "I don't know if it's the right one or not, but this is what he gave us at some point. It might have been years ago."

"I appreciate it."

"Yep." He turned and went back the way he came.

CHAPTER 27

The address he gave us was on Whidbey Island, which was one ferry ride away. The ferry terminal wasn't too much further north up the highway in a town called Mukilteo. We reached the ferry line and bought a trip leaving in twenty minutes. We got in line ten cars back and watched the massive boat slowly head our way. The salty smell of kelp blew through the open windows.

We boarded the ferry at eleven-thirty and got out and walked up to the top. You can stay in your car, but I think we both felt it was a little too tight in there considering all that had transpired between us the past few hours. I felt overwhelmed.

In the back of my head, I had at least considered the idea of a future between Francesca and me. Not necessarily some big Italian wedding and all that, but at least a good year of a gooey little relationship. You know, taking a trip to some strange city and walking the streets holding hands. Dining at little bistros, sitting at outside tables sharing bottles of wine and our deepest thoughts. Making love in a park in the moonlight. Creating some memories. Helping me remember how to love another human.

We got coffee and she got a bowl of clam chowder, and we sat

TURN OR BURN

at a table by the window watching it all go by. Precipitation was beading up on the windows.

"Don't judge me," she said. "I can feel you judging me." She took a bite of the steaming chowder.

"I'm not judging. Believe me, I am not one to judge."

"So what are you thinking?"

"About what to do if Jameson is there? We need to be careful."

I wiped a smudge off the glass with my handkerchief—it had been bothering me—and leaned back. The ferry wasn't full so the booths in front and back were empty. "Say he kidnapped the girls. Do we want to make him admit to it? Or do we want to watch him?" Francesca was half-listening so I answered my own question. "I think we watch him. What's he going to do next?"

I looked up at the television. They were showing where Dr. Kramer had been shot, in Green Lake. They flashed a letter and the caption under it read: *Soldiers of the Second Coming claim responsibility for doctor's murder.* I grabbed the keys off the table and said, "Meet me down in the car. I need my computer." I told her what I'd seen.

She stood and picked up her chowder. "I'm coming with you."

Back in the Rover, I booted up my computer and found the news online. It didn't take me long to find out what the letter said. I read it out loud:

The Lord God took the man and put him in the Garden of Eden to work it and keep it. And the Lord God commanded the man, saying, 'You may surely eat of every tree of the garden, but of the tree of knowledge of good and evil you shall not eat, for in the day you eat of it you shall surely die.'

If we continue our pursuit of eternal life on earth, God will deny us the earthly return of Jesus and we will not ever know Heaven. Don't make us sacrifice anyone else to get our point across. Let Dr. Kramer be the last.

- Soldiers of the Second Coming

I closed the computer. "You think Lucy Reyes and Erica Conway were with the Soldiers of the Second Coming?"

"Uh, *yeah*. Is a frog's ass watertight?"

I laughed out loud. You have to love it when foreigners use American sayings. "So they think these technologists are eating from the Tree of Knowledge."

"Which means no second coming of Christ."

"Hence the triskelion. Remember what you said? The triskelion may signify rebirth. Second coming…rebirth. *Ding, ding, ding.* I think we have a winner."

Francesca nodded in agreement and said, "That preacher on the tube, Wendy Harrill, was talking about some of this. The common thread among these Singularists is the pursuit of a longer, more perfect life, and that's the single greatest threat to Christianity. You know what I mean? As a Christian, life is supposed to be hard. You're supposed to struggle, and in that struggle, you learn to live the right way, and when you die, you get to go to heaven. So what if you have the choice of not dying, or not dying for a long time? Not only that, but what if the struggle goes away, too? If all these technologies come about, we're talking about living a long time without all the pains we're used to. No disease, no loss. Of course these people are pissed off. It questions the core of who they are."

I looked at her. "Are you religious?"

"I grew up in Rome. The Vatican was my second home."

"Well, I have to say your people are crazy. I should have just assumed this was about a bunch of religious freaks. Who else could it have been? No different than the people we've been chasing in the desert. A different God, but same fantasy."

"These aren't my people. They're nut jobs."

"That's a nice term for them," I said. "Singularists are working to manufacture heaven in their own way, not waiting and taking the chance that we wake up there after death. They are searching for God with science, not faith. So we've got a group of people out there so convinced this is wrong that they will break their commandments to save mankind. These people are lunatics of the highest degree. They've killed and it seems like they're going to keep killing until they get their way."

"They definitely give my faith a bad name."

"They give radical Islamists a damn good run for their money."

"I'm assuming from your cynical attitude that you're not religious."

"Lady, I don't even believe in myself. I gave up on finding answers a long time ago. I'm just keeping busy until I die 'cause I'm either too much of a pansy or too proud to kill myself. I don't know which one."

"Oh, get over yourself. You're a good-looking, smart guy. You own a vineyard and make wine. You somehow got me naked. I think there are people out there that have it much worse."

"I'm sure you're right."

"I am! You're a drama queen," she said.

Some awkwardness came rushing in, and I decided I wasn't going to say another damn word.

CHAPTER 28

I'd been to Whidbey Island many times over the years. My friend's parents used to invite me to their cabin every year, and I'd learned about the island's rich Native American culture. The Snohomish, the Suquamish, and the Swinomish, among others, had lived there long before the Europeans moved in. Whidbey is like Bainbridge, where Ted's folks lived, but it's even further out there, much like the residents. People that left the city years ago to find some peace and quiet. An island where they can be who they want to be, smoke what they want to smoke, and love who they want to love. A splendidly colorful place sprinkled with artists and activists and actors and surely a few members of the witness protection program, as well.

We drove off the ferry in Clinton and followed the GPS on Francesca's phone toward the address Overalls had given us. Lush, dense forests quickly surrounded us. It was as remote as any place could be in the United States. You can drive miles without seeing anything but rolling hills and trees and a few mailboxes and farms.

About twenty minutes from Clinton, headed north, we found what we were looking for. A couple turns had put us into a deep forest with a long, winding two-lane road twisting even deeper

TURN OR BURN

inland. We passed an old mailbox with the correct number on it. We were there: *1523 Hounds Hollow*.

We continued on, looking for a place to leave the Rover. It didn't make sense to pull right up and introduce ourselves. If this guy was behind what was going on, he was not to be taken lightly.

Francesca turned right on a gravel road with no mailbox. We parked fifty yards down, so that we were off Hounds Hollow and not as obvious.

"I'm getting hungry," I said. "You?"

"I'm okay. If you'd eat a little protein, you wouldn't have to eat every ten minutes."

"You know, you're really starting to sound like me."

"It's annoying, isn't it?"

"When you do it, yes."

She closed the door and locked the Rover. The rain was still falling and dripping from the canopy high above. We left the road, cutting through the woods toward Jameson's house. A bed of moss and leaves covered the forest floor; the leaves crackled under our feet. There was no way to be silent. But we didn't think it mattered that much, unless Jameson's friends at the woodshop had called and told him we were looking for him. But then why would they have given us his address? Matter of fact, his friend hadn't just given it to us. He ran out after we'd left and chased us down. The guy seemed to be going out of his way to help us.

"So you're going to be a Countess?" I asked, taking out my Ruger and checking the magazine. It was fully loaded. I pushed it back into the shoulder holster.

"That's the plan." She seemed exhausted by the subject.

I couldn't help it, though. "What are you going to do?"

"I don't know."

"Well, if you're going to leave him, don't do it all on my account. I could hang around you a little longer, but you don't want to marry me. Believe me."

"Don't flatter yourself. If I did leave him, it would have nothing to do with you. You were just a little side effect."

"You really know how to make a guy feel special, don't you? A complete drive-by is what you did to me."

"More like a hit-and-run."

"A come-and-go."

She laughed at that one.

Just then, a sound came from my three o'clock. I jerked my head and we both moved behind a tree. I pulled my gun out and made a couple hand signals, indicating where I thought it was coming from. She agreed. We both cocked our pistols and knelt down low, watching and waiting.

More leaves cracking. I motioned for her to stay put and I moved forward, dashing to the next tree toward the sound. I took cover with my back against the tree, then turned and looked. Nothing. I did it again.

More movement. I raised my gun and rolled around the tree.

"Deer," I said. "It's a deer."

A small doe was working her way through the forest, eating berries off a plant. At the sound of my voice, she disappeared like a bullet from a gun.

Francesca and I both took deep breaths and continued on, moving further and further into the woods, the tall trees swaying, dripping water all around us.

"Hey," I interrupted. "You smell a fire?"

She stopped and stuck her nose in the air. "Faintly."

Shortly after, we reached Jameson's long driveway. We took a hard left to follow it without getting too close. After about a quarter mile, a cabin came into view. Nothing special at all. Couldn't have been more than four rooms total. Smoke rose from a brick chimney. Three cars occupied the driveway. And you guessed it. One was a green two-door, a Honda. Just like Jess had told us. There was also a beat up Mercedes that had rusted above the wheel wells and a Dodge Ram truck.

TURN OR BURN

We both saw the dogs at the same time, and stopped and watched them for a while. Two Dobermans were pacing back and forth in the front. They were tied up.

Approaching more cautiously now, working our way toward the back of the house to avoid the dogs, we got close enough to be able to see through the window. One man was standing in the kitchen washing his hands. I motioned for Francesca to move to the other side of the house, and she went on her way. I rested behind a large tree and pulled out my Ruger. I twisted around to see Francesca working her way from tree to tree and then disappearing on the other side.

That's when I heard a woman's scream coming from inside the house. The dogs started barking, and someone opened up the front door and shut them up.

I started moving closer to the back of the cabin.

The screaming came again and the dogs resumed barking. I ran to the outside of the cabin and dropped just under a window, my back to the wall. I looked around and didn't see anyone. The woman screamed again and then broke into a cry.

I rose up, turned around, and peered through the glass. I'll never forget what I saw.

I was looking in from the far side of the main room. On the other side, maybe twenty feet away, there was a woman sprawled out on the dining room table. She was naked and lying face-up. Her hands and feet were tied to each corner, the rope disappearing behind the table. Three men were there: two watching from one end as another pulled a steel fireplace tool out of the fire. He looked in my direction and I ducked. It was Jameson Taylor, I was sure of it. Thick glasses resting on that cauliflower nose. A thick white beard. A green button-down vest over a blue flannel shirt.

I stood up a couple seconds later and saw his back was to me as he moved toward the woman. He wore heavy black boots, and I could hear his steps as he moved. Then I noticed the red glow at the end of the iron in his hand. He was going to brand her. Certainly it was the same mark—the triskelion—we'd seen on the two dead women, Lucy Reyes and Erica Conway.

No way I was going to let that happen. I stood and started running for the door around the corner. Just as I began to round the house, I caught the blur of a wooden plank coming my way.

CHAPTER 29

My vision came back to me in a blur. Giant evergreens hovered above me. I could feel my arms being tugged and could hear footsteps, and it became obvious that someone was dragging me. My heels were digging in the dirt, drawing two parallel lines. My forehead hurt badly from where they'd hit me, and I was dizzy. I turned my head side to side, grasping for reality. Licked my lips and breathed.

Then I shook and pulled, trying to get a better view of my surroundings. There were two of them. Not the same men I'd seen inside the cabin. One held my gun in his free hand. I shook some more, and he hit me in the side of the head with it, knocking me back into a daze.

"You calm yourself down," he said in a Canadian accent. He wore a golf hat and a beige shirt.

"Where is she?" I mumbled, jerking my arms.

He hit me again, much harder this time, knocking me out for a moment.

I came to with a raging headache. We had reached the steps at the front of the cabin. The dogs were barking again. The Canadian snapped at them and they went silent. The men lifted me up the stairs, my heels hitting every step as we went up. They pulled me through the door. There were five of them now. No one was talking. They dropped me on the bare kitchen floor, and I tried to sit up. One of them put a foot on my shoulder and pushed me back down. I wiped the side of my head and blood coated my fingers.

"We'll fix that," someone said, before showing himself.

It was Jameson Taylor. He appeared above me, grinning. I saw that the beard covered up some deep acne scarring. He was not a pretty man, to put it lightly. He put his big black heavy boot on my chest. "We were expecting you."

Expecting me? Had the man in overalls from the woodshop given us this address on purpose? What a fool I'd been! I twisted and looked around. All five of them were staring down at me. At that point, my only hope was Francesca. *Where was she?*

With his boot still on my chest, Jameson reached into the pocket of his vest and dialed a number. "We've got him," he said. A pause. "Agreed. See you in a little while." He hung up. Pushing another couple buttons on his phone, he lifted it, framed me on the screen, and took a picture.

As Jameson removed his foot, the Canadian took a handful of my hair and said, "You make a move, you get kicked in the face."

"You're all dead men," I said.

Jameson began to laugh. "Harper Knox. You have no idea what's going on here, do you? You've no idea what's about to happen."

"I don't imagine we're off to a church picnic," I mumbled.

He grinned. "Not quite." Then he looked back at the Canadian. "Tie him up."

Before I could resist, two of them had me on my stomach and were tying my hands together. I grunted as one of them pushed me hard into the floor. *Where the hell was Francesca?* I heard Jameson tell two of the men that their work was done, and then the door opened and closed as they left. There were now just three of us.

TURN OR BURN

They lifted me up under my arms, and that's when I saw the woman. She was still tied to the table. I'd forgotten about her. She wasn't moving.

The two men walked me to a chair that had been pulled away from that very same table. They pushed me down onto the seat, and I knew I had to make a move. I couldn't pull my hands free, but I kicked my feet out and rolled to the ground. Before I could get a kick in, the Canadian jerked me back up by the arm, threw me back in the chair, and locked his arm around my neck, cutting off my circulation. As I fought to breathe, the other one wrapped a rope around my chest and the back of the chair. After several times around, he tied it tight. The Canadian let go and I inhaled gulps of air. He knelt and tied my ankles to the chair legs, tightening the rope enough to stop the flow of blood to my feet. Then the other one pressed a strip of tape across my mouth, forcing me to stabilize my breath through my nose.

I began to gain control of my mind again and looked around. Jameson had walked over to the naked woman. Her limbs were still tied to the corners of the table, and she was unconscious. She had long blonde hair, a tall forehead, and a face covered in makeup that her tears had melted. She was a plumper woman on the top and bottom but had a tight waist. Her breasts fell to either side of her rib cage, and her thick legs were flattened against the wood. Jameson stood on the other side of the table from me. He gently stroked her face. Once the men had made sure I wasn't going anywhere, Jameson looked at them. "All set?"

They nodded.

"Good. No more interruptions."

He slapped the woman's face, attempting to wake her. She didn't move. He leaned down very close to her face, breathing on her, whispering to her. He slapped her again. "Wake up!" he yelled.

Her eyelids lifted a little.

Jameson brushed a strand of hair away from her eyes and whispered in her ear, "It's time, my darling. Time to wake up after a lifetime of sleeping. It all begins here."

Her terrified eyes opened wide and she began to plead. Jameson threw a hand over her mouth. Still speaking very calmly and quietly, he said, "Now what did I tell you about that? Don't make a peep, okay?"

She didn't move. Her eyes couldn't have been any wider.

"Okay?" he said again.

She nodded. He lifted his hand from her mouth and she said, "Okay."

Jameson stood back up and walked toward the fireplace. The poor woman tilted her head and we made eye contact. When she saw the tape over my face and the rope binding my chest, she gasped.

I pushed myself up and pulled with my hands, trying to break free of the rope. I wasn't even close, but I ended up knocking the chair over, and going down with it.

A fist came flying into my jaw, furthering the trauma to my brain. "We won't have that again, eh," the Canadian said, lifting me and the chair back up.

There was absolutely nothing I could do, and I had very little idea of what was happening, but there was a pretty good chance this woman was about to be burned.

Jameson came back into view, holding the same branding iron he had earlier. It had thick padding at the end so it wouldn't burn his hands; it looked like rags had been taped around it. The tip was glowing. "Mr. Knox, don't let me see that again."

Upon eyeing the glowing iron, the woman began pleading again. "No, no. Please. I'll do anything you ask. Just…no. Don't hurt me."

"Shhhh…" Jameson whispered. And in a creepy, slow, quiet speech, Jameson's voice took over the room. "Compared to burning in the fires of hell for all eternity, this won't hurt at all,

Ms. Dorachek. Not one bit. I'm saving your life right now." He had the iron in his left hand, and he held it high in the air. With his right hand, he reached into a bowl that was sitting on the windowsill. His fingers came up dripping with water. He threw his hand at the woman, splattering water across her body. "Let this holy water cleanse your soul and remove the darkness that has taken hold."

He reached for more water and threw it at her again. His voice grew louder and shook with vibrato. "Dear Lord Father, cleanse this poor girl in the Holy Spirit and send the darkness away. I baptize you in the name of the Holy Spirit." She was crying uncontrollably. He dipped his hand in again and threw it at her. "From this day forward, you will no longer walk the path of a sinner. You will join us in the coming days as we fight our battle against the sinners." And again. His hand went to the bowl, he cast his hand toward her, and water splashed across her face and body.

He lifted the iron.

"No!" the other guy who'd been quiet suddenly shouted. "Please stop!"

I looked over. He was much younger, maybe not even twenty. Looked like he'd walked right out of Sunday School. His words lacked any conviction, any sense of strength. His baby face and curly hair made it even worse. "Please, Jameson. This is not what God would want. You know that." His pleading sounded nearly absurd.

Jameson whipped his head toward him, gritting his teeth. Then, after a couple of seconds, he left his position and walked up to the young man. With the iron still in one hand, he raised the other hand and backhanded the young man across the face.

"Not another word out of your mouth, Elvin! She is a sinner." He shook his head in disgust. "You poor, innocent boy, you have a lot to learn."

Elvin shut up. He appeared to be way out of his element.

Jameson went back to his position and took the safe end of the poker with both hands and raised it high in the air. "*Behold He is coming with the clouds, and every eye will see Him, even those who pierced Him, and all tribes of the earth will wail on account of Him.*" Jameson crossed himself and continued, "The Father, the Son, and the Holy Spirit. The Father, the Son, and the Holy Spirit!" He repeated it several times, and the other two men standing there were crossing themselves, whispering their own prayers.

The woman screamed and her body writhed as she desperately sought to free herself. He began to bring the glowing red iron down toward her stomach, and I kicked and screamed, but there was nothing I could do, either.

The iron met her skin just above the waistline on the left side, and she screamed loud and deep. The dogs howled. Smoke rose and the smell of burning flesh assaulted me. Jameson screamed, "You are free, child! You are free!"

He removed the branding iron from her stomach. It peeled off the skin and a large blister rose up.

Her crying seemed to slow now, and she stopped pulling at the rope wrapped around her wrists and ankles. I could see blood at one wrist where she had tried to rip her way free. She was in shock, and I was surprised she hadn't passed out.

There was nothing I could do. I was utterly helpless.

Jameson returned the glowing stick to the fireplace and walked back slowly. "You see, Mr. Knox. It's as easy as that. Ms. Dorachek is free. Her path will still be rocky, but she is free now to walk it." He came around the table again and reached out and stroked her face. "Isn't that right, Ms. Dorachek?" He leaned over, staring deeply into her eyes. "Isn't that right?"

Scared, she shut her eyes, and it looked like she was squeezing them as tight as she could, as if the harder she squeezed, the further away she could be. I pulled again at my binds, but I knew I was wasting time and energy.

He continued to stroke her face. "It's time we choose whose

side we're on." Then he looked up at me. "Whose side are you on, Mr. Knox?"

He nodded at one of the men, and they ripped the tape from my face. I took a huge gulp of air, and then opened my mouth and stared at him. "You crazy son of a bitch. I'm going to kill you!"

"Now, now, that's no way to speak. I'm just asking whose side you're on."

"Look at me," I said. "Look me in the eyes. Deep in the eyes."

He did.

"*I will put a bullet in your brain.*"

"I think you need to be cleansed," he said. "You'll be fine soon. Perhaps even walk with us one day. That's the plan."

I glared at him.

"It all begins on this table," he said. He reached into his pocket and pulled out a knife. Then he began to saw at the rope holding the woman's left wrist. Speaking to the two other men, he ordered, "Gentlemen, clear Ms. Dorachek from the table and get her resting on the couch. We have more work to do."

"You're a lunatic," I said.

He looked at me again. "Mr. Knox…you're next."

CHAPTER 30

They lifted Ms. Dorachek off the table and gave her a sip of water. She nearly collapsed as they guided her to the couch behind us. I think she'd lost the energy to cry or fight anymore. I watched them tie her legs and feet, while Jameson went to the kitchen and washed his hands.

"You get his neck, Elvin," the Canadian said. "Hold him tight."

A hand went around my neck. They covered my mouth back up. Then the Canadian unwrapped the rope around my chest and freed my ankles. Elvin squeezed tight, following his orders. I'd be damned if they were going to burn that mark on my skin. Though my opportunities of getting out of it were dwindling away.

I was angry with Francesca. Where was she? If they'd caught her, then she would have been right here with me. A poisonous thought kept creeping into my head. *Had she led me to them? Was she part of it?* But that made no sense. How could she be involved in all this? Unless they had been targeting me long before Ted had brought me in, which would also possibly implicate Ted. I didn't want to believe it. Either way, I didn't need any answers right at the moment. I just needed Francesca to walk in the door and start pulling the trigger.

TURN OR BURN

They started to lift me and I went dead weight. Wasn't about to help them. Not that they needed any. They lifted me up and slammed my back onto the table. Jameson held my hair tight by the scalp while the two men tied my legs up near the corners. Then they came up and did the same with my arms, wrapping my wrists tightly and cinching them down. I could feel the rope cutting the skin, just like it had done with the woman.

I was pulling at all four corners when Jameson said, "There's no use. The Lord has a plan for you, and it begins here on this table." He leaned down and unbuttoned my shirt. "Don't bother fighting it."

I stared him in the eyes, not letting him win this battle. The other two had backed off now, watching Jameson at work. Elvin looked terrified but he certainly wasn't intervening. Once Jameson had unbuttoned my shirt and pulled it away from my chest and stomach, exposing flesh, he stepped away and went to the fireplace. I eyed the window and thought I caught a flash of movement, but I stared longer, and there was nothing. I looked at Elvin and the Canadian, and they were now calm and reverent, waiting on the ceremony.

I heard the iron being pulled out of the fire and then Jameson's boots moving back toward me. Then I saw the red glow. I pulled harder on the ropes to no avail.

I didn't have any options.

He stood on the side of the table, and just like he'd done with the woman, Ms. Dorachek, he held the branding iron high in one hand and began to dip his hands in the bowl of holy water. As he threw his hand at me, water splattered across my chest and face, and he began to speak in a near chant. "By the power vested in me by God, I now step into your life and pull you away from the path of the devil. May you sin no more!" He reached in and threw more water at me, spewing more bullshit out of his mouth, throwing more and more water.

He raised the iron even higher and took it with both hands

and began, "*He that believeth and is baptized shall be saved; but he that believeth not shall be damned.* May the Father, the Son, and the Holy Spirit cleanse your soul, Harper Knox. It is our path to save even the weak ones, so says the Lord."

I shook and pulled and screamed through the tape as I stared at the red-hot triskelion hovering just above me. Sweat was rolling down the side of my face and I turned and twisted, but they had the ropes so damn tight that I was helpless.

He kept repeating the same words, "The Father, the Son, and the Holy Spirit," as he lowered the branding iron down toward my abdomen.

You've never seen someone squirm so much in your life. I had twisted so far to the right side—away from him—that I'd just about disconnected my femur from my hip. That's when the Canadian got pissed. I felt him slam my knees against the table, straightening my legs. Then he hammered a fist into the side of my knee, which hurt like hell.

A lot of demons were coming up inside of me, stirring this nightmare. My brain was losing control. The feeling was all too real and familiar. I could hear those voices from the past, the two Afghanis attempting to interrogate me, ignoring the fact that I couldn't speak their tribal babble, hitting me with a metal bar in the shins relentlessly, bringing pain that I can still feel from time to time.

Then the burn of the branding iron hit me. Hard. Seared right up from my abdomen to my skull. For a moment, I didn't know where the iron touched me. My eyes welled up with tears, and I could hear the muffled sound of my own yells.

Jameson's eyes met mine. He was still holding the iron down, pressing it against me. My eyes went from his eyes, down the length of the iron, to the left side of my abdomen. As he began to pull away, I saw what he'd done to me. He'd marked me just like the rest of them.

It was a mark I would live with forever. The triskelion.

TURN OR BURN

I finally settled down as he stepped away from me and returned the poker to the fire. I looked at my stomach again. The blister had swollen up more than an inch from the skin. He came back and poured some water from a bottle into my mouth. I welcomed it.

As I swallowed, he said, "What happens now, you're wondering."

I looked at him. In fact, that was what I had been wondering.

"Now, your education begins. How you will be used, I do not know yet. We'll have time to figure that out, but there is plenty of work to do. We need people like you. But I know you're going to take longer to break than the others. Still, no one is unbreakable. Not for God." Jameson looked at his two men, pointed his finger at me, and said, "You keep a gun on him."

The men nodded.

Then Jameson said, "Take them home. I will see you there. Keys are in the car. I'll take the dogs." As he stepped away, he crossed himself and said to me, "See you on the other side."

With that, he walked out of the cabin. I heard a car start and then the gravel churn as he sped away.

"I don't know if I like this," Elvin, the weak one, said.

"Get over it, boy," the Canadian replied. "You're going to get yourself killed. Now, get his arms tied back up behind him." He picked up a gun off the kitchen counter and pointed it at me. "You make a move, I'll shoot you."

I was in pretty bad shape, but without the gun, I could have taken them. With it, there wasn't much I could do. Elvin cut me loose from the table and tied my hands back behind my back. Then he draped some kind of bag over my head. Everything went black. The air got tight. I slowed my breathing.

They opened the door and led me out.

"Steps," one of them said to me. After missing the first one, I found my footing and worked my way down.

They led me across the gravel and pushed me into the trunk of a car. It had to have been that old Mercedes.

"Elvin, don't just stand there," the Canadian said. "Are you an idiot? Go get her." A minute later, they threw the girl on top of me. She was awake now. Crying badly. I could feel that they'd covered her with some sort of wool blanket. I moved over so that she slid to my side. I felt her back against my chest.

Then the trunk shut.

III

"Isn't me, have a seed
Let me clip your dirty wings
Let me take a ride, cut yourself
Want some help, please myself.
Got some rope, you have been told
Promise you, I have been true
Let me take a ride, cut yourself
Want some help, please myself."

- Kurt Cobain

CHAPTER 31

I caught the beginning of a conversation as the two men made their way from the trunk to the front of the car. Elvin asked, "Do you think the Madonna will come around? What happens if she doesn't? Maybe this isn't God's plan."

"Doubt is the devil's sword, boy. It will happen soon enough. Get out of your head. Have faith."

"But—"

"But nothing! You keep your mouth shut and do as your told. You're lucky to be one of us. Don't forget that."

Their voices turned to murmurs when the car doors shut. Then all I could hear was the sound of the motor as they started the car and the woman crying next to me.

"My name's Harper Knox," I said. I could taste the mildewy odor of the bag wrapped around my head. It must have been burlap.

She stopped crying for a minute. I waited for a response. Nothing.

"I'm one of the good guys. What's your name?"

After a few seconds of silence, she said, "Leanne."

"Well, Leanne, I have no idea what's going on right now, but I'm going to figure a way out of it. Do you have any idea who these people are?"

She mumbled no.

The car started up and the driver peeled out, leaving in a hurry, taking on the bumps with little care.

Once we adjusted to the speed, I asked, "Are your hands free?"

"No. They tied them."

"We're going to be okay. People know where I am. We'll get out of this. How's the burn on your stomach feel?"

"It hurts."

"Mine does, too."

Out of nowhere, a shot rang out and a second later, we hit something. Full-blown force. I shut my eyes. The impact slung me into Leanne, and we both hit the top of the trunk as the car started to roll. The two of us bounced up and down, slamming against the top and bottom and sides. A sharp pain stung my shoulder and arm.

The car finally settled with one final jolt that threw us up into the air. We both came back down hard, and I heard the breath get knocked out of Leanne. The car was upside down.

The open door alarm was beeping repeatedly.

We both squirmed around a bit, finding—as best we could, considering the circumstances—more comfortable positions. I was closer to the lock of the trunk. She was right up next to me. I stretched out tall and felt my right shoulder swell with pain as I tried to find some oxygen in that claustrophobic burlap bag. I pushed at the trunk, hoping it might give, but we weren't going anywhere.

There was silence for a while, then footsteps. Someone was coming closer to us. Then a key in the lock and a click. The trunk suddenly unlatched and opened, sending us tumbling down onto the earth. I pulled at my bound hands and shook my body, trying to shake the bag off my head. I could not see a hint of light.

Someone came toward me. Stood above me. Pulled the bag

off my head. The sun hit my eyes sharply and I couldn't see for a couple seconds. I took deep gasps of air.

As my vision cleared, I looked up at a figure standing above me. A woman.

"You have to be kidding me," I said.

"Sorry it took me so long."

"Yeah. You're a few minutes late. What happened to you?"

"Fell into a manhole." Francesca knelt down and looked at Leanne Dorachek. "You all right?"

She nodded with tears rolling down her eyes. "What is happening? Who are they?"

"I have no freaking idea," Francesca answered, as she started to cut Leanne free with a knife. I squirmed up to a seated position. Leanne was still naked but didn't seem embarrassed about it. Must still be in shock. Once she was able, she got up and went for the blanket that had also fallen out of the trunk. She wrapped it around her.

"Are they dead?" I asked, trying to look past the trunk toward the front of the car.

"Not yet," Francesca said as she cut me free.

I finally stood. My shoulder was still hurting but I didn't think anything was broken. I walked around to the front of the car. Both men were in there and I could hear ragged breathing. I was on the driver's side. I knelt down and looked in. They were upside down. Both alive. A stream of blood trickled down the Canadian's neck and face. Elvin was moaning in pain.

Francesca came up from behind me. "I shot him. That's when he clipped the tree and you guys rolled. I didn't mean for all that to happen. I was trying to stop the car."

"Get the other one," I said to her. She went around to the other side. I reached in and grabbed the Canadian by his shirt and started to drag him out. Something kept him from moving, and I realized he had his seatbelt on. That seemed funny to me and I smiled to myself. How law-abiding of him. What a good citizen.

I reached around and unclicked him and pulled him out. The bullet had gone right in between his clavicle and his neck but looked like it had missed the major artery. He was foggy but coherent.

"You're mine now, asshole," I said. Leaving him lying on the ground, I stood up and looked around. There was a chunk in a tree where we had made impact. No other signs of life anywhere, other than the cabin with the smoking chimney back at the end of the driveway.

I knelt down again and checked his pockets. "I already got their guns," Francesca said, from the other side.

"Was my Ruger in there?"

"Yep. I got it over here. What do you want to do with them?"

"Get some answers. Let's take them back to the cabin."

I grabbed the Canadian by what little hair he had and pulled him up. He was holding the bullet wound, trying to keep the blood from flowing. "Start walking," I said, and he did. When we got close to Leanne, I said to her, "Follow us. We'll take care of you."

She stepped in front of the Canadian and punched him in the face. His head twisted, and a raw sense of justice began to take form.

"Shit," I said. "You've got a hell of a right hook."

Without saying anything, she wound up again but I put up my hand. "Hold off. You'll get your chance. We need some answers first."

She stepped out of our way.

Elvin didn't look much better off. He was hunched over and limping. Francesca was leading him our way with a gun to his back. She asked, "Why don't you take these two to the cabin? I'll go get the Rover."

"All right."

"Be right back." She handed me my gun and disappeared in a

run back into the woods. With Leanne at my side, we led our two prisoners back. Once inside, I made them sit on the couch next to each other.

Leanne came over to me with a cup of water and I downed it. "Should I call the police?" she asked.

"Let's hold off a minute. Why don't you take a load off? Find your clothes and put some ice on your burn. I'll take care of these two."

Truth be told, they weren't much of a liability. They were both hurt badly from the car flipping. I went up to the Canadian and started feeling in his pockets. His shirt was thick with blood, and he was still holding his neck. At the moment, I wasn't too worried about how much longer he would last. "Who are you?" I asked. "I'm going to get some answers out of you one way or another, so you might want to go ahead and get used to talking."

He didn't say anything.

I found a set of keys on a key ring with a cross. His wallet and a Seahawks lighter were in the other pocket. I opened up the wallet. Thirty bucks in cash and a picture of a woman. "This your wife?" I asked. "She know what you're doing?" I threw the picture at his face.

No answer again.

His Washington State driver's license didn't look much like him at all. He'd lost some weight. "Thomas Henry of Tacoma. I'll get back to you in a minute. Seems you're not taking me seriously. You're going to wish you'd never crossed the border up there. Promise you that."

I went through Elvin's pockets too. He flinched as I touched him. He was scared out of his mind and he had good reason to be. Another WA state license. A name that meant nothing to me.

"Now, I need you two to start talking. I'm going to need answers quickly. So tell me, what's going on here? Who are you people?"

They looked at each other.

"You don't need permission," I said. "I highly advise you to look at me like the man who owns your fate. I'll treat you like you treat me. One of you better start talking." I leaned over and tapped the tip of the gun on Elvin's skull. "Elvin, seems you have a little bit of sense down in there somewhere. This is your chance to find some redemption."

He looked down.

"Okay, let's see how far you're willing to take this little game. I've been here *many* times before. On both sides."

I took the Canadian by the neck and pulled him off the couch to the ground. He hit the bare floor with a grunt. Using my foot, I flipped him over onto his back and then went toward the fireplace. I reached down and pulled the branding iron out of the waning fire. Luckily, someone had stuck it back in before we left. I turned toward the men and held the iron up in front of me. "I was worried the fire was cooling down, but this baby's still glowing. I think it will do the trick."

Both of their eyes grew wide, and the Canadian scurried backward until he hit the couch. He was still clutching his neck.

"Where are you going?" I asked. "This little thing scares you? It isn't that bad. I would have thought you'd already had this done. Or is it something you just do to the people you kidnap?"

"You'll pay for this," he mumbled, spitting blood.

I clicked a few times with my tongue, like I was telling a horse to move. "I'd worry about yourself right now. You want to tell me where you were taking us? What was the new location Jameson referred to? Where is it?"

"I don't know what you're talking about."

I took a few more steps toward him.

"Stay away from me!"

I looked up at Elvin, who was still up on the couch, frozen in fear. "You think he's pissed his pants yet?"

Elvin didn't say a word. I noticed Leanne Dorachek over in a chair looking at me. I said to her, "I didn't think you'd mind if I had to get some answers from them."

"Stick it down his throat for all I care."

I smiled and turned back to Elvin, the weak one. "All right. Time's up. Where's Jameson headed?"

Nothing.

I took the iron and thrust it at him. Elvin screamed like a child and tried to move toward the edge of the couch. Below me, the Canadian was sliding away. I lowered the iron and pressed it against Elvin's thigh. His pants burned instantly and I could smell his flesh. He yelled louder. "Get away from me!"

"Hurts, doesn't it?"

I jabbed at him again, this time getting his shoulder. He screamed. The shirt burned and smoked, and his flesh sizzled as the iron burned its mark.

"Elvin, you know this shit is wrong. You have to. You're caught up in some kind of groupthink. It's not right. You know that. I'll help you out if you'll work with me. I can see the good in you."

Nothing.

I raised the iron again.

"You have to stop," the Canadian said. "He's not going to say anything. He can't."

I looked down and asked, "Why's that?"

"They'll kill us if we do. They'll kill our families."

"Who will?" I went to him. The glow of the iron was dying some.

"He will."

"Who is he? Jameson? He doesn't seem too bad. I'm going to get him whether you help me or not."

He shook his head and closed his eyes. I raised the iron and he put his hands up in a feeble attempt to protect himself. I got him in the chest. The cloth of his shirt and his flesh sizzled. I pressed hard, making sure he felt it. Making sure he'd have the same mark I had. For a long, long time. He screamed loud and his eyes rolled into the back of his head and he collapsed. Lights out.

"Looks like we lost him," I said, looking back up at Elvin. "It *does* hurt. I'll admit that."

Elvin had worked himself into the fetal position on the far end of the couch. He was terrified.

"You're going to help me one way or another." I touched him with the end of the iron. Though it was losing its heat, the tip still blistered his skin as I pressed down on his arm.

He screamed like a child.

"Okay," I said. "Where is Jameson headed and why are you scared of him?"

He closed his eyes and started saying the Lord's Prayer. "*Our Father, who art in heaven, hallowed be thy name...*"

I lifted the iron and whacked him in the ankle. More crying. "Almost as effective," I said. "Now, answer my damn question, or I'm going to tie you up and torture you like we're in Baghdad. Maybe run a wire up under your cuticles...see how far it will go. How does that sound?"

He kept his eyes closed. Kept praying. A pool of urine started to collect underneath him and soak into the cloth of the couch.

"You got ten seconds!"

"Please leave me alone!" he begged.

I raised the iron up again to hit him, but the opening door stopped me. I turned to see Francesca bursting in, out of breath. "We have to get out of here," she said calmly. "They're surrounding us. Four or five cars." She clapped her hands. "*Andiamo!*"

CHAPTER 32

"Who are these people?" I asked, dropping the iron and running toward the window.

"We'll talk about it later. We have to go."

I went back toward the two men I attacked. The Canadian—the tough guy—was still out, probably on his way to dying from his wound. I looked at Elvin. He was in the fetal position on the couch. "Tell them what I'm capable of. Tell them I'm coming for them. We'll see each other again soon." With that, I left him there lying in his own urine.

There was only one door out. We started towards it. Francesca looked at Leanne. "I hope you can run."

Without letting her answer, we took off out the door, and I'm sure I can speak for all of us when I say our hearts were pounding. As I hopped the two steps to the ground, I saw several cars speeding down the long drive.

"Where's the Rover?" I asked.

"Gone. I don't know. We're on foot."

We ran to the back of the house and that's when I noticed what Leanne was wearing: high heels. "Hold up," I said. "Give me your shoes." She looked at me, confused. "Give me your shoes! I'll rip off the heels. You can't run like that."

She pulled them off and I ripped the heel off each one. Then I helped her get them back onto her feet. The cars skidded to a stop out front.

"This way," Francesca said, darting into the deep woods. We followed her. Francesca and I had guns, but we didn't need to be putting up a fight, not with our odds. And we really didn't know what we were up against. After one hundred yards of negotiating the fallen trees and thick underbrush, I turned. Men were coming our way.

"I can't keep up," Leanne said, stopping to lean against a pine tree.

"Yeah, you can. Just think about what we're running from. We'll slow down some soon…but we have to cover some ground first. They're right behind us. You with me?"

She nodded, and we ran for another half mile before slowing down. If this had been a stroll, I might have stopped to enjoy the beauty surrounding us. You can complain all you want about the rain in the Pacific Northwest, but nature thrives in it, and what you end up with is some of the lushest landscape on the planet. It was almost rainforest, what we were running through. Some of the tallest trees in the country, plant leaves bigger than your head. But this was no walk in the park, and I wasn't enjoying myself. We were on the wrong end of a manhunt.

We'd slowed to a jog. Leanne was breathing heavily and grunting. She would have been crying, though I think she was all cried out. "Do you know where we are?" she asked.

"No," Francesca answered. "But we'll run into something eventually."

"I have to stop for a little while," Leanne gasped. "Please. I can't breathe."

We stopped. Leanne folded, sucking air. I was beat, too. I hadn't run that fast for that far in a while. I looked back and listened. I couldn't hear anything. Maybe we were okay.

"Where the hell were you?" I asked Francesca, turning to her.

TURN OR BURN

Before answering, she happened to look down—I still hadn't buttoned my shirt back up—and saw the burned flesh for the first time. "Harper, what did they do to you?"

"Yeah, you were late."

She reached out for me and touched my stomach near the burn. "I'm sorry."

"It's fine. Nothing you could do, Princess. What happened to you?"

She put her hands on her hips. "I fell in a hole. Some kind of animal trap, I think. I fell twenty feet. It took me a while to get out."

I nodded my head. "You hurting?"

"My leg hurts some but I'm alive. We have to keep going. Leanne, you ready?"

"I guess so." She still had makeup running down her face from earlier, and I could tell by the look in her eyes that she'd never shake what had happened to us today.

"You have to be," I said. "Find some strength. I believe in you."

I was thinking about how much faster we could have moved without her—though of course we would never leave her—when the Dobermans started barking.

Leanne nearly went into convulsions. "I can't do this," she said. "Please, make them go away."

"You need to have faith," I said. Oh, the irony of that statement.

We did a half mile before we slowed again. We could still hear the dogs in the distance. Francesca was doing a good job at making sure we didn't make any circles. "There's a road," she said. "Maybe we can stop someone."

I caught up, drew some deep breaths, and looked ahead. The road wound up and to the right and disappeared further into the forest. If you looked carefully, you could make out the yellow line that used to be there. "We've got to pick a way and go with it," I said. "Follow me."

We started running. Leanne was keeping up, knowing that the alternative would be deadly. A vehicle appeared; it looked like a Suburban. I went to the center of the road, getting ready to flag it down.

When the driver saw me, he sped up. He was coming towards me fast. Too fast.

"Back into the woods!"

We ran off the road and continued in the direction we'd been running. The Suburban moved faster, its engine revving. It screeched to a halt and, within seconds, they were shooting at us. We went down, scrambling behind trees. Chips of bark fell on top of us as the bullets came. They had our position, and the woods there weren't quite thick enough to protect us from being hit.

"What should we do?" Francesca asked me. Her Italian accent was stronger now, as if warfare brought it back.

"Distract them. I'll make my way around and see what I can do."

"You got it." She told Leanne not to move and then got up and started running parallel to the road, making enough noise to draw attention. She was staying low but they saw her and fired in that direction. I took off the other way.

After fifty feet, I moved left toward the road, coming up behind them. They were still taking shots at Francesca, and I tried to bury the worry in my mind. She could take care of herself.

One of the men was standing at the tree line following Francesca with his rifle. The other had his rifle propped up on the hood of the Suburban, pointing in the same direction.

As I reached the edge of the trees, I moved even more quietly. Neither one saw me. Taking a few steps toward the road, I got a clear line of sight to one of them. Thirty feet away. I raised my gun and fired at his back. The shot sent him tumbling over on his side. His rifle fell from his grip. I shot off another round. A kill shot for assurance. This wasn't a game.

TURN OR BURN

Before the other one figured out what was going on, I came around the back of the Suburban with my gun pointed at his head. "Drop the rifle!" I yelled. "Make a move and I'll bury a nine-millimeter bullet in your skull."

He turned his head very slowly toward me and verified that I had a gun.

"You know you can't get it around fast enough. Don't even think about it."

Poor bastard didn't listen to me. A quick movement in his neck gave away what he was about to do. I really wanted to talk to this guy, though, and knowing that his partner was most likely seeing angels, I decided to take my chances with a warning shot. I fired into his shoulder and ran toward him before he could do anything else. I kicked him to the ground, at the same time stripping the rifle from his hands. Then I hit him with the butt of it and he went night-night.

"I got 'em!" I yelled out into the forest. "You can come on out!"

Francesca came out down the road.

Once she got close, I said, "I'm glad you're okay."

"Thanks, tough guy."

She helped me lift the live one into the backseat of the Suburban.

"Leanne!" I yelled. "You out there? We need to move. The others heard those shots. I can promise you."

I listened. The dogs were getting closer.

"C'mon, Leanne. Let's go!"

As if it couldn't have gotten any worse, another vehicle appeared at the end of the road. They were hauling ass toward us.

I looked back to the woods. "Leanne!"

"I'm coming!"

"Run your ass off!"

I got into the driver's seat, and Francesca got in the back with our prisoner. I put the Suburban in Drive and held my foot on the brake. "Take shotgun!" I yelled through the open window to Leanne, who had finally made it to the road.

She got in just in time.

I pressed my right foot down just as a bullet tore through the side window. Two men came out of the forest, running toward us, firing. The two Dobermans were up ahead of them.

But we were moving, and only two more bullets made contact, burying themselves into the door.

I was moving the needle as fast as I could, testing the limits of the Suburban, but the vehicle behind us had too much speed. Looking in the rearview mirror, I saw a ram on the hood. It was the Dodge I'd seen at the cabin. They'd be on us in no time.

"He's dead," came Francesca's voice from the backseat.

"What?" I turned. "That bullet got him?"

"No." Francesca had pulled his head up and was pushing it away from her. Foam was coming out of his mouth. "More cyanide."

CHAPTER 33

We came to a fork in the road, and I swerved left with no idea where we were heading. The Dodge Ram was right up on us now. A gun rose out of the window, and they started firing.

"Get down!" I warned, just as the back window exploded.

"Keep it steady," Francesca said. "I'll get them."

I turned to see her loading the rifle with bullets from the dead man's pocket. She aimed and fired. Their windshield cracked. Another shot. The Dodge took a hard left and smashed into a tree.

I didn't slow down for another half mile. Once I felt like we were safe, I slowed to a stop on the side of the road. "Get him out of here," I said.

Francesca didn't argue. She stood and dragged the guy out by his shoulders, pulled him a few steps behind the tree line, and climbed back in. "You know Jacobs is going to be all over us. Won't be hard to figure out we were a part of all this."

"At this point, it doesn't matter. We're into some serious shit, and the only way out is to get to the bottom of it. Then Jacobs will give us a break."

"We hope."

I pulled back onto the road. "I know if we go to him now, he'll put us in jail."

"And without us, he's not going to get anywhere."

"Then, it's settled. We go at it alone. Ted would do the same thing for us."

We drove back to the ferry terminal and left the Suburban in the lot. I wiped down the keys and left them in the ignition. We boarded via the pedestrian walkway, looking way out of place. We got in line to get a bite to eat and something to drink, and the cashier certainly did a double take as I paid. *What, lady? A little sweat and dirt scare you? You should see the burn under my shirt.*

We hired a cab back to Seattle. First, we dropped off Leanne at a friend's place and asked her to forget everything she saw. It didn't take much convincing. She hated cops. All she needed to hear was that I'd make things right. I promised her justice.

We grabbed our stuff at the Pan Pacific and headed over to Fremont to a small motel. The front desk clerk gave me no trouble when I paid in cash. He checked my ID but didn't copy it. We split a room for safety reasons, and trust me, that was *all* I was thinking about. Safety.

I took a look outside the window. Not much scenery: a large fir tree and lots of concrete. Francesca sat on the end of her bed and started scrolling through channels on the television. "So we've lost our cars and our computers. And we have no idea what to do next. I don't, at least. Do you?" She looked up at me.

I had taken off my shirt and was looking at the triskelion they'd burned onto my stomach.

"Does it still hurt?" she asked.

"It's fine."

"I'm sorry I let them do that to you."

"You didn't."

"I tried as hard as I could to get out of there fast."

"I understand. How'd you get out?"

"Getting halfway up was easy, but then the wall curved back in toward the hole. It was like I'd fallen into a cavern. I kept digging my fingers in, trying to reach the lip, but I had no holds. It was all dirt. Finally found a root and it got a lot easier."

"I guess I believe you."

"I couldn't have made it up."

I raised my eyebrows and nodded. I guess I still trusted her.

"Turn it up," I said, noticing CNN. They were talking about Dr. Kramer's murder. We watched for a little while. They'd released more details. Kramer had died of blunt-force trauma injuries to the head. In other words, someone had hit her in the head multiple times with a blunt object, and then they had pushed her body into the lake. I realized something about it just didn't seem right.

"You know what doesn't make sense?" I said. "This isn't the same kind of murder as the others. We go from a well-planned assassination in a high-security environment at the Summit, to a sniper on the street, to some kind of hate crime. Someone *bashed her head in* with a rock. Doesn't line up."

"Well," Francesca said, "we're talking multiple murderers already. Each individual may have his or her own method. This is a group. The same group that just branded you...don't forget that. I wouldn't put anything past them."

"Oh, I won't. Trust me. I'm just saying...it seems inconsistent."

"We do have an admission of guilt. What else do you want?"

"What if someone else sent that letter claiming responsibility for Kramer's death? A copycat. Or what if there is some turmoil in the group...maybe two different factions of the Soldiers of the Second Coming. We see it all the time in the desert. Two leaders go their different ways. I'm just saying, Kramer's murder seems different than the other two. Like there was a different motivation. A different thought process. Something more personal."

"I hear you, Harper. We certainly don't need to make any

conclusions yet. That's for sure." She shrugged her shoulders and stood up. "Anyway, I'm going to go grab a few things from that store down the road. You want some meds for your burn? Looks like you could use an ice pack for your forehead, too."

"All of the above, please. And some Advil."

"You got it."

"Hey, Francesca?"

"Yeah."

"Please be careful."

She smiled. "Isn't that sweet. You're still worried about me."

"This is just almost more than two people can do on their own."

"I'll be very careful."

She left as I was peeling off my clothes and turning on the water. I left it cold so it wouldn't burn as badly. I stepped in and the water instantly dirtied at the bottom of the tub. It was a mixture of blood and dirt and sweat, and the cold felt good on my skin. I closed my eyes and let it run over my face and down my body for a while. I was nearly overwhelmed by what was going on. I didn't even know where to begin, and to tell the truth, I was losing hope.

***

Francesca came back with two bags. "Lie back," she said, pulling a box of Neosporin and a bandage out of the bag. I put my head on the pillow. She sat on the bed and applied the cold gel onto my burn with a gentle touch, covering every bit of the blister. She was close enough that I could feel her breath against the wound. Then she unwrapped a bandage, pulled the sticky part off, and pressed it against my stomach.

She patted my chest. "I'm going to take a shower."

"Be there in a second."

"Don't even think about it." She shook her head and disappeared into the bathroom. I was in desperate need of some rest. Making sure the Ruger was loaded and within arm's reach, I let my eyes close and soon drifted off.

Not too long after, the demons came.

***

"Harper!" It was a female voice. "Harper. Wake up!"

My eyes opened and the shock of reality hit like someone had dumped a cooler of ice water on me. I gasped for air and started swinging at whoever was touching me.

It was Francesca. She caught my hands and pinned them down. I stopped fighting and gasped for more air.

"You're okay, Harper. Breathe deep."

I fell silent and lay limp on the bed. I could feel the trickle of sweat rolling down my face. Francesca leaned over me and turned the light on, and curled up next to me. She put a hand on my chest. "You with me?" she asked.

"Yeah, I'm with you."

"That was a bad one, huh?"

I rubbed my eyes, feeling ashamed and embarrassed.

Francesca got up and came back with a couple hand towels soaked in water. She was wearing a T-shirt and panties. She put one towel on my chest and folded the other and laid it on my forehead. Putting her leg up over my waist and her arm around my chest, she held me tight.

I lay there, staring at the ceiling for a while. All that healing I'd done had broken down. I hadn't had such a nasty dream in two years. It felt like the dream had lasted days, but the clock said it was only 2 a.m.

I watched that ceiling for almost three hours, Francesca's touch comforting me. I was too exhausted and depleted to think about what had happened the past couple days and what she'd told me about being engaged, so I just lay there and felt her touch and thought about how nice it would be to take her back to Red Mountain.

CHAPTER 34

The Riverside Church of the Woods wasn't really in the woods. It was across the street from a shopping center near the highway in Renton. Right smack-dab in the middle of all the shit I hate about America: Olive Garden, Fred Meyer, McDonald's, et cetera, et cetera. Any kind of chain. Matter of fact, I think I hate anything that is big enough to have a CEO.

The church was a massive establishment, its property taking up two full blocks. A four-story cross rose out of the ground and reached up past the roof.

We pulled in at 10 a.m., hoping that meant they were open for business. We'd cleaned up, eaten, gone for a walk along Lake Union, and talked about what we should do next. Her contact had given us more information regarding the cabin and Jake's Woodworks. Jameson Taylor owned the cabin, and I had a feeling his wife didn't know that. Another man owned Jake's, and it wasn't a guy named Jake. We'd go see them again soon enough, though I had a feeling those involved were already far out of our reach. As I've mentioned, I'd been doing this a long time. I could smell a dead end.

Besides, a visit to see the preacher, Wendy Harrill, was long overdue. Apparently, judging by how much I'd seen her on the news lately, she loved media attention just as much as she loved Jesus Christ. We had watched quite a bit of the local and national news that morning, and Wendy had been talking specifically about the letter the Soldiers of the Second Coming had penned claiming responsibility for Dr. Kramer's death. She had gone on and on about how the pursuit of *Transhumanism*—the idea of using technology to transform the human condition—was leading us into a time that we could not control, that we were flirting with powers we did not understand. She made it quite clear, though, that she did not condone any violent acts, such as the murder of Dr. Kramer, and that the Soldiers of the Second Coming was a radical and unwelcome group amongst other Christians.

I couldn't find any news about what had happened on Whidbey Island the day before. No report of the men I'd killed. No news, period. We could only assume that Jameson and his men had cleaned it up quietly. And taken the Range Rover.

With both of us carless, we took a cab to the church. I asked the driver to wait for us across the street, and we walked up to the front door. It was locked, so we went around to one of the smaller buildings. A flower delivery guy was just coming out, and he held the door for us.

There was a welcome area with a long hallway leading to what looked like offices. A picture of Jesus hung on the wall. The flowers the man had delivered were on a tall table in the corner. They were white lilies. Madonna lilies. I knew because my mother used to grow them. The woman behind the desk was munching on a biscuit as she said, "Good morning. Can I help you?"

"I think so. My name's Salvi and this is Chess." I paused for effect, making sure Francesca heard my amazing jest, but I didn't look over. "We're thinking about joining the church but wanted to see if we could meet with Mrs. Harrill before we went any further."

TURN OR BURN

The woman smiled. "Sure. We can set up an appointment for later in the week."

"Does she have any time today? We're only in town for a few hours. We live down in Portland for the time being...moving up here in about a month. Finding a church is important to us so we're scouting them out now."

"I understand completely. You two married?"

I did my best blush. "Not married...we're engaged." I squeezed Francesca's hand, and she dug her fingernails into my skin.

"Well, congratulations. You guys are such a cute couple." She didn't look down to see if Francesca was wearing a ring. Even if she had, it was Seattle. People are into bucking trends like wearing diamonds.

I threw my arm around my "fiancée." "Don't we look great together? Her parents *love* me."

"I'm sure. Let me see what I can do."

"Thanks so much. We don't need a lot of time, just need to make sure we're the right fit."

As the woman checked Wendy Harrill's schedule, I snuck a peak at Francesca. She was eyeing me like she wanted to kick me. I gave her a wink.

"Tell you what," the lady came back. "Wendy isn't in yet, but she should be here in the next thirty minutes. If you could wait a little while, I'll see if she could see you briefly."

"We'd be happy to wait." I held back the urge to ask her some questions. I didn't want to make her suspicious of my intentions, and I had a pretty good feeling that Wendy Harrill would have all the answers we needed. "We'll walk across the street and get some coffee. Be back in just a little while."

A Tully's Coffee was across the street—a somewhat less corporate establishment than the coffee house I will not name—and we headed that way. I let the cab driver, a thirty-something Ethiopian man, know it would be a little while longer, and he didn't seem to mind. He was taking in the Steve Job's biography on tape. Besides, he was racking up a nice fare, one I wasn't looking forward to paying.

The traffic was heavy as we crossed at the intersection. Nothing triggers me more than traffic and crowds. Lots of people in one place. I hate it. I hate the people, the congestion. All the mediocrity out there, marching in line to eat their shitty fast food and buy crap from Wal-Mart that they don't need just because it's cheap. Sheep. Damn sheep everywhere!

I don't even know why this stuff bothers me. It's not that I'm above mediocrity. Hell, I'd love to be called mediocre, average...*normal*. But somehow so much of America bothers me. That's what happened after my last couple years in the desert. Whenever I'd return, I'd nearly lose my mind over the littlest of things.

Lines, the homeless, fat people, loud people, annoying people, angry people, happy people, people who didn't do what they said they were going to do, patronizing sons of bitches, loud noises, stoplights, politicians, spam mail, bad service at restaurants or wherever, having to fill up my gas tank when it wasn't convenient...even bottled water. If you're near a tap, drink the damn tap water. Quit filling up freaking landfills with useless stuff. Not that I was some tree hugger. I hated them, too.

They were all things that *didn't matter*—that I'd been dealing with all my life—but now they bothered me in a way that no civilian could ever understand. I thought I'd ridded myself of these little stresses, but they were coming back in full-force with every passing hour. I needed to be back on the vineyard, stat. I'd already exposed myself enough to Francesca, so I kept my thoughts to myself.

"So what was that you said to the cab driver when we got in?" Francesca asked.

"You mean *Selam Dehna Neh?*"

"Yeah."

"It's 'hello, how are you.' Or something like that, in Amharic."

"Very impressive."

"A good Ethiopian friend of mine taught me a couple things," I said.

After slinging yet another cup of caffeine down my gullet, feeding my growing rage, we walked back to the church. Wendy Harrill was just inside the door, taking off her jacket and hanging it on the rack in the corner. She was about to meet the not-so-nice Harper Knox, but I was intent on suppressing that for as long as possible.

"Here they are," the secretary said to Wendy, a smile in her voice.

CHAPTER 35

We both threw out our smiles again and regarded Wendy Harrill in person for the first time. She was captivatingly attractive in her blue business suit. Every strand of her brown hair was cut to the exact same length, and it fell very professionally to her shoulders, but her face was far from formal and uptight. Her young, sexy eyes made her look younger than she probably was; I guessed a little over forty. Probably a man-eater back in the day. Maybe she still was. She was certainly still in great shape, and carried herself with supreme confidence.

The top two buttons of her shirt were undone, and a sliver of a gold necklace traced down her chest and disappeared in between her breasts, which I tried not to look at as I started to walk toward her with my hand extended. She smiled and came toward me. I summed it up in my mind. Wendy Harrill was a master of looking hot yet sternly conservative and religious, almost papal (though these people weren't Catholics), at the same time.

"Welcome, welcome, welcome," she said. She was so captivating she almost made me want to explore Christianity for a minute. Then I remembered that my life was shit, and I was going to die and there wasn't much to look forward to until the coffin closed, and I quickly dropped my need for religion.

TURN OR BURN

"Thank you, thank you, thank you," I said with great enthusiasm, the thespian in me shining.

"Please come with me. We can go into my office."

"Thanks for making time for us."

"Oh, it's my pleasure. I had a few free minutes this morning."

"You do seem busy. We've seen you all over the news."

"Oh, yes. Lots of work to be done right now."

We followed her back outside and she led us to the main building. She bowed at the altar as she entered. Francesca and I did as well. I felt like I'd take anyone's help at that point. Take away the massive cross out front, and the church could have just as easily been confused for a medical clinic or an attorney's office. The pews were designed so that the congregation sat in a half-circle facing the altar, as opposed to the usual straight rows in the church that my folks dragged me to. The design almost suggested a more liberal view of the Lord, but from what I'd seen of Wendy on the tube, that was far from the truth.

Wendy took a seat in the front pew and motioned for us to join her. We all sat looking at the altar, which was a table holding a four-foot tall golden cross, surrounded by an arrangement of flowers that my mother would have called "darling" or "exquisite." She did flowers back at our little Episcopal Church in Benton City.

I sat between the two women. Wendy was almost uncomfortably close. She twisted toward me and put an arm up on the back of the pew.

"This is my office," she said with a smile, beginning to work the magic that had no doubt won her a congregation of the devout.

She started her spiel and it was more like a performance than a discussion. It disgusted me. "I understand you live in Portland and are moving here," she said. "So you're searching for a place to worship. I used to live in Portland. I'm an Oregon Duck through and through."

I nodded excitedly, showing a lot of teeth, thinking how my last nerve was fraying quickly.

"Let me tell you a little bit about what we do, what we believe. I've been here for fifteen years and—"

Boring! It was my turn. "Before you go on, let me interrupt you." My words almost startled her. "I think I can sum up why we're here pretty quickly."

"By all means."

"A friend sent us here."

"Who would that be?"

I looked her in the eyes. "Jameson Taylor."

All I was hoping for was some sort of recognition, so I could push her if she tried to lie. What I got was one seriously terrified look. It only lasted a second before she composed herself, but it was clear it was way too early in the morning for her to have been prepared for such a perfect blindside.

I decided to continue. "Now, let's not waste anyone's time with you trying to deny that you know him. I know you do. He told me," I lied. "We're not here to get you in trouble. We're here for some information."

She started to stand. "Look, unless you're the cops, I have nothing to say to you. I've already told them what I know."

I grabbed her arm. "Please sit back down."

She wasn't very quick to move so I pulled her down. Gently, of course. She didn't like it, and I could see some fear creep into her.

I got very close to her, still gripping her arm. "I don't think you're involved with what's going on here in this city, but I think you might have some information. No, I'm not a cop. Nor is my partner here. We lost a friend a few days ago because of this, and we're trying to find some answers. You are our only hope right now. I apologize for grabbing you, but we can't walk out of here without the truth. I'll do whatever it takes, if you know what I mean. Don't make me be that guy. So you can tell us what you know about Jameson Taylor and this group he's running with, and we'll walk out of here and you'll never see us again, or you can try some kind of dance, and I'll have to include you as one of *them*. And by that, I mean my enemy. I can be ruthless to my enemies, as you can imagine."

A tear fell from her eye, and she wiped it with her free hand.

"Don't be scared," I said, "but I'm glad I got your attention. I'm not here to hurt you. I'm here to find some bad guys. What do you think? You feel like talking?"

She nodded.

Of course I had no intentions of hurting her. I was simply doing what needed to be done.

"Thank you," I said. Then I did something really out of character. I reached up and wiped a second tear from her eye. Harper Knox, the King of Compassion.

"Tell me about Jameson."

I had just crumbled this poor woman. She took a breath and then leaned over with her elbows on her thighs. "I've already told the cops all of this."

"That's fine. I have an inherent distrust in our justice system. In short, I feel confident that I can get more done than they can. So please…"

"Jameson started coming hear about a year ago and got very involved. Quickly. Within six months, he was the head of our vestry."

"What's the word: *vestry*?" Francesca asked.

"It's the administrative committee. They do the stuff that lies on the more political side of our church. He became more controlling than I liked, and extremely radical, and I asked him to leave. Simple as that."

Francesca continued. "How did he become a problem specifically?"

"Well, it seemed he wanted my job. He was trying to undermine me. Change the way I do things."

"Like what?"

"He didn't think homosexuals should have any roles of authority in our church. He wanted a man that had been with us for five years to stop teaching Bible Study."

"You didn't agree?"

"Not in the slightest. We are not on this earth to judge. I also got the feeling he didn't think that, as a woman, I should have any authority, either."

We heard a door open and looked back at the entrance. A janitor was coming in, pushing a mop. I turned back around and asked a question of my own. "Where can we find him now?"

"The cops asked the same question. I have no idea. I made him leave and he hasn't been back."

"Don't lie to me, Wendy," I said. "You don't want to do that. There has to be something you can remember. Some way to find him."

She sat up. "I'm not lying." She glanced at the janitor, who was working his way through the pews. "I'm not lying," she said again. "I have the address he put on file with us. I gave that to the cops, too. That's all I have."

"Do you know anything about his personal life? Did you meet his wife?"

"No. I never met her. He said he was trying to bring her in, but she wasn't ready yet."

"What does that mean? 'Wasn't ready?'"

"That's just what he said."

"Was anyone else close to him here? Anyone we could talk to?"

"No one was close to him that I'm aware of. Everyone seemed to gravitate toward him at first, eating up every word he said, and then by the time I asked him to leave, no one disagreed."

"What were his feelings on the Singularity? I know you've been extremely vocal publicly about it. Did it ever come up between the two of you?"

TURN OR BURN

I studied her as she responded. She looked me directly in the eyes and without flinching, said, "We never discussed it. This was long before the Summit was announced. It was something I hadn't discussed much with my congregation until afterwards."

We grilled her hard for another fifteen minutes and then decided that the well had gone dry. I felt liked we'd gotten the truth. I gave her my number and we left her sitting in the pew.

It wasn't until we got back into the cab and had gotten close to the highway that I noticed someone was following us.

CHAPTER 36

"Take this exit," I told the cabbie. Then to Francesca, "Someone's on our tail. That red wagon, five cars back. VW or something. Been onto us since before we got onto I-5."

The cab driver moved to the right lane and exited a half mile down. The wagon followed us. As we came to a stop at the red light, I waited for the wagon to come up behind. It was a busy exit; several cars were between us. A truck drove up, sandwiching our pursuers, and I took the opportunity to make a visit. I opened up the car door.

"Be right back." I stepped out and started walking toward them. Two male white drivers sat in front. As soon as they saw me coming their way, they started making a move.

The driver threw it in reverse, slamming into the truck behind them and pulling out onto the shoulder on the other side. I ran in between two cars to get closer to them. Thought about drawing my weapon but didn't want to start firing on people without knowing who they were. For all my luck, it was some of Dick-tective Jacobs's plain-clothed lackeys.

They hauled ass off the shoulder into the grass, moving toward a gas station forty yards out. As the car turned, I could see the back end; I looked for a tag, but it didn't have a license plate.

TURN OR BURN

I cursed out loud.

They hit a bump over the curb, reached the asphalt, and peeled away. I ran back to the cab and hopped in, closing the door. "I'll give you two hundred bucks to go after that red wagon," I said.

"No way. You're crazy. I got a family, man."

"Three hundred."

"Get out!" He turned toward us. "You get out of my car! Now! I will call the police."

The light turned green and someone started honking.

"Oh, no you won't," I said. "Give us a ride up to the U District and we're good. I'll give you an extra fifty bucks, cash. Let's not have any trouble. Not a good idea on your part."

He turned around, mumbling something in Amharic, and put the cab in gear. We got back onto the highway and got him to drop us off in the U District.

"*Amesege'nallo*," I said, flaunting more of my linguistic skills.

"Yeah, whatever. Just get out of my cab."

"I'm sorry," Francesca said to the man. "He has the epitome of a dysfunctional life. Lost his parents when he was younger. Came back from the war with PTSD. Now, he's an asshole. He forgot how to treat people."

I was out of there before I heard what the driver said. I glared at Francesca once she got out. She tilted her head down and raised her eyebrows. "What?" she said. "Did I cross the line? Am I wrong?"

"You're not wrong."

"At least you know it."

We got out of the car and walked over to Jake's Woodworks. Last time we'd gone by, they'd sent us to Whidbey where they'd burned the triskelion on my skin and we'd nearly died. I figured I owed them one.

No one was there except for some kid in his twenties. He said he was the only one working and that the owner was out of town.

He didn't know where. Not surprised, we went on our way.

We walked around the U District wondering what the hell our next move would be; we were running out of options.

"I don't know about you, but I sure am getting tired of this cab thing. Want to come buy a truck with me?" I asked Francesca.

"That would make things easier."

"I think so. And at this point, it's hard to guess how long we're going to be in town. I'm not feeling much closer to the truth than I was three days ago."

Francesca agreed.

***

We left the Toyota dealership around 4 p.m. with my new ride: a white, three-year-old Tundra truck with twenty-seven thousand miles on it. The white would help fight that desert sun, which was going to start delivering 100-plus degree days out at the vineyard soon. Hopefully, my insurance would cover it. I felt like they'd agree my old one was totaled. We went by Jameson's wife's house again. She let us in but we learned pretty quickly that she didn't have much more for us. She did confirm that the cops were looking for him, too. I didn't mention he had branded me the day before.

After that, we went by Apple and bought a new computer. The one I'd left in Francesca's Range Rover, I was sure, was long gone. I will spare you the details of how annoying I was to haggle with during the day's purchases. I'm pretty sure none of the sales guys I'd worked with would go home thinking good thoughts about me. And it felt good to spend a ton of money I didn't have. If I ever see Ted in the afterlife, I'm going to collect on whatever the common currency is. This pro bono retribution work was for the birds.

We got back to the hotel at 6:30, and I said I would go find us

TURN OR BURN

some food. Francesca was going to start mulling through some Internet blogs and see if we might make any progress that way.

I needed a walk anyway. I strolled over to Thirty-fourth and walked into the PCC Market, which is something like Whole Foods, but more Seattle-hip. Still full of tree huggers and yuppies walking around with yoga mats, but hell, you can't take a step in Seattle without running into three of those types anyway. I picked a few things up from the deli: roasted beets, couscous, spinach salad, falafel, some other picks. What I call "medicine food." For all the hell I give them, the yuppies do know how to eat. That's for sure. I hoped Francesca could handle not eating meat for a night, though her body might break down due to a "lack of protein," as my meat-eating buddies love to say. She sure as hell wasn't going to get any sausage from me. I chuckled at my own joke.

As I was leaving, I popped over to the wine section. The past few days had been a lot to deal with, and I had a strong desire to get drunk. I don't drink California wine because, if I'm drinking domestic, I'm going to support my home state. Besides, I think you can always find better deals in Washington. I ran my eyes up and down the shelves, noticing many wineries I was familiar with, some winemakers I'd run into over the years, and then plenty of others that I'd never heard of. Wineries were popping up like crazy, and I couldn't keep up.

I finally found what I was looking for: Red Mountain. That's where I lived and it ran through my blood. I had been raised on Red Mountain, and in a way, it had raised me. Back when I was a kid, there were no vines. I was a boy when John Williams and Jim Holmes planted the first vineyards on the mountain, back in the seventies. They came in and cleared out the tumbleweeds and dug holes for irrigation and planted baby vines, and the magic of Red Mountain was discovered.

The bottle I took off the shelf was a blend made by the Hedges family, who lived right up the road from me. They'd come to the Mountain in the early nineties, back when I was head banging to Pearl Jam, and within a few years, they had picked up more than one hundred acres near the top of the mountain. Anne-Marie was from Champagne, France, and Tom was from right down the road in Richland, and they had done a great deal for Red Mountain and for Washington State wine in general. And they were good, honest, hardworking people making top-notch wine that was full of soul. They'd certainly taught me a lot over the years.

In an almost-happy state, I grabbed two bottles of the Hedges Family Estate Red Mountain wine, paid the lady, and bid her a *Namaste* on the way out.

***

Francesca was leaning up against the back of her bed looking at the computer. She'd showered and put on an A.S. Roma T-shirt and sweatpants. Women love to get comfortable when they're not out and about. Apparently, even female soldiers were like that. It didn't occur to me until right then what kind of trouble I was asking for by introducing alcohol into this equation. I think it was my subconscious playing tricks on me, screaming to the real me: *you need to get laid!*

"What'd you get for us?" she asked.

I set the bags down on the desk. "Vegetarian heaven. You won't believe it."

"Great. I would love to dive into a plate of leaves. Sounds delish."

"Hey, I'm looking out for you. Can I fix you a plate?"

"Sure. Or I could just stick my head out the window and nibble on some fir branches."

"True. Or you could go downstairs and find yourself a patch of grass to munch on. Bovine style."

"Tempting."

TURN OR BURN

"I did get some wine. I have an urge to get drunk tonight. You're welcome to join me."

"Is that how you plan to get back in my pants?"

"Absolutely not. I'd like those pants to stay on tight tonight."

"Good…because like I said, you've gotten all you're going to get."

"Believe me, I am in no way interested in being the reason the royal highn*ass* of Palermo gets dumped before his big wedding day. You can consider yourself safe here."

"Good. All business then."

"All business. You couldn't even tempt me if you tried."

"Nice try. You're extraordinarily smooth." She pointed her finger toward the bathroom. "Go wash your hands so we can eat."

"I'll be right back." I prowled slowly as a lion, shaking my extraordinary derrière. Self-proclaimed, of course.

"*Dacci un taglio*," she said, laughing. I didn't know what her words meant, but it was the kind of laugh that warms you up. I wished I could bottle it and save it for the lonely days that I knew were coming.

And I'll admit. I sure did like knowing I could make her laugh. Does wonders for a man's confidence.

CHAPTER 37

I fixed us both plates and handed her one. Then uncorked a bottle of the Red Mountain. "Would you like a glass?" I looked at our options for stemware. "Or, I mean, a plastic cup."

She smiled. "I won't let you drink alone."

"That's my girl."

I poured some into two plastic cups and ended up on the other bed, watching the local news and devouring vegetables. We both agreed that the wine was outstanding. She asked about it and I enlightened her. She knew all about *terroir*, the word the French use to describe a grapevine's environment as the grapes come to ripeness. She told me that the Italian word is *ambiente*. Many things contribute to a wine's terroir: the soil, the climate, the people, the philosophy, the story…and it's what I was afraid we'd been losing in America for years. So many wines taste alike these days. They lack individuality, adapting an almost robotic nature. They lack *terroir*.

"Tell me about your own wine," she asked. "Do you sell it?"

"The little bit that I've made so far, yes. I've planted about fifteen acres but it's all young vines. Third leaf, meaning it's their third year in the ground. I bottled some last year but this year will be my first real crop."

TURN OR BURN

"What did you plant?"

"I've got five acres of Merlot, six acres of Cabernet Franc, and four acres of Syrah."

"And you're going to blend them."

"Yep."

"Does it have a name?"

"Knox Vineyards."

"So clever."

I smiled. "There's something to respecting the old world in such matters. Your wine represents you and all your blood ancestry before you. You honor your line by putting your name on the bottle."

"You're preaching to the choir, *piccolino*. I used to steal Barolos from my father's closet. When I was a young, young girl. So when can I taste your wine?"

"Soon. Perhaps I'll send you and Sir Salvador, the sovereign of the Sicilian throne, a bottle as a wedding gift. I'll even sign it."

"You're funny when you get a little wine in you."

"Just wait until later."

"You're making me regret telling you about him."

"No, don't. It's probably best. If I'd known you were single, I might have tried to pursue you and that wouldn't have worked out well. I'm sure you can imagine what it would be like to be with me. For an extended period of time, I mean."

"I think it would be nice. If circumstances had been different, I might have given you a chance. Aside from your hard edge, I think you're a good man."

I let those words sink in. The room got very small very quickly.

"Thank you," I said, almost whispering it. I poured myself another glass.

In a desperate attempt to change the subject, I said, "Ted's funeral is tomorrow."

"I know. I think we should go."

"I do, too."

"They might be looking for us."

"Who?"

"The bad guys," I said.

"Good. Then we can stop running around trying to find them."

The wine continued to flow as we both scoured the Internet on our computers. My new Apple was light years faster than the old one. We found some good stuff. Plenty of people speaking for and against technology and the Singularity and even the Summit, but nothing that could be directly related to what the Soldiers of the Second Coming was up to.

I spent some time researching Wendy Harrill. Seemed she'd been a public figure most of her life, starting in college as the editor of her school's paper and then her class's president. I'd watched a couple of her most recently uploaded videos. She was very well-versed in the arguments surrounding the Singularity, and made strong points regarding her pessimistic view of what could happen if we didn't put a leash on our scientific advances.

In the end, I concluded that because I valued life so little anyway, it would be fun to see just what would happen if we let technology get the best of us. If it's time for us humans to go, then so be it.

***

"You want to go for a walk?" I asked, closing my computer and standing up from the bed. The clock now read 9 p.m. "I need a break."

"Me, too."

She dressed, and we went out into the Seattle night. We'd moved on to the second bottle, and I carried it in my hand, wrapped in a paper bag. People were out and about, looking for trouble under the nearly full moon that was sneaking in and out of cloud cover. We worked our way past the grunge bars to the water. I could hear some pretty heavy tunes coming out of one door, but it didn't stir my interest.

I led her to Gas Works Park, which was about a twenty-minute walk. Back in the early part of the twentieth century, it had been a working gasification plant until they lost a need for it. The city had turned it into a park but hadn't torn down the plant, which had rusted and taken on a deep orange. A lush green lawn that went all the way to the edge of Lake Union surrounded it. The park was closed but that didn't mean anything. It wasn't hard to figure out a way in. Especially not for a Green Beret, the elite of the elite...

We took a seat in the grass down near the water. The city surrounding us was still bustling, cars speeding south on I-5 high up on the bridge to our left. The city lights flickered in and out like thousands of lighthouses lost in the fog. Along the shore on the east side, the houseboats gently rocked in the current.

"We came here one year on the Fourth of July to watch the fireworks," I said, reminiscing, trying not to think too much of my mother.

Francesca took the bottle from me and took a swig. Wiping her mouth, she said, "You're doing a pretty good job."

"At what?"

"Getting through to me."

"I don't know what you mean."

"You know exactly what I mean. Harper, you have quite a romantic side when you want to. You're really something under the damaged goods exterior."

"Hey, I didn't take you out here to get romantic. Our friend's funeral is tomorrow, and that's what is on my mind. It better be on yours, too."

"I haven't stopped thinking about Ted since the second I saw him on that floor. Don't try to get all holier-than-thou on me."

"Holier-than-thou is what got us into this in the first place." I took the bottle back from her and drank. "Sorry."

Then, to the surprise of both of us, we turned toward each other and kissed. She tasted like the grapes of Red Mountain. Bing cherry and fresh-picked mint. Bumps rose on my skin. Her hand brushed my cheek and the late spring's night chill ran through me. Our lips grazed lightly, then we pulled away. She grabbed my head and pulled me in, closing the space between us. She traced my lips with her tongue and then playfully entered my mouth. I held my lips ajar, letting her tongue taunt mine, then closed them, sucking softly on her bottom lip.

I turned my body toward Francesca even more and slid my arm around her back, allowing her to relax backwards to the ground. I leaned over her, ever so tenderly kissing her cheeks and forehead. Then I held my cheek to hers. It felt like warm satin and evoked something deep down. Somehow, I felt trust, like we had become very dear to one another. The connection was so damn real.

"What's wrong?" she asked. I was still holding my cheek to hers.

"Nothing at all," I said, pulling back to look at her once again.

I put my knees on either side of her waist. She let her arms fall to her sides, and once again, I felt a trust between us. I slowly unbuttoned her shirt and the moonlight began to illuminate the delicate mist collecting on her skin. She wasn't wearing a bra. I kissed her and tasted the rain, moving down as each of the buttons released. I opened her shirt when I reached the bottom. Her nipples were hard from the wind that was blowing over the water.

I rose for a moment and pulled my shirt over my head. I felt the cold. She touched the bandage covering my burn. I took her hand and pressed it there. Our eyes locked with conviction.

She reached for my belt and unbuckled it. Unbuttoned and unzipped my jeans. I felt her cold hand reaching under the band of my boxers. Her touch made my eyes roll back; I released a deep, uncontrollable sigh. We kissed as she touched me with her magic fingers. I touched her in eager reciprocation. In no time, I was inside of her, each of us moving in time under the dark of the heavens.

***

When we finished, she sat in between my legs with her back against me, and I wrapped my arms around her, keeping her warm. We listened to the city moving around us for a long time before I broke the silence.

"You're doing something to me," I said, opening myself up again.

I let those words float out over the water.

She pulled my hand off her breast. "I'm going to tell him," she said.

"Why?"

"There was never any question. I knew from the second our lips met that I would have to tell him."

I reached over and grabbed the bottle. A sip was left. "Then what?"

"I don't know. His heart will break."

I asked the question I wasn't sure I wanted an answer to. "Will you leave him?"

"I don't know. I might not have a choice. He may never speak to me again."

"That's probably better than marrying him for the wrong reasons."

"I know." She pressed up from the ground and began to collect her clothes. I could see the change happening before me. "I feel so dirty right now."

Now, I know very little about women, but I do know that I don't always say the right things, so I chose at that moment not to say anything more.

We both got dressed. Whatever moment there had been was long gone. Welcome back, awkwardness. We walked to the hotel in silence. After we returned, she grabbed her phone and told me she'd be right back. She was about to break a poor man's heart.

***

I'd been lying in bed thinking when she came back an hour later. The lights were out. She went into the bathroom in the dark, then a few moments later, slipped into her bed.

I tried not to toss and turn until I thought she was asleep. I found myself thinking about Jameson marking me again. The anger—even hatred—I felt toward him had in no way subsided. And it bothered me even more that he'd done it to those helpless women. Forget about me. I'd been beaten and tortured before. But the others…no telling how many there had been. I began to revisit the day before, how they'd pulled me off the table once they were done, tied me up, and dragged me to the trunk.

That's when their conversation—the one between those two men—hit me, and something started to make sense. I opened my eyes and turned on the light.

"Francesca," I said. "You up?"

She opened her eyes. "Yeah."

"We need to go."

CHAPTER 38

I was knocking on Wendy Harrill's door thirty minutes later. Francesca had dialed her contact—who was apparently open twenty-four-seven for service—and given us the preacher's home address. Wendy had money, and I didn't know if that was from her husband bringing in the dollar bills or her failed attempts to walk the path of the frugal while preaching the Gospel. The house was up on a hill outside of Renton, looking back towards the lights of town.

After a couple knocks on the red door, she peaked through the side window. I waved and said, "Wendy, I need to talk to you. Please let us in."

"It's late," she said. "Please go away." I could barely hear her through the glass.

"Open the door or I'm breaking it down. Don't even think about calling the cops."

She looked at me with angry eyes.

I pointed toward the door handle and whispered, "Open up."

She turned the dead bolt and opened the door. "Why are you here?"

"Can we come in?"

"Are you giving me a choice?"

"Not at all."

I felt bad about scaring her again, but I was quite sure she had lied to me. And if so, then I didn't feel *that* bad.

"Is anyone else here?" I asked, pushing open the door.

"No."

"No kids?"

"My daughter is out. Why the hell are you here?"

"Uh...isn't that a curse word in your profession?"

"Yes, I'm sorry. But you have invaded my home."

Wendy wore a cotton robe cinched tight. She was still very beautiful without makeup. Perhaps even more so, I thought. We stood, looking at each other in the foyer.

"Here's the deal. I've met some of these people that are doing these bad things in our city." I pulled up my shirt and ripped the bandage off. The blistering had gone down, and the triskelion was well-defined. She looked at it and then back at me. I wasn't done talking. "As you can probably surmise, this was done without my consent, and I'm not happy about it. Now, during my time with them, your name came up. It became clear that you know much more than you are letting on. Were you sleeping with Jameson Taylor?"

"What are you talking about? I told you what I know."

"You're not hearing me. This group of people—the Soldiers of the Second Coming—or whatever you want to call these weirdos, is responsible for the death of my only dear friend in this world. A man I fought next to for twenty years. Not only that, but they've also killed at least two very innocent women, and it seems to me they have only just begun. I am trying to get answers and I'm tired of looking." I raised my voice and pointed my finger at her. "I'm tired of having people waste my time! You know more than you're letting on and you're going to start talking. Right now." I took a step toward her. "*Right now!* Do not make me get it out of you. I don't care if you're a preacher. I don't believe in God. I don't care if you're a woman. I don't believe in chivalry. All I believe in is true justice and I will get it. I will find every single one of these bastards and cut their throats. So open your mouth and start spitting out the truth. Waste no more of my time!"

Francesca took hold of my arm, trying to calm me. I shook her off.

Wendy remained silent, perhaps weighing her options, perhaps considering calling me on my bluff.

"I am warning you now," I said. "Don't make me get ugly." And I knew she could see the steam rising.

The alpha female there before us lowered her head but I knew there were tears. More tears. It was the second time I'd made her cry in twenty-four hours. She dropped to her knees and then the real crying came. "They're going to kill her," she said. "Please leave me alone."

"Kill who?" Francesca asked, kneeling next to her, putting a hand on her shoulder, speaking in a gentler tone than what I'd laid down.

I'd just shown Francesca what kind of temper I really had. Not only that, I'd also shown her what kind of man I really was. It was simply uncalled for to speak to the woman that way and I knew that. But I'm not a boy scout. If there is good inside of me, it's buried under a lot of bad.

All that being said, from the words that had just come out of her mouth, it appeared I was right. Wendy had lied to us.

"Who are they going to kill?" Francesca asked again.

"My daughter," Wendy said in a fresh eruption of tears. "You must leave. If they know you were here, they will kill her."

"We're not going anywhere," I said.

Francesca threw up her hand at me, telling me to shut up. And I obeyed.

She turned back to Wendy. "How old is your daughter?"

"Eight."

"You have to tell us everything you know. We can help you.

We can help her. This is what we do for a living. I'm assuming the cops know none of this?"

She shook her head no.

"I'm going to get you a glass of water. I want you to take a seat and tell us everything. You need our help. Trust me. I've been in this situation plenty of times and they're lying to you. Your daughter may get hurt either way." Francesca patted her shoulder and stood, going into the kitchen.

"Can I offer you a hand?" I said, reaching out to Wendy.

She looked up at me. "Stay away from me."

We got her onto the couch and let her sip some water. "How did you know I was lying to you?" she asked, once she'd gotten herself together. Such a narcissistic question, I thought. Around everything that was going on, her first concern was why she hadn't gotten away with lying.

"A very long shot," I said. "I heard the men who burned me talking about you. They said something about the Madonna, asking if she would come around. The only other time that word has crossed my mind, in years, was this morning, when I saw those Madonna lilies that were delivered to your church. They sent them to you, didn't they?"

She nodded.

"It doesn't matter. Start talking."

"You'll bring Rebecca home? Promise me."

"We'll bring her home."

She took a deep breath. "They said they were watching me. If they are and they know I'm talking to you, they'll kill her."

Francesca touched her leg and I thought I'd better take a backseat. "You tell us everything you know, and we'll find your daughter. We're your best hope."

"His name is Daniel Abner."

"Who is he?" Francesca asked.

"The leader of the Soldiers of the Second Coming."

"It's not Jameson?"

TURN OR BURN

"No, of course not. Jameson is a pawn. Abner controls everything. He owns these people. He is their savior."

"You need to back way up," I said. "Who are these people? What is happening?"

"Are you familiar with David Koresh?"

"Of course."

"Then you're on the right track. But this man is much crazier. He's going to hurt a lot of people. I don't know what they're planning, but he told me that many people would have to be sacrificed so that the world could understand the severity of where we are headed. He quoted Matthew 5 more than once when we were together."

"What's that all about?" I asked.

She closed her eyes. "*If your right eye causes you to sin, tear it out and throw it away; it is better for you to lose one of your members than for your whole body to be thrown into hell. And if your right hand causes you to sin, cut it off and throw it away; it is better for you to lose one of your members than for your whole body to go into hell.* This is how he feels about the people he's going after."

"I see. So the targets must be technologists in some way or another."

"I don't know."

"How are you involved in all this?"

"They tried to recruit me. That's why Jameson joined our church. To somehow befriend me and bring me in. I started meeting with them. It's a very spiritual group with deep beliefs. I met with them several times over the course of a few months."

"Why did they care about you?"

"My message. We agree on a lot of things, especially regarding technology. We're both Terrans. We're biblical literalists. We're terrified of the future."

"*Terrans?*" I asked, hearing that word for the first time.

"It's what the Australian AI researcher, Hugo de Garis, started calling us. Terrans oppose the development of artificial intellects, or *artillects,* as he calls them. I think it's an appropriate name so I've adopted it. Many of us have."

"I see."

"I thought that was why they contacted me. Because of our similar beliefs. That was part of it. But there was more. He eventually told me he wanted to marry me."

"Jameson or this Abner guy?"

"Daniel Abner. He wanted me to help lead his people. He'd been eyeing me ever since my divorce. I was attracted to him at first. We spent a couple months speaking privately, discussing the future of our world. Like I said, our core beliefs were totally in line. In a way, he began to captivate me. I nearly left the church." She shook her head. "But that's when he began speaking about the Christ child. He told me that he was put on this earth to father the child."

Francesca and I exchanged a glance. Now we were getting somewhere, albeit somewhere *way* off the reservation.

"I knew then," Wendy continued, "that he had been sent by the devil and I had been tempted. I stopped meeting with him."

"Where did you meet?"

"Different places. The first time we met was here. Then he wanted me to come pray with his group, so I did. I went out to Jameson's cabin on Whidbey Island and joined them. Maybe twenty people. It was a very magical experience, and we met several times after that. The larger group, I mean. Then he began to court me, sending me flowers, showing up here." She looked at Francesca. "I fell for him."

Francesca offered a look of compassion.

Wendy clasped her hands together in her lap and looked down before continuing. The difficulty of recounting the story was becoming more and more obvious with every word she spoke. "A week ago, he came to see me at my house and told me the rest of his thoughts. That we were destined to have the Christ child together...that I would bear his child. He asked me to marry him, and he told me of his plans at the Singularity Summit…that he was going to kill Dr. Sebastian. He also said he had something even bigger planned soon. He made it very clear to me that God had chosen him to do such things."

Wendy looked back at Francesca, this time with a little glimpse of her old self, the strong woman that had fought through a male-dominated profession to become a leader in Christianity. "I told him to get out, that he'd been taken over by evil. I screamed at him, saying he'd been sent by the devil." She gritted her teeth. "I said that I wouldn't dare bring his child into this world. He broke down in tears. Before he left though, he got very angry. He backhanded me and threatened me. He said he'd kill Rebecca if I ever mentioned his name or spoke of what he'd told me."

"Where was she?" I asked.

"At a friend's house in Seattle. As soon as she left, I called her phone. Jameson picked up. They'd anticipated me saying no. He told me that she wouldn't be hurt but they had to take her until everything was over. To make sure I kept my mouth shut. I had to lie to Rebecca's friend's mother, so she wouldn't freak out."

"Why would they take her and not you?"

"I asked him that. I begged him to take me instead. He said they still wanted me out there preaching about the dangers of technology, sharing my beliefs. He said my words would have a great impact on people all over the world soon and that he'd hurt her if I didn't stay vocal. What choice did I have?"

"What are they planning?" Francesca asked.

"I don't know. I didn't even know that they would kill Dr. Kramer. But I know this is serious. Abner told me that the child we would have together could only survive if our Lord and Savior allowed it to, and He only would if we as a race would stop chasing God with science." Wendy began to cry again, barely able to speak. "I wanted to tell someone but I couldn't. She's just a little girl. She's everything to me."

"We will find her," Francesca said. "I promise you. But you have to help us find them. How do we do that?"

We let her cry for a couple minutes. Once she'd gained control, she said, "I don't know. They have a farm somewhere. He told me he wanted to take me there for our marriage. I don't know where it is. He said it was beautiful and he couldn't wait to share it with me. I don't even know what town. That has to be where she is. I don't know how else to help you."

Francesca offered her a tissue.

"I don't want to be responsible for more people dying but I can't choose them over my daughter. You have to understand that."

"You must know something," Francesca said. "That's why they took your daughter. They must be worried that you could expose them. That you know something about how this can be prevented."

"I don't even know what *this* is!"

"I know. But you spent time with them. You know their names. You know his name. Daniel Abner. That's a start. That could help us. Do you have any idea when or where they plan to do something?"

"Soon. Here in Seattle. That's all I know."

"How many of them were there?"

"Out on Whidbey Island? Maybe twenty...but I got the feeling there were a lot more at this farm. Like maybe they had some sort of community. You have to leave...please. They'll see your car."

"They don't have to know you spoke to us. You tell them we came asking and you didn't say a word. And you try to find out more. It sounds to me like you are very important to him. If you are to carry his child, you will certainly hear from him again soon, and it might not have anything to do with you meeting with us."

"Maybe he found another woman more willing."

"Maybe so."

TURN OR BURN

I stood, thinking this was much too big to try to fight on our own. It would have been selfish not to bring the cops in. Jacobs needed to know what we'd found out. So despite our promise to Wendy to keep it between us, I felt like we had to reach out to the detective and let him know something bad was coming soon.

CHAPTER 39

"What the hell is going on here?" I asked Francesca as we got back into the truck and pulled out of the driveway. Aside from the headlights of a few moving cars, the night was dark and depressing. The never-ending mist was still falling, reminding me of the two of us in the grass earlier.

"This is the craziest thing I've ever heard," she said.

"Me, too. I think we need to call Jacobs. You agree?" I reached into my pocket for my phone.

"Call him."

I got his voice mail. "Jacobs, Harper Knox here. Call me now." I hung up.

Francesca took her phone out and said, "I'll put someone to work on figuring out who this Daniel Abner is." Her guy promised to get her something quickly.

"Daniel Abner has to be monumentally delirious to think that he is going to father the next coming of Christ."

"Yes. Even to think he can stop technology, he's crazy. What's that all about? He really thinks something he has planned is going to convince the world to stop using cell phones?"

"We're going to find him and find out."

Back at the hotel, we put some effort into Googling Daniel

Abner. Couldn't find even a mention. I dialed Detective Jacobs again, figuring he was asleep. Still no answer.

While we were waiting on Francesca's contact to send information, we lay in our beds with our eyes closed, trying to get a little rest. We both had a feeling things were going to start moving quickly. One way or another, we were going to find out what this Abner guy was up to, and I hoped desperately it wasn't by watching it on the news.

"You spoke with your fiancé?" I asked.

She didn't answer for a little while and I figured she'd fallen asleep. Then, "Yeah. We talked."

"How'd that go?"

"Great. He's looking forward to meeting you."

I smiled a little. "I *am* rubbing off on you. That's good."

"He's hurt. Of course."

"Is it over?"

"I don't know. We talked for a while. He wants to think about it."

"I don't understand why you wouldn't end it."

"I don't care, Harper, whether you understand or not. Why would you? You're not in my shoes. Quit trying to understand it. You're only wasting your time."

"Well, I'm sorry if I have feelings for you that I can't just toss out the damn window. I think that if you go back to him, you're a fool."

"Harper. It doesn't matter what you think. At. All."

I sat up. "It does. I think you and I have something that you and the prince never had."

"You don't know that. Quit calling him a prince, for God's sake. I knew I shouldn't have let you into my life. It was a mistake."

I raised my voice. "A mistake? You call the past few days a *mistake*?"

"Yeah. I think you and I lost a dear friend and we found

comfort in each other. It happens all the time. When you share a traumatic experience with someone, a bond develops. And I'm not sure that bond is valid in the real world. It doesn't hold up. We're experiencing loss together. And you were already struggling before I even met you."

I stood up and walked toward the door. "You are so damn clueless. Go marry your prince. Go live your life. Go make your mother happy. Do *not* go psychoanalyzing our relationship or me in general. You're way off the mark with this one."

"*Basta! Basta!* I've heard enough!"

"Way off the mark!" I slammed the door and went out into the night.

***

"You done whining?" she asked, finding me sitting on the curb down the steps twenty minutes later.

"I'm sorry I yelled at you," I said, not looking up.

"Sorry I belittled us. I didn't mean to do that. You have become special to me. More than I wanted you to. I didn't intend on having these feelings, and it's really making things confusing. I don't know what's going to happen next. You don't either. Let's not worry about it right now. I just got an e-mail about Daniel Abner. I have an address. How about we go save Seattle and worry about love and loss later?"

"Yep." I stood and followed her down the steps. "You're going to have to introduce me to this dude one day…your contact, I mean. He does good, fast work for you."

"Of course you would think it's a dude."

CHAPTER 40

"Jacobs," I said, "It's Harper again. Trying to get in touch with you. The guy behind all this...his name is Daniel Abner. Something is going down. I have no idea what. And for the record, I am still not running my own investigation. Just ran into this information and figured you'd want it. Get your ass out of bed and *call me*." I hung up.

Fifteen minutes later, we were at the address from Abner's driver's license record. He was renting a home in SeaTac, the low-rent district near the airport. It was a white, one-story ranch house on a quarter-acre lot that desperately needed painting. He clearly wasn't living above his means, and he certainly was not much into working in the yard. The grass was high and the landscaping was non-existent. A rusting Pontiac lay on concrete blocks on the side of the house. It was not going anywhere anytime soon. It was like we'd stumbled upon the set of *Sanford and Sons*.

We parked the car two blocks down and walked over. We were both well aware that the cops could show up any minute if they hadn't been there already. I'd thought about calling the police station and sharing what we'd learned about Abner with whoever picked up, but it didn't feel right. I did not want a bunch of clumsy cops blowing the only lead we had. But I knew Jacobs needed to know. He could help.

No lights were on, but of course it was just past 4 a.m. and most people on the block were sound asleep. We went around the back, both packing guns. A part of the chain-link fence had come out of the ground and fallen down; it was easy to step over. I knew from the last time we'd tried to sneak up on these guys that we had to be careful, so we weren't taking any chances. "Keep an eye on things, please," I told Francesca. "Let me go check it out."

Francesca hung back and disappeared into a very black area in the corner near a small shed. I went up to the first window and looked inside. A streetlight from behind gave me some light to work with. A sprawling spiderweb covered the upper corner of the window on the inside. A banana spider was resting in the middle. There was an overflowing pile of dishes in the sink, and the chairs around the table were out of place. The house didn't look habitable, but then again you never know with some people. Along with years in the Army comes a neurosis for cleanliness. If Daniel Abner was in fact living here, he certainly had not been in the armed forces.

I looked through two more windows but the streetlight was too far away to help me see inside. I needed to go in. Pulling on some leather gloves, I went to the back door. It was locked. I went around to the front. Locked too. Returned to the back and used the butt of my gun to break that window with the banana spider. The glass shattered inward. I flicked the spider off its web and unlocked the window and pushed it up. I listened for a little while. Nothing moved. I pulled myself inside.

I felt like I was at grandma's house. All the furniture had the wear and tear of thrift store finds. A musty odor filled the air. With my gun drawn, I began to work my way through the rooms. It was the kind of scene that, if you watch too much *CSI*, would make you expect to find a body. Except for the kitchen, the rest of the house was carpeted, and I was able to creep quietly. Not that it mattered at that point. Anyone in there would have heard the window break. I started moving faster, knowing I didn't have much time. Went into the last room, the master bedroom. No sheets on the bed. An empty dresser. I pushed open the closet. Nothing. No one had lived there in a long time.

I dialed Francesca and told her to hold on a little longer. She said everything was good on her end. I did a quick search, hoping I might find something that could tell me more about this guy. There was nothing. No papers, aside from a stack of warrantees and directions for the appliances.

Leaving out the back door, I joined Francesca and we left the yard. We moved quickly back to my truck. I told her what I'd found.

She went around to the passenger side as I pressed the unlock button on the keyless remote. She hadn't quite gotten to her door when I heard her murmur something and then drop, like she'd fainted. Instinctively, I dropped to a squat and looked around. My heart picked up its pace.

At that instant, something flew by my head. A bullet?

Moving low, I ran around to the other side of the truck next to Francesca. She was facedown on the ground. A heavy wave of anxiety and confusion tried to debilitate me. Whether she knew it or not, she was changing my life. She was healing me and reintroducing me to love. I could barely handle the idea of her experiencing any pain at all, let alone being shot or killed. Whispering *please, please, please,* I grabbed her arm and dragged her into a grass ditch off the side of the road.

"Francesca," I said. "You alive?"

She didn't respond.

"C'mon, Fran. Please get up." My cheek quivered as a monstrous sadness swallowed me.

I looked around, knowing they were coming after us. A line of tall bushes blocked the streetlight, so I couldn't see much of anything. With my eyes scanning the dark landscape and my gun out, ready to fire, I began searching for her wound.

I had no idea what I was up against, but I decided they should know I was armed. I fired up into the air.

Then I listened.

Nothing.

I cursed to myself, still trying to find the wound. I was having no luck. No wetness. No blood. I felt her mouth and nose. She was breathing.

"Francesca," I said again. "Tap me if you're okay."

Still nothing. I fired another shot up high, hoping it would keep them off my back. "I could really use you right now, Jacobs," I said, talking to myself.

I pushed Francesca onto her side and touched her mouth again. No blood.

Finally found it. A tranquilizer dart was embedded in the side of her neck. I ripped it out. Some of my anxiety dissipated, and a sense of relief soothed me. There was no way I could handle losing her right now. She'd become too important to me.

I didn't have much time, but I needed to center myself, so I closed my eyes and breathed easy for a moment, picturing sunshine and Francesca's smile. A few seconds made a huge difference; now I was ready to fight.

Knowing there was nothing more that I could do for her at the moment—other than get us out of this mess—I left her on her back and began to crawl up out of the ditch and toward that line of bushes ten feet away. Lights were coming on in the nearby houses. It was the kind of neighborhood where many people probably had a gun or two in their home, so I didn't want to run into someone's yard right off the bat. Besides, I didn't want to get too far away from Francesca. No way they were taking her without taking me out first.

Moving low around the bushes, with my elbows in the dirt, I looked down the street. A man was standing under the streetlight staring at me. I couldn't make out his face. He made no move. He didn't look like he was armed. I had no idea if he was an enemy or a civilian, so I didn't fire. I watched him for a moment and then kept looking around. No one else was nearby.

I rolled to the other side of the bushes and looked down another road, the one right in front of Abner's house. Another man was standing there. Unarmed. Not moving. His arms were crossed. It was beyond terrifying.

I kept looking behind me, too, with no freaking clue how many men were out there. Or, out of respect to Francesca, I should say how many *people* were out there. The truck helped hide my position somewhat but they knew I was there. If I could only get Francesca into the truck bed, I might be able to make it to the driver's seat and get away.

As if they had been reading my mind, there were four quick shots from a gun with a silencer. The bullets tearing through the air were louder than the shot from the gun. All four of my tires began to wheeze, and the truck drooped and eventually settled on the rims.

I lowered myself back down into the ditch. I wasn't 100 percent by any means, but I was functioning with control and clear thought. Protecting Francesca gave me strength. I took out my phone and dialed 911. I told the operator I was an Army guy, gave her our location, told her the situation, and hung up. Depending on response time, if I could keep us safe for five to eight minutes, I figured we'd be okay.

I noticed a drainage pipe, which was starting to look like my only option. It was barely big enough to crawl through. I weighed the possibilities for a moment. How could I get Francesca in there and move us both quickly enough to escape? And what was in there? How far could we go?

CHAPTER 41

As I saw things, there were two options: attempt to negotiate the drainage pipe or stay where we were and try to hold them off.

It was not an easy decision to make. The biggest problem with my first option was having no idea where the pipe led or even if it lead to anything. I had no light, so there was no way to tell. I had a feeling that by the time I could get Francesca in there and start dragging her, they'd be onto us. A couple quick shots would be all they'd need to take us out.

So I had my answer. I needed to hold our position until the cops showed up. At that point, all I cared about was saving Francesca. The want for retribution paled in comparison. Put me in jail for all I cared. Just get her out of here.

I took the gun from her shoulder holster and found an extra clip in her jacket. I listened for a minute, peering up out of the ditch. Didn't hear a sound. Couldn't see anything moving.

I fired into the darkness, emptying the magazine of her Glock, spraying shots in every direction. Seventeen in all. Enough to wake every neighbor within a half mile. The more 911 calls made, the better. Needless to say, I was also hoping the spray of bullets would at least keep anyone from making a run at us.

While loading another magazine, a voice pierced the silence. It was a man and he was speaking loudly, probably from fifty feet away. "Mr. Knox. I've got ten men surrounding you. Your friend has been hit by a tranquilizer, but we do have much deadlier weapons pointed at you. I'm afraid we will use them unless you'd like to surrender to me. I can assure you neither one of you will die."

"Cops are on the way!" I yelled back.

"I'm sure they are." He didn't sound worried.

"Who are you?"

"We don't have time to discuss such things. If you'll come with me, we'll have all the time in the world. What say you?"

"No, thanks."

"We have night vision goggles. You will not get out of this alive if you choose to fight. Your friend will suffer terribly if you make the wrong decision."

I rose to my knees and fired two shots in the direction of the voice. I went back down to my stomach.

Silence.

"That answer your question?" I yelled.

"No, no, no, Mr. Knox. Not a good idea." The voice was coming from somewhere else now.

I was over the conversation. Crawling on my stomach, I eased my way out of the ditch and moved back under the bushes. Looked around, searching for some movement. Someone fired a shot and it hit somewhere in the dirt behind me. But it was close. Too close. I didn't have much time. I slid back down into the ditch, grabbed Francesca's torso, and pushed her into the pipe headfirst.

"Mr. Knox. You're not listening to me. Come out of that hole with your hands high in the air. I will give you ten seconds. Then I will order that my men kill you both."

My mind was racing. I was about to stand when I heard the sirens.

A ray of hope.

I pushed Francesca further into the ditch while trying to watch my back. It wasn't the easiest task. Her body wasn't cooperating. It would have been easier to get on the other side of her and pull, but I wanted to stay in between her and any bullets.

Footsteps. Many of them. People running toward me. I turned and saw a man coming around the back of my truck. I fired. He dropped. Another man came running and I put him down, too.

I got back to my knees and looked for my next target.

Something hit the back of my neck. A sting. I reached for the wound and felt a dart. I instantly felt a flush of confusion and blurriness, and the last thing I remember was falling face-first into the grass.

IV

"The water in which the mystic swims is the same water a madman drowns in."

- Joseph Campbell

CHAPTER 42

I came to with no earthly idea of time. No idea of where I was. Everything in my body felt wrong. Everything in my head felt wrong.

The drug was working its way through my system, blurring my thoughts, wrenching me away from any sense of clarity. Soft organ music played in the background. I was on my back. I could feel that my body was tilted, elevating my legs above my head. I tried to move them but they were restrained. My arms were also strapped down at the elbow and wrist.

I opened my eyes. Still darkness. Something was covering my face.

Something was in my mouth. I bit down. It was a wet cloth. I did my best to spit it out but I couldn't. Another cloth was draped over my face. I could feel the wetness on my cheeks. I'd been in this situation before but it took me a few more seconds to figure it all out. The drugs had slowed the recognition. But the truth came to me in an overwhelming way.

Even with the drugs mushing up my mind, the idea of being waterboarded was sobering and absolutely terrifying. I felt my body losing control again, in an attack so powerful that nothing I had learned could fight it. Paranoia and anxiety and helplessness all blended into one high-octane cocktail. *Just let me off! Make it stop!* I silently pleaded, like a patient at a hospital who had overdosed on LSD.

I had been waterboarded before. Never by the enemy. Only by choice. The first few times were during training. The others were amongst fellow soldiers, whether we were making bets or drinking or whatever. Yes, that was our idea of fun at one point in time. Even when you know who is doing it to you, even when you know you're going to be okay, it's a nightmare. It is not a simulation of drowning. It is drowning. You *are* drowning. You are dying a terrifying death.

Scared out of my mind, I took some deep breaths through my nose and tried to break my restraints. Nothing budged.

Then it began.

"Harper, this holy water will begin to purge the demon," a voice said. "It will be a slow process to make you one of us, but it will happen. First we must break you and cleanse you of the past. It began with our mark on your body, and it will end with forgiveness and rebirth. See you on the other side."

A hand went to my forehead, holding me down. I felt the pressure of the water as it hit the cloth covering my face and began to drip into the other cloth in my mouth. Tapping into what I'd been taught, I focused on relaxation and began to inhale very slowly through my nose. It was the only way to last.

You couldn't imagine how on edge I felt. I wasn't thinking about PTSD specifically—it's not like that—but that's what was coming out of me, surging through my veins, making my heart over-pump, making me relive all the pains of war, all in fast flashes. My body *or* mind wasn't equipped to handle torture anymore. At one point, I could have dealt with it, and I had. But not now. Not ever again.

And yet…there wasn't a choice.

My body finally acquiesced. I had to breath out. That's when the water began to rush in. Water filled my mouth and throat and nasal passages and even went up into my sinuses. It was excruciating. I might as well have been thirty feet underwater. The pressure in my head became overwhelming and it felt like the blood vessels in my brain were close to rupturing. I needed oxygen so badly but there was none. The screaming inside my head was so loud.

At the moment when death was becoming a welcome escape, someone pulled the rag out of my mouth and removed the hand from my forehead. I sucked in air with everything I had and felt the comfort of oxygen replenishing me, filling up my lungs, passing through my veins, and reaching all the way up to my brain. A glimpse of clarity washed over me.

"Do you know why you are here?" a man asked.

He slapped me on the cheek.

"Hey, are you listening?"

I nodded, still feeling the replenishment of deep breaths.

"Do you know why you are here?"

I shook my head and cursed, but my words came out weak and hopeless.

"You chose the wrong side of this war."

His hand went back to my forehead as he pushed the rag back into my mouth.

The water came again.

Three, four, five seconds.

At seven seconds, it was unbearable. At around ten seconds, my body gave in again and the water filled my head. *Kill me, fucking kill me*, I kept thinking. I could hear the gurgling coming from my mouth. I tried to yell but I had no power at all.

I started to lose it, but just as I was fading away, he pulled the rag from my mouth. I filled my lungs with oxygen and coughed up water that ran down my cheeks. The anger I felt earlier was gone. No threats came out of my mouth. I wouldn't beg, but I wanted to die. All I wanted was this guy to finish me off.

"It's not easy paying for your sins," the voice said. "Many

people have been in this room, and they've all been saved."

I recognized that voice but I couldn't place it. But I started to realize what was going on, what all of this was about. Singularity. Soldiers of the Second Coming. Jameson Taylor. Daniel Abner. They had us pinned down at Abner's place. Francesca had been hit. *Francesca!*

The rag hit my mouth again and I shook my head, maybe saying "no" out loud, maybe just pleading to myself. I don't know.

They repeated the process several more times, maybe ten more, but I'm not sure. Enough to where I was sure my brain was going to give out, even without drowning.

They did their work well and beat all the fight out of me. The depth of the nightmare became indescribable. I heard screaming and gunshots and IEDs and bodies exploding around me, and I could taste blood and smell death.

So much so that I eventually found myself pleading to them when they jerked the rag from my mouth.

"Fucking kill me," I said. "End it!"

A little laugh. "I think we're getting somewhere."

"I'm sorry, Ted. I'm so sorry. Please kill me." I'd been broken.

"Sorry. Not yet."

"What do you want?" I asked.

"For you to become one of us."

"Who are you?" I asked, and it was barely audible.

No answers. All they kept saying to me was something about paying for my sins, having to learn the difference between good and evil, having to break me, making me one of them.

They finally stopped. They unstrapped my arms and then put my wrists together and cuffed me. A taste of freedom came over me as the other straps binding me to that bench or table were loosened. I suddenly found a little urge to live again.

Someone grabbed my arm and pulled me off the table. I tried to get my feet under me but I fell down hard, my knees crashing

TURN OR BURN

into the floor. My eyes were still covered. A man lifted me up and said, "Come with me."

Not that I had a choice. I followed his lead and walked for a while. He opened a door and pushed me in. I fell to the floor. He closed the door, and I was alone. No more sounds. I lay on my back and breathed for a while. Once I got a grip, I reached up and pushed the blindfold off my eyes. I was in a walk-in closet of sorts with white walls.

I pushed myself up against a wall and took in more breaths, savoring what we so easily take for granted.

CHAPTER 43

Minutes, hours, days later. They'd taken me in and out of that closet several more times, subjecting me to further waterboarding and several beatings. Then, I'd finally drifted off from pain and exhaustion. Finally, some peace.

They'd put fresh, clean clothes on me, though I didn't remember them doing it. Some very soft cotton beige pants tied at the waist. A white shirt of similar fabric. No shoes. I was clean, too. They must have bathed me. I sat up and felt the pain in my side from where'd they kicked and punched me. Maybe even hit me with something. I couldn't remember.

I was now in a bedroom. No windows. The walls were stacked logs, like those of a log cabin. No paint anywhere. The queen bed had clean white sheets. The room was bare, save the slippers waiting for me on the floor and the small bedside table with a book on it. It was the Holy Bible.

I sat up and ignored the slippers as I stood. The room began to spin and I let myself fall back onto the bed. I rubbed my face and a couple minutes later, decided to try again.

Where's Francesca? I wondered.

I stumbled to the door. There was no handle. I realized that a bit late as my clumsy hand went to turn it, grasping empty air. I

TURN OR BURN

tried to peel the door open by pushing my fingers through the cracks but it was sealed.

I had an urge to beat on the door but held back. They were probably waiting on that. Perhaps I had a few minutes to collect myself. See if I could get out of there. Nothing is truly foolproof. First, I looked for a camera or microphone. Were they watching me? I couldn't find anything. Come to think of it, it was extremely quiet. No sounds from the outside. Dead silence. I touched the wood of the walls. The more I looked, the clearer it became that I wasn't getting out of there unless someone opened that door.

I went up to it and hammered on it with my fist. It didn't make much noise, the wood absorbing my strength. "Hey!" I yelled. "Hey...you want to let me out of here?"

No one answered.

I went back to the bed and sat down. Tried to run this all through my mind...well, my half-mind. How had they known we would go to Abner's place? Had Wendy told them? How long had they been waiting? What had they done with Francesca?

A click pulled me from my thoughts. Someone opened the door. It was a young, petite Korean woman, dressed similarly to me. She couldn't have been much more than five feet tall. "Hi. My name is April. I need you to put these on. You can keep your hands in front of you."

I smiled for the first time in a while. "You think I'm going to put your handcuffs on? You kidding me?" I stood.

"I am not kidding. It is best for you to comply. We removed them so that you could get a good night's sleep. Now, please. It will make things easier for all of us."

"Where am I?"

"There are three large armed men outside the door who will be happy to put these on for you." As she said that, two of the men appeared at the door. "We also have Francesca Daly. You are in no position to disagree with me. You have seen what we are capable of. If you make this difficult, you will only waste your energy and perhaps lead to her harm. We know who you are. We are fully prepared. Now put your hands out, okay?"

"I see why they sent you in. You're quite convincing."

She smiled again as she latched the cuffs around my wrists. "Put your shoes on and follow me."

I nodded, thinking that I was going to have to make a move sooner rather than later but I had no idea what that would be. Hell, I didn't even know where I was. I limped out the door, past the three men—who were indeed armed and bigger than me—and I followed the woman down a hall. She pushed open a door and rays of sunlight flooded in. She held the door open for me and motioned for me to come.

I limped outside into the cool air and almost into a dream. The drug was swirling through my blood and dragging me down, making it all seem like some sort of twisted fantasy. The setting sun shined through a line of evergreens, lighting up ten to twelve acres of farmland that was cut into a valley of trees surrounded by mountains. I turned and saw the building I'd just walked out of. It was a newly built, one-story log cabin reaching back toward the tree line. There were other cabins, too, lined up like barracks. I could hear the gentle movement of a stream nearby.

On the other side of the farm, there was a larger house—some kind of Victorian—that looked like it had been there long before the other buildings. Past that, there was a dilapidated barn. People were spread about across the field in the center of the property, and it became evident that this was a commune of sorts. A group was sitting in a circle in the grass talking. A little past them, two women were on their knees with trowels working in a well-maintained garden. A boy was playing fetch with a black lab. A couple was strolling through a patch of wildflowers. Near the trees, Elvin, the young man from the cabin, was doing a bad job at chopping some wood. At that rate, he'd be at it all day. Each of them stopped what they were doing and stared at me for a moment before going back to their own business. I'd seen some crazy things in my day, but this place had to top it all. It was a creepy reminder of how strange and delusional people can be, how groupthink can manipulate your mind. They probably thought they were the normal ones.

"Harper," I heard a man's voice say.

I turned and saw the man who branded me. Jameson Taylor.

He'd tied a red bandana around his head. "Have you been treated well?" he asked with a slight crack of a smile. The two Dobermans were at his side.

"Where is she?" I asked.

"Francesca is safe and resting. We'll go by and see her later. She's got a big night tonight. I'm sure you have lots of questions. Follow me and we'll talk. Someone wants to meet you."

As he spoke those words, I knew it was him who had been speaking to me while they had me strapped down.

I looked behind me. The woman who'd led me out had disappeared. The three men were still there, though, standing at the door looking at us, making sure I didn't do anything unacceptable. Truth was, there wasn't anything I could do. Between the heavy lethargy and confusion still lingering from the tranquilizers, and the fact that my hands were locked up and that I was outnumbered, I had been rendered useless. Besides, they'd beaten all the fight out of me. I was a shadow of the man I'd been days ago, weeks ago, years ago. A picture of human decay.

We took a well-traveled trail leading into the woods. The dogs ran ahead and the armed men followed us, hanging a few feet back. The leaves high up were dripping water from a recent rain. "How did you know where to find us?" I asked.

He grinned. "Wendy Harrill called. Said you'd shaken her up some and that she'd told you Daniel's name. Wasn't too hard from there. I knew you'd go to his house. I also had a pretty good feeling you wouldn't be calling the cops, so we knew it would be a good time to grab you. Even if you had called the cops, we would have just waited until our next opportunity."

"You know I am going to kill you, right?"

"I don't see how that is possible, but I am prepared to die."

"Good. Good."

We reached a clearing near the stream that I had heard earlier. A man was standing over a wooden table, working. As we drew near, he stopped and turned around.

The man before me turned up one corner of his mouth, recognizing me. "Welcome, Harper."

I eyed him. "Abner," I said. He acknowledged my greeting with a widening smile.

CHAPTER 44

Jameson walked away, leaving the two of us standing alone in the woods. Daniel Abner looked very much like a professor, from his slightly long hair to the John Lennon glasses to the hint of beard from his lazy shaving habit. He was a tall guy, maybe six foot three, and was in good shape. His dark brown hair was tucked behind his ears but wasn't quite long enough for a ponytail.

With two hands, he held up a very ornate cross that he'd been carving. A detailed and clean effort, though I held back my praise. There was a triskelion in the center where the two pieces of wood met. It was identical to the one above my waist.

"I think I'm done," he said. "Just in time for tonight."

"Good for you. That makes me really proud. My friend is dead, and now my comrade and I have been kidnapped and locked up by you kooks, and you shove your little hobby in my face like I give a damn. What are you doing, Abner? What do you want with us?"

I could see a hint of rage light up deep behind his blue eyes, and I thought to myself that he'd certainly lost his mind. But he held back like a good man of the cloth. "You got in the way. Both of you did. I can't have that. You running around all over town trying to figure out what we're up to. Trying to punish us for killing your friend. That's absurd. Your friend was a casualty of war. We all know that. You forced us to bring you in. But I've realized the two of you have come into our lives for a reason. Now, you are in the process of being saved. I am sorry it is so uncomfortable, but it's the only way. One day, you'll look back on all this and thank me. You will have found your way. We may even be friends."

"That's why you tortured me? So you could *save* me?"

"That's why we are and will continue to torture you. Until you are one of us."

"That will take a long time."

He nodded his head and sighed. "I'm afraid you're right. Longer than the others for sure. But in the end, they've all come around. You will too."

"You people are out of your heads."

"They say such things of all prophets."

"Prophets...that's what you call yourselves. What war are you fighting, Abner?"

"All in time. Let's walk. I'd be happy to answer your questions." He motioned with his hands. "Please follow me. Humor me for a little while." He began walking back into the forest, finding another trail. I followed him.

"Are you a man of God?"

"No."

"That's a shame. You will be, though. You have the triskelion on your skin now. It's a mark of continuity and progress and rebirth. But I'm sure you know all this by now. All of those we have marked have come to see the light. You are on their path. Jesus said, *Be thou faithful unto death and I will give thee a crown of life.* It's not too late for you. Not too late for any of you."

Turning his head toward me, he changed the subject. "I saw pictures of you before the Singularity Summit at Dr. Sebastian's house. We figured you were a new member of the team. You

TURN OR BURN

almost caught one of my men the first day you showed up. He said you saw him in a neighbor's window. That would not have been good."

"Why were you after the doctors?" I asked. "Why did you kill Dr. Kramer?"

"I'll tell you something now that you will not believe. We didn't kill Dr. Kramer. We did try to get at Dr. Sebastian at the Summit. That was more of a test run, so to speak. To see how dedicated our new soldiers were. Turned out I was able to trust the women to attempt it, but they still weren't ready. They failed at their mission. Instead, they killed your friend, Ted, which caused me great problems. You suddenly found a need to get involved. I tried to warn you, too. You had nothing to do with this, and you've fought for our country, so I offered you a way out."

"By blowing up my car?"

"You needed to know I was serious."

"What do you mean, you didn't kill Kramer?"

"We had nothing to do with it." He said it in that kind of prideful, confident way that told me he very well could be telling the truth.

"Who did it then?" I asked, not believing anything he was saying.

"It's not important."

"Are we done here?"

We'd taken a loop through the woods and were closer to the main house. The sun had dropped behind the trees and it was cooler now. Toward the middle of the field, in between the house and the cabins where they had tortured me, there was something going on. People were gathering. He asked me to sit in the grass with him and I did so.

"That's my home," he said, pointing toward the white Victorian. A cylindrical tower on the left side reached well past the rest of the roof. "We've been here a long time. We used to all try to cram into the house but eventually we outgrew the house and the barn. That's why we built cabins like the one you were in. It's really a healing kind of place." He sighed. "So this is us...The Soldiers of the Second Coming."

"Your own little asylum."

He gave a fake laugh. "You have no idea why we're here, do you?"

"Let's see...from what I've gathered so far...you people are scared of cell phones. You kidnap and abuse prostitutes. You brand people. And you think your son is going to be Jesus Christ. That about sum it up?"

He soaked that in for a moment. "That's a jaded way of looking at it. We are not scared of cell phones. In fact, we do use cell phones. We are not scared of technology. We fear God and that is all. I know that we, as a race, are on the wrong track. Technology is a dangerous game. Up to now, we've used it to enhance our lives in a more sterile fashion, in an organic way. Cell phones make it easier to communicate. Anesthesiologists make the pain go away. Computers make communication easier. But there has come a time now where technology has become the end and not the means." He turned to me. "So you wonder why we are here?"

"Enlighten me."

The scripture started coming out of his mouth and his voice changed. "*And God saw that the wickedness of man was great in the earth, and that every imagination of the thoughts of his heart was nothing but evil.* We are here to work our way to heaven. Technology is now getting in the way of that. Our imagination is dredging up the devil. There are biologists finding ways to alter our chromosomes in order to stop degenerating. Changing the way God made us...trying to keep us from dying.

"Scientists, like Sebastian and Kramer, are trying to unite man and machine, encouraging some sort of radical evolution that I can assure you will end with the Lord's abandonment. Engineers

TURN OR BURN

are attempting to create nanobots that can multiply on their own. *Multiply on their own!* We are just asking for machines to take over. To kill us off."

He fiddled with a stick that he picked up off the ground as he continued. "We are not Neo-Luddites. We are conservative bioethicists. We are the ones who will make sure other humans don't cross the boundaries, that they won't worship false idols. Christ will come again, by my seed, and He will come soon, and we will beg God for this honor and will plead for His mercy and ask that He forgive us for who we have become."

"Good talk," I said. "I strongly advise you get on some medication. Never before have I met someone more screwed up than me. Until now. Where is Francesca?"

"Close by."

"Is she okay?"

"She's being treated with the utmost respect."

"You need to let her go. She has nothing to do with all this."

"She has everything to do with all this!"

"You are out of your goddamned mind."

"We'll see about that."

CHAPTER 45

As a blanket of blackness swallowed the farm, Daniel Abner led me back into the camp. My mind was still loopy from the pharmaceuticals, but what came into view as we approached camp was beyond even the most severe of hallucinations.

Out in the field, we came upon an outdoor church of sorts, lit up in great splendor with torches standing free in the ground. A wooden cross—the same one Abner had been working on earlier—stood on an altar amongst hundreds of multi-colored flowers. Two women in white stood next to it.

The benches were full. It must have been everyone in the camp, maybe one-hundred-and-fifty strong. They all rose and turned as we drew near. A woman came up and helped Abner slip a white pulpit robe over his head. Then she handed him a silver stole that he took and placed around his neck. He looked at me and smiled. "See you in a little while, my new friend."

Jameson appeared and took me by the arm. He led me back behind the benches, and we stayed standing, watching the scene. Everyone's eyes followed Abner as he approached the altar. He motioned for them to sit. I hadn't paid attention to the two women in white until that moment. They were standing together on a diagonal, facing the people. Two men stood directly behind them, and it was clear the women were not there of their own accord. They held bouquets of white lilies in their hands and more lilies in their hair—those same Madonna lilies—and it looked like their hands were tied in front of them.

The one closest to me was Francesca. The uneven and sporadic light of the torch made it hard to read her face but I could see her fear. Luan Sebastian, the doctor's wife, stood next to her, sharing a similar look, both looking into the night with glassy eyes. What was Luan doing there?

"They look beautiful, don't they?" Jameson asked.

I knew Francesca wouldn't have been so cooperative had she not been fully convinced that there was no other way. We had to play the game for a moment. Surely, at some point, we would find a window of escape. She had to have the same thought. The opportunity would come sooner rather than later if we showed them that we were easy to control. We would build trust with our captors, and then they would let down their guard—if only for just a second. I would be there to take advantage. So for now, I had to comply quietly and observe this disturbing horror without interfering.

A man pinned a microphone to Abner's silver stole and then went back to his seat in the front row, where he put on headphones and picked up a professional video camera, resting it on his shoulder. It was the kind of camera you might see during the filming of a movie. Much larger than anything for personal use. He and Abner communicated for a moment, testing the mic, and then Abner turned his back to us.

What was I about to witness?

CHAPTER 46

"All rise," Abner said loudly, raising his hands, still facing the altar. It was clear the microphone he'd put on earlier was only for recording purposes. He didn't need a mic. His voice carried well over the pews and across the open field.

The people stood.

He led them in a hymn I'd never heard before. Jameson, standing next to me, joined in with his low, gravelly voice. He was surprisingly on pitch. Though I have pretty strong pipes, I didn't know the words. They sang, "*Lo! He comes with clouds descending, once for favored sinners slain. Thousand thousand saints attending, swell the triumph of His train. Hallelujah! Hallelujah! Hallelujah! God appears on earth to reign.*" You get the idea.

Francesca couldn't see me, as there was no light where we stood. I wondered what they'd done to her. It was out of some dark nightmare, what I was looking at, and I knew she felt the same way.

As they finished singing, Abner turned and motioned for his flock to take their seats. They obeyed.

He clasped his hands together. "*Blow ye the trumpet in Zion,*" he began, "*and sound an alarm on my holy mountain. Let all the inhabitants of the land tremble. For the day of the Lord cometh, for it is nigh at hand.*"

TURN OR BURN

He spoke with all the power and grace of similar preachers I'd seen on television. He'd clearly found his calling, so to speak, and I could see very quickly how he'd captured these people's hearts. He'd turned them all crazy, and I kept thinking about David Koresh and Waco, Texas, and all his wives and children, and Jim Jones and the Jonestown he created in Guyana, Africa, where almost one thousand people committed suicide. Those were the kind of people I'd dealt with all my life, but most of my enemies had been of other religions. The extremists I'd been fighting had been Muslims, but they were no different than Christian radical extremists. *Misled* is the word that comes to mind first.

"Brothers and sisters," Abner said as he lowered his hands, "the day of the Lord is coming, and we have been chosen to be the soldiers of His return. I can think of no greater honor and I accept with all my heart. I believe we all do."

A round of Amen's ran around his congregation.

He lowered his voice. "As many of you have heard me say before, I am not a Neo-Luddite. I don't have a problem with technology, but there has to be a line. Right now, there is not one."

He paused and the people nodded.

"We must draw a line because there is a point of no return—an *event horizon* as these Singularists call it—and we are *not far from it*. We are toying with forces that we will not be able to control. We are eating from the Tree of Knowledge. We are trying to become God!" He backed off. "I'll tell you right now that I don't want to know what's on the other side. It's not God's Kingdom. I know that. It's the end of our race. It's the end of our chances of ever walking along beside Him in Heaven and seeing our loved ones again. Jesus said, *But he that denies me before men shall be denied before the angels of God.*"

Abner went quiet for a moment and looked around at his people, who were captivated by his words. Even the young children were wrapped up in them.

"I believe in the good in people, and I believe that we can get through to—" he pointed at the camera, "many of *you*, who have no idea what is going on. You don't know about the Singularity. Some of you don't know what the future might bring if we don't pull back the reins of technology. Well, I am here to warn you. Tomorrow will be a wake-up call. Many will suffer, but it will save so many more. We do this for our Lord and Savior Jesus Christ as it is our duty." He whispered, "Amen."

They came back with a quiet, "Amen," and I wondered what the hell he was talking about. What was going to happen tomorrow?

He looked directly at the camera. "I'm hoping some of you who see this video find this as terrifying as I do. I'm hoping you do your homework and figure out that I'm telling you the truth. They want to take what makes you *you* and find a way to upload it into hardware. Then from there they can load you into some kind of virtual world where you can live in a video game, or you can be installed into a non-biological substrate or carrier and have a robotic body that will never age. They want to find a way we can live longer. A way we sinners can sidestep the pain and suffering that is our responsibility to endure. We're here to *learn lessons*, brothers and sisters, not to find shortcuts. Some of you will think I'm crazy, but these are facts."

I thought he was crazy, whether they were facts or not.

He shook his finger and raised the pitch of his voice. "Go look into what DARPA is doing. The Defense Advanced Research Projects Agency. Go find out what they're up to. They're the ones funding Dr. Sebastian and Dr. Kramer's work in combining man and machine. And guess where that money comes from. From *you*! From the taxpayers! If there is a promise of building a stronger soldier, a promise of winning the next war, then our government will find a way to fund it. Even if that means reconstructing a soldier's DNA, playing with forces that are undoubtedly evil. We are counting on the fact that you

TURN OR BURN

didn't know that. You didn't know that we as a race are trying to play God. Well, wake up!"

Abner kept talking and I was growing weary of it. I looked around. Someone was looking at me from the congregation. I squinted my eyes and made out the face of Elvin. He saw that I had noticed him and quickly turned back around.

"The Lord has come to me recently. He has affirmed these things that I pass on to you. Jesus Christ is coming back." Abner thrust his arms into the air. "He's coming to take us home!" The people cheered.

"God has chosen me to give you your savior. To offer the seed of the Christ child. This doesn't make me any more special than any one of you." He looked through the crowd. "Like you, I'm simply part of the plan." He turned to Francesca and Luan. "As are these women here, who God has chosen for my wives. One of these two will carry the child. We can't know which one, and it doesn't matter. All that we can hope is that God sees it fit to allow this baby to live and flourish and thrive and soon become our leader. He must know that we're down here fighting for Him. Can I get one final, everlasting, eternal *Amen*? Let's let Him know we're down here waiting."

"Amen!" they shouted, like Roman soldiers following their Caesar.

"I can't hear you!"

"*Amen!*" The word echoed through the camp and out into the night.

Abner led them in another hymn, which everyone knew by heart.

CHAPTER 47

What happened next was beyond anything my imagination could have come up with. Another man with a robe and stole came up to the altar and proceeded to marry Abner and the two women. And there was nothing I could do.

This marriage was done in a more quiet fashion, much less of a show. The cameraman had set down the camera. I couldn't make out what was being said, but I could fill in the blanks. Abner said his vows and put rings on the women's fingers one at a time, kissing them both on the mouth. They weren't fighting back, and I knew Francesca was still waiting for an opportunity. She'd been through a lot worse than getting kissed by some maniac in the woods.

She was a big girl, a warrior, and I had to keep telling myself that.

After they were done, Abner looked back at his people. "It all begins now, brothers and sisters. Let us go forth to love and serve the Lord!"

The people stood and clapped and cheered. Men escorted the women away, and Abner disappeared behind them.

Jameson took my arm. "Let's go," he said. "Show's over."

He jerked me away and I lost sight of Francesca. Holding a

flashlight, Jameson led me in the opposite direction of the crowd. Two men followed. I recognized one of them as the Canadian, and when he turned toward me, I could see the bandage on his neck from Francesca's bullet.

"Where's he taking the women?" I asked.

"To plant the seed of the Christ Child."

"You don't really believe this nonsense, do you?"

"With all my heart."

I couldn't hold back any longer. I went for Jameson's throat. My cuffed hands came up fast and jabbed him hard underneath his chin. I didn't get very far. The other two men had me on the ground in seconds. I heaved for breath as I tried to fight off the two men. The Canadian hit me in the jaw with a punch that I think he'd been thinking about for days. I ate the dirt. They jerked me back up by the arms.

Jameson was rubbing his throat as he said, "For that, I'll make sure she is first in line."

"You bastard."

He grinned and slapped my cheek. "Now, let's take you back to the barn. We've only begun working on you. One month from now, you will be a new man. The Lord will help us wash away this evil."

CHAPTER 48

As they escorted me further away from the crowd, I found it terribly difficult to put one foot in front of the other. I was broken, mentally and physically. The thought of more torture terrified me.

The barn came into view in the moonlight. It was on the verge of collapse. Jameson slid the front door open and shined his light inside. It was the size of basketball court. The floor was covered in hay. The men led me toward the back as the hay crunched under my bare feet.

The Canadian took me by the hair and shoved my head in between two pieces of wood. There was a cutout of a half circle on either one, making room for my neck. It was like some medieval guillotine of sorts, hopefully *sans* the blade. He slid the top piece of wood down and it pinched my skin as it locked my neck into place. I heard a metal lock close somewhere around my head. I was just high enough that I couldn't rest my knees on the ground, and I was forced to stand there in a very awkward and uncomfortable position.

Jameson threw a fist into my side, and it knocked the wind out of me. As I gasped for air, he said, "We'll break you soon enough, but we have more important things to attend to now.

TURN OR BURN

You'll have some company though, if he's still alive. See you soon."

I didn't say anything. There wasn't a point.

They went out the way we came in and as the door slid closed, they took most of the light with them. As my eyes adjusted, I listened for a while. It was quiet, save some crickets chirping outside. Then I thought I heard a groan and breathing. "Hello," I said. "Someone in here?"

Nothing.

"Hey! Someone in here?"

"Yeah," a voice said behind me. It was barely audible.

"Who are you?" I asked.

"You first."

"My name's Harper Knox."

He laughed some, but it was a weak laugh. "Harper," he said. "I should have figured. It's Coleman Jacobs."

"Detective Jacobs...what are you doing here?"

"Hanging out."

I grinned darkly. "Do they have you locked into one of these contraptions?"

"Yeah. They beat me pretty badly, too."

"How long have you been here?"

"A couple days maybe. I'm not sure. You?"

"No idea. Maybe the same. You have any idea what's going on here? I called you, you know. Left a message."

"I didn't get it. They took me from my house. I was sound asleep. They came in and knocked me out. I woke up here. Been locked up in this damn building ever since. I have no idea where we are."

"It's a barn. We're in some kind of commune. Way out in the woods on a big farm."

"What are we dealing with?"

"I don't know exactly." I told him about the sermon and the wedding I'd just seen. "I know they're up to something tomorrow but I don't know what. That preacher Wendy Harrill told me it's going to be bad. She said lots of people are going to die." Then I told him about Abner's plans for Francesca and Luan.

"So he's going to rape them?"

"Yeah."

"I'd say we'll be able to stop it," Jacobs said, "but I'd be pumping you full of bullshit. I don't think we're getting out of here. No one has any clue where we are. I think I'm going to die in this barn."

***

Time passed.

Maybe two hours. I'd gone through every leg position I could think of in order to relieve some of the stress. I was thirsty, too.

"We there yet?" I asked.

He didn't respond.

"Jacobs!"

"Yeah," he said after a few more seconds. "I'm fading. Need water." He didn't have to tell me. I could hear it in his voice.

Right then, the door of the barn cracked open.

Footsteps.

It was only one person this time and he was coming for me. The footsteps grew louder and the flashlight in his hand brighter. It was a man with an axe in his hand. I couldn't see his face, just his torso and the steel of the axe and a shotgun slung around his back. He set the light down, pointed it toward me, and raised the axe.

"You need to think about this," I said, trying not to close my eyes.

He wasn't listening to me. The axe came down quickly.

Payback is a bitch. I'd been thinking about killing myself for years, but now someone was finally doing me the favor, and I didn't want it. Not that I was scared. I just didn't want to die

TURN OR BURN

anymore. Was that because of Francesca? Hell, I don't know. But the fact was that I didn't want that axe to end my life. I wanted to live. At least I had that going for me if all of a sudden I woke at the base of the pearly gates and needed to defend my existence.

CHAPTER 49

The sound of steel meeting steel clashed near my head and I lost sound in my left ear for a moment. I opened my eyes. He had missed but he was going for it again. I turned my head just as the axe came toward me.

Metal on metal again. Sparks flew. Either he had the worst aim in the world or he was helping me. "What are you doing?" I asked.

"Shut up and keep your head turned away. This is making enough noise as it is." I turned away and he swung the axe several more times until I heard something pop. He pulled a chain through a hole and slid the top piece of wood up, and I stood, rubbing the flesh around my neck and enjoying the feeling of straightening out my legs for the first time in hours.

I finally got a look at him. I loved seeing that little baby face. Once the ringing in my ears ceased, I said, "Thank you, Elvin. Can you help me with these cuffs?"

"Yeah. Turn around and put your hands on the wood."

I did and he raised his axe. I grimaced, ready to lose an arm. "Be careful."

He swung three more times and the noise was absurdly loud. Someone had to hear it. The cuffs finally separated. I reached for

TURN OR BURN

the axe. "Can I get that from you?" I took it from my new friend and limped over to Jacobs near the opposite wall. Elvin followed me with the light. Jacobs was in the same contraption I was. His eye was nearly swollen shut and his face was covered in sweat. He looked like he'd lost some weight. Some of that balloon gut had deflated and his face had thinned up. Using the axe and making way too much noise, I set him free and he fell to the ground.

I pulled him up by his arm. "Can you walk? They'll be coming after us."

"We'll find out." He rubbed his neck, finding his balance. They'd dressed him in similar attire, and like me, he had no shoes on.

I looked at the shotgun Elvin had brought with him. It was a Mossberg with an extended magazine tube. "I don't suppose you want to lend this to me, do you?" I asked him.

"You can probably work it better than I can."

I took the gun and some shells that I stuffed in the pocket of my linen pants. I handed Jacobs the axe and looked back at Elvin.

"Where's Abner? Where are the women?"

"In the main house. Up in the tower bedroom. Everyone from the camp is there, surrounding them."

"How many are armed?"

"Almost everyone. All the men at least."

"Okay. We need to get out of here."

We made our way out of the barn and snuck into the woods. It was black outside.

As she'd told me and proved, Francesca could take care of herself. As hard as that pill was to swallow, I had to accept it. Saving her from being raped had to come second to figuring out what else Abner was planning.

Oh, keep telling yourself that, Harper. Truth was, all that mattered to me was Francesca not getting hurt. But I forced myself to choose. If I could prevent both, I would, but first and foremost, I had to save people's lives.

Once we were behind the tree line, as Jacobs tried to get himself together, I whispered to Elvin, "What is Abner planning? I mean, other than making a baby?"

"Car bombs. Lots of them. I don't know where. He wants to draw attention to what we're up against. We've been training these people for months. Reprogramming them like we started with you."

"You mean the prostitutes?"

"Not all of them are prostitutes."

"Where are they?"

"They're already gone."

"Where?"

"I...I don't know. The locations were kept secret. I don't even know who knows other than Abner. He might be the only one."

"Do you have a phone?" I asked.

"No," he said.

"Can you find one?"

"There's only a few in camp. Only a couple people have them. Abner. Taylor. I don't know who else. They don't trust us with them."

"Where is Jameson?"

"Protecting the house."

"Where are we? I mean, location-wise?"

"We're in Ashford. Just outside of Mt. Rainier National Park."

"How far is the closest town?" I asked. "Closest place we might find a phone."

"Maybe five miles. Unless you catch someone on the road driving. There are not many houses out here."

Jacobs spoke up. "We need to call it in. I'm with you."

I looked back at Elvin. "Can you run?"

He nodded. "Sure."

"I want you to find a phone. Call 911. Tell them that Detective

TURN OR BURN

Coleman Jacobs is here. Tell them everything you know. Make sure you tell them about the car bombs. And tell them Jacobs and I are going to find out more and will try to call." I put my hand on his shoulder. "You can save a lot of people today. Can I count on you?"

"Yes."

"Do you know where we can find more guns?"

"They're locked up in the main house, where Abner is."

"Shit. Well, run your ass off. We're going to need some help."

He mumbled something and was gone. We could only hope he would follow through.

As he disappeared into the forest, I looked at Jacobs. "You in this with me? We need to get Abner. No matter what."

"We can at least try."

CHAPTER 50

We crossed the camp cautiously. As we got closer to the main house, we heard singing. We kept moving, staying in the shadows.

The white Victorian farmhouse came into view, with its steep roof and wraparound porch. The tower on the left side reached another story past the rest of the house. The lights were on. Abner had the women up there.

Torches lit up the grounds surrounding the house. That's where the singing was coming from. The entire front lawn was covered with people, like it was some kind of pilgrimage. A few men were standing guard closer to us, so it wasn't going to be easy to get inside. Especially with an axe and a shotgun. But we had no choice. "Let's try the other side," I whispered.

Staying far away, we moved low through some high grass toward the back of the house, but we discovered quickly that the house was completely surrounded by worshippers and guards. They had no intentions of letting anyone disturb this moment.

I squatted next to Jacobs. "I've only got six shots. We have to get more weapons."

"But they're all in there."

TURN OR BURN

"Then let's walk right in like we're part of them. See how far we can get."

"I don't think we have any other choice. I'll go first. Watch my back."

"Yep."

Concealing the axe against his chest, he started toward the crowd, his short legs holding up his belly and the rest of his bulk surprisingly well. Though I would rather have had Ted by my side, Jacobs had the concentration and confidence of a seasoned veteran. I stayed back a minute and then began moving. A few other people were walking the grounds so we didn't look *that* out of place.

I got there ten seconds after him, hiding the shotgun as best I could against my body. I worked my way under the torch light past the people who were sitting on blankets and in chairs on the grass looking up toward the tower. Some were holding up crosses and bibles, saying prayers. The young children were sleeping. Many of the people were singing, "Jesus Loves Me," and truthfully, it freaked me out. Stephen King would have had a field day.

No one noticed us at first. They were all so focused on what was going on inside that house.

Jacobs did something that surprised me. As he got close to the porch, he took a seat on the grass. Like he was one of them. I kept going.

Once I got near him, I made the only call I could. Two men were sitting on the porch with guns on their laps. In some weird way, I felt like I was the evil one, like I was killing people during a church service. But these people were different. There was nothing right or good about what was going on.

Raising the shotgun, I ran up the steps and started firing. I put a hole in the chest of the first guy before he had even gotten up. I killed the other one just as he got off the chair. The screaming began behind me.

As the drugs wore off, a surprising thing was happening. I felt shockingly on top of my game. I hadn't felt so focused and relaxed amidst chaos in more than three years. Looking back on it later, I realized that the love I felt for Francesca Daly had crushed my fear. Nothing, including my monkey mind, was going to get in the way of protecting her. If only for a night, love had conquered my PTSD.

I heard footsteps running up behind me and turned. Almost pulled the trigger. But I heard, "It's me, it's me!"

Jacobs was working his way up the steps.

I looked past him at the people.

Some were coming after us; others were running the other way. I fired a couple warning shots, hoping I didn't have to shoot anyone else. The ones coming our way slowed, but a round flew right by my face, implanting itself in the front door.

"We gotta keep moving," I yelled, turning. Jacobs picked up a handgun off one of the dead men and followed me as we forced our way into the house.

Someone in a room off to the left was firing at us as we got into the foyer. But we didn't have the option of moving slow. They were coming after us from the yard, too, like zombies after our flesh. I slid onto the floor, simultaneously turning onto my back. I held the shotgun steady with both hands and searched for targets. I had two shots left.

A man was coming from around a corner. I pulled the trigger, and the pellets from the shotgun ripped into his neck. He fell. Jacobs was right behind me and moved toward the dead man, prying away his gun and disappearing behind a wall. Shots were coming from the top of the stairs, so I took cover.

"This way!" I followed Jacobs into another room and found a box of shells on the table. Was that a sign of good fortune to come? I loaded up. We had no idea how many men were up those stairs but had to move quickly. Like everything else, time was not on our side.

TURN OR BURN

I motioned to Jacobs to cover me and ran out of the dining room back into the hall, working my way to the wooden stairs. A man saw me up top and hid back behind a wall. As I was about to make my move, someone pushed open the front door, coming in from the porch. Jacobs came out of nowhere and smashed his shoulder into the door, knocking the people back. He twisted the dead bolt.

"Ain't coming in this way, fuckers!" he said, as the zombies on the other side began to kick it down.

"I'm going up," I said.

"Go! I gotcha."

A window broke downstairs. They'd found another way in.

Trusting the fact that I was the most battle-hardened person in the building, I had a feeling that by staying aggressive, I could stay alive. Whoever was up those stairs had probably not ever been shot at before. They weren't used to the adrenalin rush. How draining it could be. How it could confuse you.

So, taking a chance, I started up the stairs, firing the shotgun every couple of steps. I would certainly run out of shells but at least I could get to high ground. The stairs creaked below me as the shotgun cracked and holes exploded in the wall at the top. I heard more shots below and knew Jacobs had run into trouble.

Jameson Taylor appeared at the top and fired at me a couple times. I didn't bother ducking, just climbed the steps faster and fired back. I fired again and again until I was out of ammo. The symptoms of my PTSD were trying to get at me—the blurry thoughts, the blurry vision, the flashbacks, the increased intensity—but I pushed them away and reached deep down into my soul for focus. Too many lives were at stake. I couldn't let them win. I couldn't let *it* win. I reached the top and didn't slow down.

Jameson was waiting on me. He fired, and I tried to dodge it, but he got me in the arm. A sear of pain ran up my left side. I didn't have time to even think about it. I threw my good arm out in front of me and batted away his gun. It fired into the ceiling as I tackled him onto the wood floor of the hall at the top of the stairs. He hit hard and lost his breath. I swung a few punches that hit their mark, busting his face up nicely. He was damn strong, though—old-man strength if you know what I mean—and he pushed me off him. Lying on his back, he kicked me several times with those heavy boots. One of the kicks hit my left arm, the one that had been shot. It hurt like hell. Another kick got me in the temple.

I finally caught his foot and tried to break it. Just as I was about to snap a bone, someone started yelling at me. "Get off him!" It was the Canadian.

I kept twisting the leg and Jameson yelled. The Canadian fired a shot into the floor. "Get off him now!"

"Shoot him, you fool!" Jameson yelled.

I turned just as the Canadian pointed the gun right between my eyes.

It was a good try, Harper. You did your best.

I saw movement. Jacobs was coming around the corner up the stairs. He'd been quiet about it. And he saved my life. He fired a shot at the side of the Canadian's head and he was gone. It wasn't pretty.

The body dropped on top of me, the gun still in his hand. I reached down the length of his arm, feeling for it. Not in time, though. I heard a shot and turned to see Jacobs falling backwards. Jameson had gotten him.

I didn't bother peeling the gun away. Instead, I wrapped my hand around the Canadian's fingers and aimed at Jameson. But Jameson was already firing a shot.

The Gods were on my side that day, though. The bullet shot into the body of the Canadian, embedding into his chest with a thud. I didn't give Jameson time to fire another one. I shot at his face.

But I missed and Jameson was up and moving toward me,

TURN OR BURN

getting ready to fire again. I didn't miss the second time. The bullet entered Jameson Taylor's right eye and he was dead instantly.

I pushed the Canadian off me and got to my knees, heaving for breath. I looked down at Detective Jacobs. A stream of blood was soaking his pants.

He was panting as he looked up at me. "Get Abner," he said.

"I'm okay."

"The hell you're okay."

"Go!"

I didn't hesitate. Grabbing a gun, I ran down the hall toward the tower. I reached a closed door. Thinking it might be the way upstairs, I twisted the knob; it was unlocked.

Luan Sebastian was in a robe, her right leg chained to a large wooden bed. She was lying on top of the covers. There was Duct tape across her mouth. She peeled her eyes open and I saw defeat and sorrow. I cleared the room, making sure no one else was in there, and then said to her, "I'll be back. You're safe." I reached out and touched her leg to try to comfort her, but she jerked away. I had no doubt that Abner had raped her.

Going back into the hall, I finally found the stairs leading up to the tower. They were at the far end. Moving cautiously, I went up the twenty stairs and reached a locked door.

I kicked it open, expecting to see Abner holding Francesca hostage. That is not what I saw at all.

CHAPTER 51

On a tall four-poster bed reaching almost to the ceiling, Abner was on top of Francesca. He was nude. He turned toward me, shock on his face. I put his forehead in the sight of the gun. Felt that hairpin trigger start to give. But I held back.

Francesca was tied down. He'd stripped her naked. Like Luan, a strip of tape covered her mouth. Our eyes met.

A savage rage came over me.

I let go of the gun and it hit the floor as I nearly flew across the room and onto the bed. Abner had already figured out that he would have to kill me to get any further. He was sliding off the other end as I came over the bed after him. I reached for him with my good arm but missed as he disappeared onto the floor. I scrambled over Francesca and fell on top of him. He was pulling a gun up but he didn't have a chance.

I ripped the gun from his hands and hit him in the ear with it, and he fell onto his back, losing consciousness.

I pushed myself up and went to her, wishing I could cradle her in my arms like a child and take her home. How could something so evil happen to someone like her? It was terrifyingly sad to see those brown eyes, so damaged by what had happened. Yet *sad* doesn't come close to capturing it. I wanted to break down right then but I couldn't. Beside the fact that I had lost touch with being human, I still had a job to do.

"It's over," I said, putting my hands on her cheeks. "I'm here now."

She acknowledged me with her eyes, and I saw a strength that, in my entire life, I had seen only a few times. What a woman. What a soldier. I kissed her on the forehead.

The thick string that they had used was too thin to untie. It had cut harshly into her wrists as she had attempted to fight her way out, something I'd experienced at the cabin. I pulled at the string but it wouldn't break. I looked around for something I could cut with, knowing I had to get her out of there. There was no telling how many more were after us. The house was still echoing with gunshots.

"You still there, Jacobs?" I yelled down the steps.

"Yeah!"

"Buy me some time."

He answered with his gun.

I went to the pile of clothes on the floor and went through Abner's pockets. Found a set of keys and a phone. I used the keys first and sawed through the string. She sat up once I freed her arms. She peeled the tape off and took some deep breaths.

I cut the string around her ankles next, and she was finally free. She started to get up, and I grabbed her leg and squeezed hard.

"Are you with it right now?" I asked. "I need you to be with it."

"I'm all right."

And I knew she was. "More of them are downstairs. We need to be smart. Okay?"

She nodded and climbed off the bed. I turned back to Abner as Francesca dressed. He was coming back to life, his eyes opening and his hand moving to his face. Using the same string he'd used to tie up Francesca, I tied his wrists to a leg of the bed.

He wasn't going anywhere without ripping his hands off.

I went for the phone, an iPhone no doubt. Oh, the irony. I found the map and GPS'd my location, never having loved technology more in my life.

When the 911 operator picked up, I said, "My name is Harper Knox. I have a critical situation right now. Many lives are at stake. Detective Coleman Jacobs has been shot."

"What's your location, sir?"

I told her and said, "A group of people are about to set off a series of car bombs around Seattle. I don't know where yet. I'm hoping I will soon. You need to get the bomb squad, SWAT, anyone who can mobilize. Have them ready. I'm going to try and get the locations. Stay on the line. I'm setting the phone down."

I didn't bother waiting on her response. I threw the phone on the bed and looked at Francesca. "Go downstairs and help Jacobs hold them off. I'll get Abner to talk."

"No, I'll take care of Abner. I'll get the locations." She wasn't going to let me argue.

I joined Jacobs, taking position on the other side of the steps. He was hanging in there. The men below were still coming up, no care for their own lives, destined to save their savior. I killed two more of them, and the bodies down below were piling up. I leaned against the wall. "Let me see your wound."

Jacobs raised his hand a little. The bullet had entered his hip.

"You keep your hand on it," I said, "and you're going to be fine."

"Don't act like you Green Berets know more about getting shot than the police. I know I'll be okay."

"I like you, Jacobs."

The zombies stopped coming up the stairs for a minute. We sat there in silence. Then I heard the first scream. It was Abner in the bedroom. Another scream, and then howling. Near guttural roars. Francesca was having her way with him. It was hard to listen to.

TURN OR BURN

Sirens finally sounded in the distance, and I started to have some hope that we might get out of there.

***

Francesca came back down a few minutes later. I saw the soldier in her at that moment more than I ever had. I knew right then why she had chosen to be one. She had no choice. She was born, just like I was, to be one.

"It's done," she said. "Nine locations. I told the operator. I think we stay out of the rest of it."

"I think that's a good idea," Jacobs agreed. "I'll take it from here."

"Is he alive up there?" I asked Francesca.

Francesca's face darkened and without any emotion, she said, "I don't know."

"I have one more question for him. Be right back."

I ran up the stairs to the tower. The bedroom door was open. Abner was on his knees, crying. There was a path of blood where he'd crawled across the floor. Good God, what had she done to him? I felt no pity, though. Believe me.

Using my foot, I pushed him over and he tumbled helplessly onto the hardwood, like a submissive animal. He put his bloody hands up and begged, "Please…no more."

"You said you didn't kill Dr. Kramer. Who did?"

He was so shaken up that I wasn't sure he could hear me. I put my foot on his rib cage and pushed hard. He shouted in pain and grabbed my foot with both hands. Keeping my voice calm, I said, "Who killed Dr. Nina Kramer?"

"Luan."

I had been thinking that something was off about Kramer's death, how the method of murder didn't match the others, so I decided to go with it, though what he said sounded slightly absurd. "Tell me more. Tell me everything."

His words came out broken, his sentences detached. "We'd been watching Dr. Sebastian and his family for weeks before the Summit. We knew he was having an affair with Kramer. My people followed them to a bed-and-breakfast in Anacortes. Luan had followed them, too. But she didn't do anything about it. Just watched them from her car for a few minutes and then drove away. When I heard Kramer had been killed by blows to the head, it didn't take me long to figure things out. Luan had finally gotten her revenge."

I pushed down on his ribs again, coming close to cracking them. "You're lying."

"No. No! She admitted it to me tonight. Think about it. It was the perfect opportunity to kill Kramer. After what had happened the day before with Dr. Sebastian, Luan knew people would immediately suspect us."

It was making sense...too much sense to be a lie. "So you claimed responsibility so that you could have her for yourself." I wasn't asking.

He nodded yes and I walked out the door, hoping I'd never see his face again.

CHAPTER 52

They stopped all but two bombs from going off. The nine people Abner had sent to do his dirty work were caught. One bomb that did go off was at the University of Washington, right outside of the Computer Engineering building. Another was at the Microsoft Campus in Redmond. But no one was hurt. They had blocked off the areas in plenty of time. We found Wendy Harrill's daughter in one of the cabins. She was completely unharmed and was safely returned to her mother.

Over the course of the next week, they caught almost everyone involved. Abner went to jail. Jameson Taylor and the Canadian were gone forever, perhaps meeting their maker. Thirty of the others were still out there but they'd eventually turn up; many had turned themselves in. The biggest discussion at the moment was where the children involved would go. They'd been brainwashed badly and there wasn't much hope for them.

During that time, we had slowly put some of it together. Abner had raped Luan but hadn't quite gotten his chance with Francesca.

She saved a lot of people by doing what she did, and I would have done the same. That's why we were both contractors. We bend the rules and sometimes we ignore them. But we get the job done.

I may never be a religious man, but I do believe in good and evil, and I know deep down that Abner was evil.

The strangest turn of events was what they found in the compound. As he had told me, Abner and his crew had been watching Dr. Sebastian for quite some time and had been videotaping him. The cops found a video of Sebastian and Kramer doing something in a parked car that wasn't part of the their research for the Fusion Project, if you know what I mean. On my lead, prosecutors were searching for evidence that Luan had been involved in the murder of Dr. Kramer. Abner, of course, was now denying what he had told me the day before. Maybe she'd get justice one day, but there didn't seem to be much of a case. Stories don't always wrap up nicely. Poetic justice is not always served.

Another tape had surfaced, too, and it was a YouTube sensation. Abner's sermon from the night before. One of his people had released it to the media, and needless to say, it had consumed the interest of the world. Nothing like it since Waco, Texas, the talking heads said. Perhaps it was enough to remind people that those folks that live in the Middle East aren't that different from us. Though I'm not a believer, I know the vast majority of the believers out there are good people, no matter whom or how they worship. But there are lunatics in every bunch, and you can't judge the whole group by a few. I know, I know. I'm shutting up now.

***

Back to the vineyard on Red Mountain I went. In a way, retreating; and in a way, revitalized.

The leaf canopies were large and healthy and soaking up the sun like they're meant to do, helping the now tiny green grapes grow to ripeness.

All was right with my world. All but her.

TURN OR BURN

Francesca had gone back to Italy. She had checked in on me at the hospital the following afternoon and then said good-bye. It was a sad one. She said what she'd been saying all along: that it wasn't going to last, that it would never happen again.

I told her I was in for the long haul if she changed her mind, and she said she already knew that. But sometimes we put ourselves second. For better or worse, we do. And she took that plane to go please her parents. I had no doubt in my mind that she loved me. No doubt at all.

So a week after it all went down, I found myself right back where it began. She wasn't there, but so it goes. I still had Roman. He was watching me dig the fifth hole of the day, trying to find a leak in a stretch of PVC pipe that fed water to my Merlot. Unfortunately, he only dug on his own terms, so he wasn't much help other than keeping me company. That's more than I could ask for anyway. Poor dog would have to put up with me the rest of his life.

I stabbed my shovel into the dirt and felt the sting in my left shoulder where Jameson Taylor had shot me. But I thought of Ted and smiled. We'd had some good times over the years. He and his brother were two of the finest men I'd ever met, and I'd miss them until I was in the ground.

The phone began to ring in my pocket. Like every other time it had rung the past week, I hoped it was her. I hoped that somehow she'd landed in Palermo and looked the honorable Prince Salvi in his eyes and instantly realized she'd made a mistake.

Ha ha, Harper. That's a good one, my friend. The sun don't shine on a dog's ass that often. No offense, Roman. Anyway, I answered.

"Harper, it's Jacobs. You won't believe this. You heard they brought Luan Sebastian in today, right?"

"I hadn't heard that."

"It's true. But that's not what I had to tell you."

"What is it?"

"Luan's pregnant."

A quick flash of Abner's face came to me, and I saw Luan chained to that bed again. I had no words.

"Abner got her pregnant. Can you believe that?"

"Jesus Christ," I said, not thinking of what I was saying.

"Yeah, exactly. Jesus Christ."

***

An hour later, I'd found and fixed the crack in the pipe. As I was tossing dirt back into the hole, my phone rang again, making me almost feel popular. I pulled my gloves off and dug it out of my pocket.

"I'll be damned," I said to myself. It was *her*, and all of a sudden my heart was racing like someone was shooting at me.

"Hello," I said, acting like I hadn't looked to see who it was.

"*Ciao*, Harper. It's me."

"Who's 'me?'"

"Francesca."

"Francesca who?"

"God, you're a riot."

"Haven't we already established that? Anyhoo, what are you doing, little lady? How's the prince and princess of Palermo?"

"I don't know. I haven't seen him."

"Why not?" I acted like this wasn't the biggest news since the moon landing.

"Well...I just haven't gotten around to it yet. I'm driving through vineyard country and it made me think of you. I wish I was drinking one of those Red Mountain blends you speak so highly of."

"That right? You know that Chianti crap is rubbish, don't you? The Italians make better cheese than wine."

"That's funny and *not* true. No, really. It makes me want to live on a vineyard one day."

TURN OR BURN

"Well, I'm sure Prince Poppycock could make that happen."

"I was actually hoping *you* could."

Right that second, I heard Roman growling. Then I heard a car swinging a left onto my driveway, just like Ted had days before. Roman started running. "That's you, isn't it?"

"Me? Where?"

I watched a little rental car start coming toward me, spitting up dust. And I could see her face through the windshield, and I felt her like a warm wind.

"You're in so much trouble," I said.

"I'm here, Harper."

"For how long?"

"That's up to you."

That's when I dropped the phone and started running toward her. She threw her car into Park and climbed out. When she saw me running, she started running, too, and it felt so damn right.

We embraced and held each other and I kissed her like I've never kissed another woman. Over the next few hours, I shared my wine with her and we spoke of the past and of the future. We watched the sunset and made love on the porch and in the dirt below the vines. Right there and then, we became part of the terroir of Red Mountain.

Right there and then, it all became whole.

Acknowledgment

Mikella Walker, I am humbled and honored to call you my wife and best friend, and I will never stop chasing you. Thank you for your love, support, and presence. This book is as much yours as it is mine.

Made in the USA
Charleston, SC
25 February 2014